The Secret Lives of Baltimore Girls

The Secret Lives of Baltimore Girls

Katt

www.urbanbooks.net

Urban Books, LLC
300 Farmingdale Road, NY-Route 109
Farmingdale, NY 11735

The Secret Lives of Baltimore Girls
Copyright © 2019 Katt

ISBN 13: 978-1-62286-260-3
ISBN 10: 1-62286-260-0

First Trade Paperback Printing October 2019
Printed in the United States of America

10 9 8 7 6 5 4 3 2 1

Distributed by Kensington Publishing Corp.
Submit Orders to:
Customer Service
400 Hahn Road
Westminster, MD 21157-4627
Phone: 1-800-733-3000
Fax: 1-800-659-2436

Prologue

Emerson pounded the door like her life was about to end if she didn't get inside. The side of her fist ached, but she wouldn't stop pounding. Sweat wet her hairline and curled her hair into fine balls at the base of her forehead. Appearance be damned at that moment. Emerson was on a mission. Her heart threatened to escape her chest through her throat. Everything around her buzzed loudly. That was her rage playing out in her ears.

Mikayla yanked Charlie's front door open so fast and hard she stumbled back a few steps. She couldn't understand who would be banging like the police about to conduct a raid.

"Girl, what the . . ." Mikayla immediately swallowed her words when she saw Emerson's red-rimmed eyes, hair like a wild bird's nest, and heaving chest.

"Eme? What the . . . What's wrong?" Mikayla screamed, shocked at the sight of the third member of their trio in front of her. Emerson's chest rose and fell like a beast on the attack. She had jagged black lines of mascara running down her cheeks, making her look like a bad version of the Joker from the last Batman movie. Her fists were clearly balled, and her nostrils opened and closed like a bull on the charge.

"Where's Charlie?" Emerson growled hoarsely. "Where the fuck is she?"

Mikayla's already-big, round eyes were about to pop completely out of her head. She hadn't ever seen cool, calm, collected Emerson Dayle look like this. Emerson was the sounding board of the group, the usually level-headed one with all of the good advice. She was usually the one with her shit together. Not today.

Mikayla wasn't a fool. She stepped aside to let this bull in a china shop move past her.

"Charlie is in the kitchen. Eme, what is the matter?" Mikayla asked again, her eyes still wide as saucers.

Emerson stormed into Charlie's house and past Mikayla, refusing to answer her question. Emerson could hear what she thought was laughter coming from the kitchen, and the sound assailed her ears like nails on a chalkboard. Charlie had to be on the phone, and with whom? Who would be making her giggle like a schoolgirl? The thoughts swirled in Emerson's head like a double-eye hurricane. Emerson felt herself floating. She was having an out-of-body experience, and this usually happened when she was off her square.

"Why, Charlie?" Emerson boomed as soon as she crossed the kitchen's doorway in a fury.

Emerson had assumed correctly. Charlie was on her cell phone. The sight of her crazed friend caused Charlie to end her call without another word to whoever was on the other end. Charlie's face flushed and her mouth dropped open slightly. "Eme, what's—"

"Out of everybody, I never thought you! You? You, Charlie? You were supposed to be my best friend! I was there for you when every single nigga crushed you and your heart. I was there for you when your mother turned her fucking back on you and called you a whore! I was there for you when you were on the streets of Baltimore, bed hopping just to have a warm place to stay! And you turn around and do this to me? You don't have respect for the code? Our code? You fuckin' bitch!" Emerson rattled off so breathlessly her head felt light. Her body shook uncontrollably.

Charlie's eyes filled with tears. She put her hands up in front of her and shook her head. She knew this day would come. She had wanted to explain it all before it blew up in all of their faces. It was too late for that now. "Eme, wait," she started. "I can explain."

But Emerson couldn't hold back any longer. The dam of reasoning in her mind had finally broken, and red-hot rage rushed out so fast and furious it flooded all of her senses and sensibilities.

"Urgg!" Emerson growled. She rushed into Charlie so wildly and unexpectedly that Charlie's body went crashing to the floor with no way for her to break her fall. The back of Charlie's head hit the hard ceramic kitchen tile with a loud, sickening crack.

"Oh, my God! Emerson! Stop!" Mikayla screamed, rushing over to the body tangle that was her two best friends.

"Why, Charlie?" Emerson screamed through tears as she wildly slammed her fists into Charlie's face. "Why didn't you tell me? Why would you do this? You are not my fucking friend! You never were!" Emerson shouted through tears, suddenly growing weak.

Charlie's eyes were shut and her head hung to the side limply. Blood leaked out of her nose and drained onto the floor. She was defenseless against Emerson's attack.

"Emerson! She looks really hurt! You have to stop! Please." Mikayla grabbed at Emerson's clothes, trying to pull her off of Charlie. It was too late. Charlie looked dead. Blood covered her face and drained out of her left ear.

"Why did she do this to us?" Emerson managed, allowing Mikayla to pull her off of Charlie. Emerson fell to the side of Charlie, sobbing.

"We were best friends! She knows what I went through! She lied to me every single day for the past six months!"

"Oh, my God! She won't wake up! Call 911," Mikayla screamed through tears. "I don't care what she did! You can't just kill her, Emerson! We are sisters! This is a sisterhood! You can't just kill her!"

Emerson threw her hand up to her mouth and gagged. She was frozen as she looked over at her lifeless friend.

"Charlie! Wake up!" Mikayla yelled, shaking Charlie's body. "Help! Help!"

Chapter 1

Charlie

Six Months Earlier

Sweat rolled down Charlie's back, causing her T-shirt to stick to her skin. Even her air conditioner couldn't help the heat that her body generated on its own. The heat of the moment. The heat of anger. The heat, period. It had taken over all of her senses. She beat her nails against her steering wheel impatiently and gnawed on her bottom lip.

"I've been a fucking fool for the last time out here. These niggas keep trying me," she grumbled to herself.

The traffic in downtown Baltimore was horrendous, bumper to bumper, and Charlie certainly didn't have time for this while anxiety crept into her mind. The call she'd received had sent her spiraling. Just the thought of it made Charlie's skin crawl like a million spiders were on her. She laid on her car horn again. Even that sound ground her nerves down to a pulp.

"Oh, my God, fucking drive!" Charlie screamed as if all of the stopped cars could somehow hear her. Traffic only inched forward. "Ugh! Come on! Fuck!"

Charlie had been here before, in a crazed-mind state over a dude. It was the story of her life—meet a dude, fuck a dude, find out dude ain't shit, get heartbroken by dude. Charlie shuddered just thinking about it. She couldn't understand why this had become her life script. Was she just totally unlovable? She'd asked herself that time and time again. What was it about her that made her an easy target? Charlie wasn't sure she even knew the definition of love. Even her mother hadn't ever told her she loved her. Charlie hadn't received hugs or kisses or love as a child. Emerson, one of her best friends, had once told Charlie that she was so desperate for love because she'd been lacking it all of her life. Charlie had dismissed it, but now she was thinking maybe it was true. She was never going to find real love.

This time though, Charlie had thought her new man, Jace, was the one. He had all the makings of the perfect guy for Charlie. Jace was tall, dark, handsome, and paid. He was a music producer and he drove not one but two luxury cars. Charlie had been immediately smitten when she'd met Jace. He'd approached her like a perfect gentleman, and once Charlie had noticed his blinging Rolex watch, she was all in right then and there.

Charlie had tried her best not to chase Jace, a mistake she'd made in the past. Charlie had even switched it up. She'd waited six whole weeks before she gave Jace some ass. Emerson and Mikayla had applauded her for waiting so long. Well, so long for Charlie's past record. But now Charlie was crushed. She'd taken off a day of work just like Jace had asked. Charlie had bathed in her special almond-scented shower gel. It was Jace's favorite. She'd ordered some breakfast from Corner Bakery for them and set a good romantic scene for them. Jace worked at night, so Charlie often saw him early in the mornings. Charlie had changed her sexy lingerie four times before her cell phone had rung. Dancing to Monica and Keyshia Cole's song "Trust," Charlie had picked up her phone and answered slightly out of breath.

"Hey, baby," she had said. She'd seen Jace's pet name, New Bae Forever, on the screen.

"This ain't your baby," a woman's voice filtered through Charlie's cell phone speaker.

Her heart had jerked. "Hello?" Charlie replied incredulously.

"Are you fucking Jace?" the woman's voice had barked in Charlie's ear. "Because I'm his girlfriend, and I find it strange that your number comes up in his call log even though he has you saved as 'client four.'"

Client four! Charlie's legs had threatened to give out, and she flopped down on her oversized couch. Her insides felt like a grenade had gone off in the center of her chest.

"Jace never told me about you," Charlie said too weakly for her liking. She had felt weak as soon as she said it because there was nothing stronger to say. It had happened again. A dude had duped her. This was not the first time Charlie had been in this hood bullshit situation with some bitch calling her about a man.

"Well, I'm telling you about me, bitch," the woman had barked in Charlie's ear.

Charlie was back on her feet and bouncing like a boxer. "What? Don't call me a bitch because you can't control your dog-ass man!" she retorted. "How stupid do you sound calling me? You should be asking your man about me, bitch!"

"I will fuck you up! Straight up, I'm from West Baltimore proper, not Baltimore County, you bird bitch!" the woman shot back.

"Oh, a'ight. You think you fucking with a weak bitch! I'll be right there to see just how fucking bad you are, bitch!"

"I'm waiting, too!" the woman shot back.

"Wait then, bitch! I'll be there in a flash!" Charlie had screamed.

Charlie had spun in circles trying to find something to put on. Fighting clothes. She hadn't worn fighting clothes in years, maybe since her early high school days. Charlie's heart was crushed and her ego was bruised, so she wasn't thinking straight.

Now just thinking about that earlier conversation and then looking out into the traffic made her blood pressure rise. "Fuck!" Charlie screamed again.

Charlie's phone rang again. When she saw Jace's pet name appear on her car's screen, Charlie's head felt like it would explode. She hit the answer button.

"Listen, bitch," Charlie answered, her voice quivering with anger. Jace's voice came through the speakers and filled Charlie's car. Charlie felt her scalp itch like someone was stabbing her with little pins. She narrowed her eyes as she listened. Just hearing Jace's voice reminded Charlie of the earlier call from his woman.

"Listen, Cee," Jace said evenly, calling Charlie by the nickname he had given her. "I . . . I can explain this whole thing." The car speakers vibrated with the sound of Jace's voice, and Charlie thought her head would explode.

"Explain? Nigga, you're a piece of shit!" Charlie exploded, biting into the side of her cheek. Charlie wished she were in front of Jace right then. She would've loved to give him the world's biggest bitch slap across the face.

"It's complicated," Jace whispered, which told Charlie his bitch was still there.

"Oh, well, it's about to get much more complicated. I'll be there in a few minutes because nobody, I mean nobody, makes me out to be a punk bitch," she said through clenched teeth.

"You can't come here," Jace said. "Just don't. It won't go well for you."

Charlie slammed her fists on the steering wheel. She felt like Jace had reached into her chest and snatched her heart out. She was crushed. But she needed to see him one last time. Charlie didn't know if she wanted to spit in his face, punch him in the face, or just lay eyes on his face.

That's how she was. She always needed closure no matter how painful it was. Seeking closure had cost Charlie
lots of painful experiences over the years. With the end
of this relationship, Charlie would be right back where
she'd started when she met Jace—alone, depressed, dick-
less, and with her biological clock ringing the alarm. The
mere thought of it made Charlie want to get to Jace and
his bitch even more.

"I hate you," she grumbled under her breath. Her
thoughts spurred her actions on even more. Charlie
swerved her car out of the lane she was in to try to ma-
neuver through the gridlock. She didn't care anymore.
She needed to get this ass whooping she was about to
hand out over with. Charlie hit the gas, swung right, and
accelerated forward. A horn sounded from somewhere,
and Charlie hit the gas again just as her car collided with
another with a loud bang.

Charlie screamed as her body flew forward. She felt
like someone had kicked her in the chest. Charlie was
shaken up. She felt like she'd just taken a beating before
she'd even gotten a chance to get to the fight. "What the . . ."
she huffed, her head immediately spinning.

Suddenly, Charlie heard loud screaming and banging.
She blinked her eyes, trying to get them to focus. She
couldn't seem to locate the source of the noise. Maybe it
was the pain stabbing through her head or the tightness
taking over her chest.

"What the fuck are you doing? You stupid-ass bitch!"
A large, scowling, man-looking woman came into focus
in front of Charlie's windshield. The woman's facial
features were hard, and she looked like she was out for
blood. Charlie heard more banging and noticed there
was another woman banging on the other side of her car.
The women pounded on Charlie's car hood and screamed
profanities at her. Her heart throttled up.

"Now you just fucked us even longer in this traffic!" the big woman boomed. "And you fucked up my car!"

Charlie's heart leapt into her throat when the driver's side door of her car suddenly flew open. Before she could react, Charlie felt herself being forcefully dragged from behind the wheel by the two women. She tried to hold on to the steering wheel as her anchor, but her grip was too weak. Her body was pulled from the car like she weighed nothing.

"Get off of me! Get the fuck off of me!" Charlie shrieked, swinging her arms wildly to defend herself. She was prepared for a fight, but not this kind of fight. Charlie tried to duck back into the car, but the first woman gripped her tightly while the other one got in her face. Charlie wasn't prepared or else she would've grabbed her stun gun from the car's middle console.

Charlie kicked her feet and caught the first woman in the gut. Charlie's kick didn't do anything. It wasn't like when she'd learned to kick men in the balls. A man hit in the balls would fold like a house of cards, but a woman who looked like a man . . . well, the kick didn't do a thing.

"You stupid bitch!" the second woman snarled, grabbing a fistful of Charlie's hair.

"Get the fuck away from me!" Charlie howled, punching the second woman somewhere close to her chin. That caused the woman to let Charlie go. The smaller woman hadn't bargained for all five foot nine inches and 170 pounds of Charlie Dixon. She'd learned really young in the hoods of Baltimore how to defend herself.

"You fucking hit my car!" the first woman spat.

"And now I'ma fuck you up!" Charlie screamed. "Get the fuck away from me!" Charlie bounced on wobbly legs, with one sneaker missing, trying to compose herself. She smoothed down her T-shirt with her trembling hands and reached up to her hairline to assess the damage to her head. The impact of the accident and these chicks had her head spinning. Charlie got into a fighting stance, and that backed the two women up a little bit, but it didn't do much to send them back to their car.

"What the fuck were you doing coming over to my lane?" the man-looking woman growled, jutting an accusing finger in Charlie's face. "You should learn how to fucking drive, you dumb ho!"

With sweat beads running a race down her back, Charlie shifted her weight to the foot with the sneaker still on and stood her ground. Her lips curled upward, and she put her hands on her hips. "I was trying to get you fucking pussies to drive out here! You think somebody got time to sit in traffic? I got somewhere I need to be! You want to look like a man, act like one and drive, bitch!" Charlie said indignantly, not letting these women intimidate her. She even ignored the pain in her head and chest.

"Somebody needs to shut that big mouth of yours," the other woman said, putting her hand up in Charlie's face.

"It won't be neither one of y'all," Charlie snapped back, boldly swiping the woman's finger from her face. The woman curled her hands into fists and moved in on Charlie. The other woman moved in too, like Charlie should know they planned on taking her down together.

Charlie steeled herself, lowered her stance, and put her fists up like a mixed martial arts fighter. She was waiting for those bitches to flex. She'd taken hits in her lifetime from dudes bigger than them. Charlie was fearless. She clenched her jaw, waiting for the first blow. She'd set out an hour earlier ready to fight anyway. These chicks didn't know just who the fuck they were messing with. Charlie had all kinds of angry energy coursing through her body at that moment.

"Charlie?" a man said from behind her. "Is that you?"

Charlie recognized the voice but only slightly turned her head toward it because she didn't want to risk the two women sneak attacking her.

"What's going on here? You all right?"

"Mason. Oh, my God. Can you believe these bitches are trying to jump me?" Charlie said, her words coming out on puffs of relieved breaths. Her body relaxed a bit at the sight of Mason. "This man-looking bitch actually dragged me out of my car, and now they both want to fight me!"

"Were the two of y'all really going to jump on a lady half y'all size?" Mason asked the two chicks. "BPD. I'd back it up if I were the both of you," Mason said, flashing his Baltimore Police Department badge.

"Yeah, back it up." Charlie smirked, feeling vindicated in the moment. Mason wasn't in uniform, but still his authority could be felt. It wrapped around Charlie like a warm blanket. It was an odd feeling, but it lingered with her for a few minutes. It was kind of like the feeling of being saved by a knight in shining armor.

"She . . . she hit my car," the big bull woman stammered, her voice a low murmur. It was a much softer tone than she'd used with Charlie just seconds before. Charlie loved how that little tin police badge reduced the Big Bad Wolf to a baby pup.

Charlie rolled her eyes. *Punk bitches!* If it didn't make her look simple, she would've stuck her tongue out at the women. "How fast our tune changes," Charlie mumbled with attitude.

"Why don't we just get you two to exchange information for insurance purposes and handle this civilly before a bunch of squad cars show up and everyone gets arrested? I'll take all the information and create a police accident report when I'm back at work. You'll both get a copy. No harm, no foul," Mason said calmly, clearly commanding the situation.

Charlie smiled a little. Who knew Mason was like this? Mason Dayle had been married to one of Charlie's besties, Emerson, for years, but Charlie had never really paid him close attention until now. Charlie had listened to Emerson complain about Mason over the past year, but in that moment, Charlie wasn't seeing any of the things Emerson had been bitching on her husband about. From Charlie's vantage point, Mason was really a strong man's man. He was kind of sexy, too.

Charlie shook her head a little. What was she thinking? She couldn't be attracted to Mason! *Mason? He's Emerson's soon-to-be ex-husband, for God's sake!* Charlie had known him for years but never really knew him. He was like a brother to her, just like Emerson was like her sister. Charlie shook her head again. Mason can't be sexy in her eyes. Those were the rules of the girl code she shared with Emerson and Mikayla. Period.

After the information exchange, Mason offered to drive Charlie's beat-up car to the nearest repair garage. He said she could follow in his car, but he warned her not to wreck his car. They both laughed.

"Thanks so much, Mason. Either I was about to get laid out or those two bitches was about to get dragged together, and ultimately we were all going to jail," Charlie joked.

"It's what I do, keep the peace," Mason said, winking at her. They were both probably thinking the same thing: just not at home.

There was a minute or two of awkward silence between Charlie and Mason. It was like something unknown hummed around them. It was strange, but Charlie shook it off. She was used to that, too, pretending her feelings didn't matter or just ignoring that she could feel altogether.

Charlie cleared her throat to help herself swallow the crazy lump that had developed in it.

"I can give you a ride to wherever you were headed before the accident," Mason offered.

Suddenly, Charlie remembered that she was on her way to kick Jace's girlfriend's ass. Her face lit up red with shame. She shook her head in shame and bit her bottom lip.

"What? What did I say?" Mason asked, noticing.

Charlie let out a long sigh, still shaking her head. "Promise you won't laugh if I tell you."

Mason raised his right hand. "Promise."

"No, like double promise," Charlie said, hands on her hips.

Mason chuckled. "Well, damn. Okay. I doubly promise not to laugh."

"I was going to beat a bitch up," Charlie said, almost whispering.

"Huh? I can't hear you," he said, leaning in toward her mouth.

"I said, I was going to beat a bitch up," Charlie said louder. She closed her eyes and shook her head.

Mason busted out laughing.

"Oh, my God! You said you promised," Charlie whined, half laughing too.

"I'm sorry," Mason said through his laughter. "Are you serious? You were in your car, driving to beat a bitch up?" he asked, repeating the last part of what she said verbatim.

Charlie rolled her eyes. "Crazy, right?" she mumbled. "I need a damn life."

"Join the club," Mason said, exchanging a long stare with Charlie. They both knew what he meant by that.

Charlie lowered her eyes to her one sneaker. *What are you doing, Charlie? What are you doing?*

Chapter 2

Emerson

Emerson lay on her side in the dark, staring out of her bedroom window at the night as she had done every night for the past few months. She hadn't gotten much sleep since she and Mason had separated and decided to get a divorce. Emerson was so used to him coming in and climbing into bed at night that she didn't realize how hard it would be to sleep without him. The divorce was in the process of being hammered out, and Emerson was sure it was what she wanted, but that didn't change how hard it was to really get to a new normal. Mason was the only man Emerson had ever known. She actually couldn't remember far back enough to a time when Mason wasn't part of her life.

Emerson and Mason had grown up together. They'd been born a few months apart, were neighbors who played together, got educated together, dated when they'd gotten old enough, and then married one another. Emerson couldn't remember one day since she was about three years old that she didn't see Mason or at least speak to him. They were real childhood sweethearts. Over the years, they'd loved hard, and as of late, fought even harder. But nothing beat the very last fight they'd had. That night, Emerson knew things had gone beyond repair with her and Mason. Emerson shifted uncomfortably on the bed, closed her eyes, and thought about it now.

"This event is going to be packed with all A-list celebrities. It took years, but I've finally busted through that glass ceiling," Emerson bragged as she moved in and out of her big walk-in closet, trying to pick the perfect outfit for her very first real celebrity event. *"It just feels like I am finally being blessed for my years of sacrifices. I mean, I needed this, finally stepping out with something I can call my own, you know? It feels damned good, too. Everyone is so proud of me. But nobody is prouder of me than me."*

Emerson was going on as she stepped out of the closet and turned around to find Mason still lying in bed. *"What time are you going to get ready, Mason?"* Emerson paused, frowning. *"Why aren't you getting dressed? I picked up your tux and it's ready."*

"Because I'm not going," Mason droned flatly.

"What? What are you talking about, Mason?" Emerson asked, annoyed. She wasn't even going to give him a minute to add anything to the conversation. *"Just stop playing. I don't have time for antics today. This night is very important to me, so end of story,"* Emerson grumbled, walking over to her vanity, picking up her perfume, and spraying it all over in a show of defiance.

Things had been tense with her and Mason since she'd miscarried for the fifth time and told him she wasn't going to try anymore. Instead, she'd started an Instagram page for fashion and gossip blogging that had taken off like a rocket. Her social media presence was her new baby. Her new celebrity status was giving her the life she'd always dreamed about. No more being just someone's wife and accepting the scraps of his notoriety.

"Antics? I'm serious. I'm not going. I worked overtime, and I don't feel like being around a bunch of phony internet celebrities who don't really live like what they put out there," Mason grumbled. *"I see real-life shit in my*

real job every day. I can't stomach all that fake-life shit. People out here on the streets dying, and y'all worrying about posting what you ate for breakfast for likes? Nah, I can't do the phony shit. Not today. I'm not going. But I wish you the best, Emerson. I really do."

Emerson had finally stopped moving and stared straight across the room at her husband. The knot that had formed in her chest finally unraveled like a ball of yarn pushed forcefully across a shiny floor. "The hell you're not. You're going to get the fuck up and get dressed right now. I will not attend such a big media event without you. This is important to me. Something of my own, finally. You will not put me under your foot anymore. Isn't it bad enough that you don't support me at all? I can't share anything with you. I can't confide in you. I can't get you to support anything I do. Let's not even mention that you live, eat, sleep, and shit your piece of shit real job while it was my fake internet money that got us through when that funky-ass department wouldn't give your dumb pawn ass a promotion." Emerson spewed her feelings, her finger jutting accusingly at Mason. She wasn't holding in her feelings anymore for his sake. His sake was what had made her waste so many years to begin with.

Over the years, Emerson had grown tired of being referred to just as "Mason's wife." She had tried being a stay-at-home wife with no career of her own so that he could feel like the man. But those days were over. She was independent, and she was expecting him to respect it and respect her.

"Oh, I'm a pawn now?" Mason repeated, sitting up on the side of the bed. "That's what you're going with, Emerson? I bust my ass to give you everything, and I'm a pawn out there risking my fucking life?"

Emerson saw hurt flash in his eyes. Emerson recognized that look, but she didn't care. He needed a dose of the truth, and she was tired of living her life sugarcoating shit.

"That's what I said! You're a fucking pawn! I've given up a lot of years like the good wife, but big, bad you, cop extraordinaire, couldn't support me, not once," Emerson spat. "Not even once! For years I sat by and let you try to be the big man. I put on a happy face in public. But what about me? Your job is all you care about. I have been the glue holding us together all these years. Well, fuck that. No more! Now you will get the fuck out of the bed and get fucking dressed and support me for fucking once!"

Mason closed his eyes and exhaled a windstorm of breath. Emerson could tell he was trying to compose himself.

"Really?" he snarled. He was up now. "You're going to act like everything is my fault? I wanted a family, but you don't see me saying anything about you as a woman not being able to give me one. Is it so hard, Emerson? Is it so hard to follow your vows and be an obedient wife, give a nigga a few kids, and make house?"

Emerson chortled to keep from doubling over at the waist from Mason's low-cutting words. He had hit low for the last time. Everyone saw Mason as Mr. Nice Guy, but Emerson knew he had a mean streak that couldn't be matched. He knew the right words to say. But so did she.

"Maybe my body just didn't take to your blighted sperm, Mason. You ever thought about that? Maybe God didn't think a man with an unfit mother and a drug-addicted father should reproduce! Maybe it was God's will I never carried a pregnancy to term, and you know what? I'm fucking glad I never did," Emerson spat

maliciously. She wanted to hurt him back. In that moment, Emerson didn't care if they'd ever recover from the word stabs they exchanged that night.

Mason jerked his head back as if Emerson's words had landed like a professional boxer's uppercut to his chin. In one swift motion, Mason was in Emerson's face. "Don't you ever throw dirt on my mother's name," Mason said through gritted teeth, breathing in her face, tears rimming his eyes.

Emerson slapped him across the face and then pushed him hard in the chest. Out of pure instinct, Mason grabbed her by the collar of her dress and held her tightly.

"Let me go, Mason!" she screamed. "Get your fucking hands off of me!"

"Don't do this, Emerson," Mason grunted in her face. Then he released his grip on her with a shove, sending her stumbling back. He shook his head.

"I can't believe this is us. All of these years . . . Do we hate each other this much? Huh, Eme?" he croaked.

Emerson sobbed so hard it took her a few seconds to gather herself. "Yeah, you made us come to this. You did," Emerson cried.

"Me? I made us come to this? So you're innocent, Emerson? You never made any mistakes in this thing we call a marriage?" Mason asked, lowering his voice into a growl. Mason swiped his hands over his face.

Tears leaked from Emerson's eyes, and she couldn't move for a few minutes. She could barely catch her breath, and her entire body felt tense. Mason was distraught too. Although he had only grabbed her roughly, she could tell he felt terrible. As a cop, he'd seen hundreds of domestic violence incidents. He'd never envisioned himself reduced to that. Mason had never done anything like that before.

"You will learn," Emerson rasped, barely able to get the words out. "You won't ever have to put your hands on me again," she proclaimed. Then, as if she were possessed by a devil, Emerson rushed into their closet and began pulling all of Mason's clothes from the hangers. She whirled around, swiped his watch collection off the shelf, and tossed his high-priced sneaker collection out the door. "Get out!" Emerson screamed. "I don't want you here! I don't love you anymore!"

Mason was stunned. He put his hands up, immediately sorry for grabbing his wife roughly. But it was too late. Emerson was ablaze. She stalked out of their closet with an armful of Mason's things. She tossed them over the banister and down the steps.

"I said get the fuck out! I swear, Mason, I will set all of this shit on fire. I will burn it down!" Emerson had screamed. The thin string of sanity she'd been grasping at in the weeks leading up to that day had finally popped and curled over. The entire scene was like some shit out of Waiting to Exhale. *It was the kind of shit that happened in movies, not to her.*

Emerson carried on. She kicked and flailed her arms and cursed and spat. Inside she felt like dying. She'd been struck by a sudden burst of angry energy that had no place else to be released but on Mason. She behaved like a woman possessed by an evil spirit. It was over. She was sure of it then.

Mason tried to reason with her, but nothing would stop her. Emerson swiped the tears off her cheeks roughly and stalked over to a pile of Mason's things. She scooped up an armful while he watched, still too stunned to really react. Emerson ran down the stairs of their home, opened their front door, and began tossing all of Mason's stuff outside. She did that until sweat covered her entire body.

"I can't believe you're doing all of this," Mason said, wounded.

"This is just the beginning, Mason Dayle!" she screamed from the door. Emerson had lost it. Not even medication could help her in that moment. She didn't give a fuck who had heard her. She was a woman possessed.

Now, in the darkness, Emerson flipped over again. The thoughts of that night haunted her almost every night. She played out several ways she could've prevented it or ways Mason could've just complied with her wishes and attended the event. How hard was it to support your own wife? How hard would it have been for her to calm her own temper? Emerson had to admit to herself, it was the first step backward mentally she'd taken in years prior to losing it that night. She had felt deep down in her soul that there would be no coming back from it. Fast-forward one month, twenty days, and sixteen hours later, and she was right.

Emerson twisted over onto her right side and picked up her cell phone to check the time. 2:11 a.m. She sighed. There was no use fighting it. Insomnia had won again. She'd had acupuncture earlier that day. She'd heard it helped with insomnia. No such luck. Even a full day of work and planning more business strategies hadn't helped. She was exhausted, but sleep wouldn't settle with her at all.

Emerson sat up and looked over at the empty spot on the opposite side of the king-sized bed. It was where Mason had slept for the six years they'd been in their new house. There were a lot of nights Emerson had slept alone when Mason had to work a double, but there was something about the finality of it now that made her a little uneasy inside.

She hugged herself and sighed, then threw her legs over the side of the bed and slid her feet into her plush slippers. She shrugged into her sleek robe and headed out into the hallway. She wouldn't need this big house after all. Emerson shrugged. It didn't matter how much life planning she'd done when she was in her twenties. Everything in her life was totally different now.

Downstairs, she flipped on the kitchen light and walked to the refrigerator. She wasn't hungry, but maybe a glass of warm milk would make her sleepy.

"Damn. Mason usually does the shopping," Emerson grumbled as she held open the refrigerator doors and scanned the barely there contents of her refrigerator. She shook her head in disgust, finally reaching in and grabbing the fat-free organic almond milk. Emerson put the container up to her nose to make sure it was still safe to drink. She turned around for a glass.

"Ah!" She jumped so hard the milk slid from her hand onto the floor with a splash. "Oh, my God, Ma. You scared the hell out of me," Emerson gasped, moving in circles to find something to clean up the spilled milk.

She'd forgotten that her mother, Anna, had come to stay with her for a little while. Her mother had been worried about her with everything going on with Mason and the whirlwind of her new celebrity career. Her mother was an alarmist, but sometimes Emerson indulged her "mothering" so that she could eventually get rid of her.

"Um no, you scared the hell out of me," her mother huffed, rushing over to help Emerson clean up the mess.

"Why are you up?" Emerson asked, genuinely flummoxed by her mother's presence in her kitchen at two in the morning.

"Couldn't sleep," her mother complained. "Took an Ambien and even that didn't do the trick. I guess it's being out of my own bed. Or maybe worrying about you."

Emerson stood up with the last of the dripping-wet paper towels held out in front of her and rushed to the garbage can. "Join the club," she said. "I don't think I've had a good night's sleep in weeks."

Her mother looked at her through worried eyes with arched eyebrows.

Emerson held up her hand in front of her. "I'm okay, Ma. I have a handle on things, and if I need to, I'll take the medication."

Her mother's shoulders slumped slightly with relief. "What's the doctor saying about it?" her mother pried, regarding her daughter suspiciously as she climbed onto one of the barstools that sat in front of the kitchen island.

"He's seen me often and knows that I know what to do if I get into crisis. You know he's good like that," Emerson lied, avoiding eye contact with her mother. "I'm telling you, I have a handle on it. No crazy thoughts. No blue moods. A little insomnia, but that's about it. Definitely not the manic mania episodes you're probably expecting."

Her mother tilted her head slightly and studied Emerson for a few seconds. She crumpled a piece of paper towel in her left hand: her go-to nervousness tic.

"You know, Eme, I had that same vacant, empty look in my eyes when I was going through my divorce from your father. I couldn't stand spending all of my nights alone. The hurt and pain back then of knowing you'd be in a broken home, the thought of people talking about me . . . But I also didn't suffer from severe depression with suicidal ideations or have any signs of bipolar disorder, you know. I never had to worry about that sort of thing when I got sad," her mother said levelly. "And not taking your medications—"

Emerson whirled around on the balls of her feet. Her eyebrows were low on her face, her lips flattened into a straight line. She hated that her mother wouldn't just let things go. The past was the past. "What? What are you talking about?" Emerson retorted. "I . . . I don't—" she started.

"Listen, sweetheart. We've pretended long enough."
Her mother eased down from the barstool. "I know you
haven't been on the medication. I'm your mother. I know
when you're different. I know when you're suffering,"
her mother said straight, moving around the counter
toward Emerson. "You're even doing the thing with the
food again. And, remember, the insomnia is the biggest
indicator."

Emerson's face flushed red. She opened her mouth
to speak, but her mother continued without letting her
say a word. "I know all of the signs. I see the mania in
your eyes. I hear the fake joy in your words," her mother said, placing both of her hands on Emerson's shoulders. "We've been here before. Remember? I am aware
of who you are at all times. You're my baby, Emerson. I
just want you to be okay."

Emerson swallowed hard and pulled away from her
mother. She had ten different defenses on the tip of
her tongue, but she couldn't speak. She shook her head
from side to side and turned her back toward her mother. She pointed, but the words wouldn't come out. Tears
welled up in her eyes.

"I know what you want to say, but understand my plight
as a mother watching you suffer. I won't do it, Emerson,
unless I absolutely have to. But you have to do your part,"
her mother said, looking at Emerson's hunched shoulders.

Emerson sighed loudly. She'd seen this coming as soon
as her mother had arrived. It was always the big elephant
in the corner of the room. Her secret. Her past. Her
Achilles' heel. It was always swirling around them like a
hive of attack bees. The secret. Her secret. A secret that
she couldn't afford to get out there now that she was a
celebrity of sorts. Her perfect persona had to stay intact.
It was how she made her living now, and nothing and no

one could destroy that. Emerson closed her eyes, took a deep breath, and let it out loudly.

"Listen, I am your mother. Do you understand? I am your mother, and I will not stand idly by again and risk losing you, Emerson. Do you understand what I am saying to you? Do you?" Her mother shook her head, her jaw going stiff as she spoke her words through tears.

Emerson's cheeks were streaked with tears. She swiped at them roughly. "Why are you bringing up the past right now?" Emerson croaked. "I'm past all of that. I'm currently the biggest thing on the internet. I have over two hundred thousand people following me and using my life as an example. I get paid to be an example now. Why would you want to bring up that old stuff and ruin it?" Emerson said through clenched teeth, still not looking at her mother.

"What happened to you affects me every day, Emerson. I'm always worried. Even when Mason was here with you, I worried and worried. But now, with everything, with you being alone with no one, I can't stand to think of it," her mother said.

"Stop it! Okay? Stop bringing it up! It's the past!" Emerson said through gritted teeth, her nostrils flaring. Every time her mother was upset with anything, she'd bring up the past. Emerson wanted to move beyond it forever.

Her mother swallowed the lump in her throat. "You're right. I'm sorry, baby girl. I just get so worried. I've always wanted better for you, Eme. Looking at you now, I'm worried. I won't lie. You won't even eat like you're supposed to. I realize it is my fault you never saw a happy marriage. It's my fault you don't even know what a happy home looks like," her mother said sadly.

"I'm fine. Marriage is not for everyone. Fortunately, I am not you, and he is not Daddy. I'm getting a divorce because I want to. You got a divorce because Daddy left you. There is a difference," Emerson spat cruelly, spinning around to face her mother.

Her mother flinched, and her back went straight. "That is just your pain talking," her mother said firmly. "You don't mean that."

Emerson's eyes hooded over. She'd had enough. "No. This is *your* pain talking. I've watched you pretend to be happy my entire life. You never let anyone outside of your marriage know if things are not right. You make believe until you believe it yourself. You said that," Emerson growled, pointing at her mother's face.

"If he hadn't left you, you would've continued to be married although you weren't happy. I believed everything you said. I took your lessons and learned how to put on a brave face each and every day. I stayed with Mason for years knowing we had outgrown one another. You can't come into my home and try to fix anything for me. I am the only one who can. And about my past, you better keep it to yourself. I have a whole new life, and that is not a part of it. That is my private business, and it not for public consumption. I am changed. I have a handle on things whether you want to believe it or not," Emerson hissed. "You can go home when you're ready, because what I won't do is pretend that I really want you here."

Her mother's mouth sagged at the corners. "Eme," she whispered gruffly, her voice filled with pity and her eyes rimmed with tears. "That's your sickness talking, sweetheart."

Emerson laughed a raucous laugh that was so out of place in that moment it sent chills down her own spine. "Oh, I'm the only one who's sick? Trust me, you were sick long before I was, Mother," Emerson said emphatically. "For one, I'm not a pathetic slug of a woman with no mind of her own, no friends, whose highlight in life is wishing a mental breakdown on her only child so she can have a purpose in life. Is it so hard for you to believe that, for once, I am in control of my life? Me! Not you. Not Mason. Not Daddy. Me. That's something you could never say about yourself," Emerson said harshly.

Her mother bristled and took a few steps backward like Emerson had actually slapped her in the face. "I just want to help—" her mother started, reaching her hands out toward Emerson.

Emerson put her hands up, halting her mother's touch. "You know what? You've helped me enough." Emerson squinted her eyes into dashes. "I think you should consider a hotel or maybe a trip back home. That would definitely help," she said firmly. With that, she stormed past her mother and out of the kitchen. Emerson closed her eyes, and her jaw rocked feverishly as tears of hurt danced down her face.

"I'll leave, but that doesn't mean I'll give up. I will not see you hurt again!" her mother yelled at her back.

Emerson paused her steps for a second. She clenched her fists so tightly her nails dug moon-shaped craters into her hands. "Go home!" Emerson yelled back. She was in control. For now.

Chapter 3

Mikayla

Mikayla sat at her kitchen table, staring out of the glass patio doors that connected to her back deck. The sun was shining, but somehow it still seemed like a drab day to her. Mikayla had never imagined her life would turn out this way. She had thanked God as many times as she could. It was a good life, and when she thought about where she'd come from and where she was now, something inside of her gave her the strength to keep fighting through, no matter how hard things got. Mikayla often wondered if, had she done things any differently, she would be sitting in a house with everything she needed. Mikayla had daydreamed of living like this as a child.

She heard the toilet flush upstairs. Mikayla looked at the clock on the wall oven and scrambled to her feet. "Fuck," she huffed. She was late with her regular routine. That might not go over so well. She rushed around the kitchen and started preparing breakfast. Mikayla made sure to put 110 percent in everything she did. She wanted to always make sure she was that perfect mother and perfect wife, even if it wasn't always appreciated.

Mikayla's cell phone buzzing on the table startled her. Someone calling her at 8:00 a.m. would surely send off a red flag if Charles heard it. "Hello," Mikayla whispered into the phone. "Damian?"

Mikayla's heart began pounding in her chest. She furrowed her brows, confused. She removed the phone from her ear to look at the small display screen. It read, unknown.

"Damian?" Mikayla inquired again. Suddenly the sound of the voice and the words that followed seemed to slap Mikayla in the face. A flash of heat came over her body, and her hands shook.

"What? What do you mean?" she whispered, nervously looking around for any sign of Charles.

Mikayla closed her eyes and held the phone so tightly her knuckles turned white. She wanted so badly to hang up, but something inside of her wouldn't let her do it. The phone call was one she knew would be coming sooner or later. Mikayla understood that she could run from her past for only so long.

Mikayla listened, although her ears were ringing. Mikayla stood with her back turned and her eyes closed, pain and memories flashing through her mind. Damian was her little brother, and he had been the person with Mikayla for some of the most horrible things she had been through, but he was also the person who had ultimately sacrificed it all for her.

Mikayla was lost in thought. Just then, Charles touched her shoulder. She almost jumped out of her skin.

"Good morning. Is breakfast ready?" Charles asked, looking his wife up and down strangely.

Mikayla knew him so well she could almost predict what his next question would be, so she was one step ahead of him. "Yes, you can just hold the cupcakes for me, and I will be there to pick them up in an hour," Mikayla said deceptively into the phone receiver. "Yes, I will be there when you open," Mikayla said, her hands so sweaty she almost lost her grip on the phone. She held the phone to her ear a little longer. Her mind raced with questions, and her nerves were rattled, but she had to pull it together.

"What are you ordering cupcakes for?" Charles asked suspiciously.

Mikayla knew he really wanted to know who she was on the phone with. She took a deep breath, did her best to calm her nerves, spun around, and continued her lie. "It's teacher appreciation at Zuri's school. I wanted to do one thing for all of the teachers at one time," she fabricated on the spot.

"Do that stuff on your own time. I'm late as it is, and I don't have all day. I need breakfast," Charles said sharply, cracking his knuckles.

"Sorry," Mikayla said, lowering her eyes. She hurried, going about the business of preparing Charles's breakfast and making sure not to make him any more upset than he appeared.

All the way back from dropping off her kids, Mikayla's hands shook. The call that had come into her cell phone earlier still had her shaken up. She couldn't really focus, haunted by thoughts from her past as she sped home. She forgot all about her daily errands, including picking up Charles's suits from the cleaners.

Mikayla had made Charles breakfast and rushed up to her bedroom after the call. She'd sat in silence, dazed and unable to move for God knew how long. That meant she was late getting the girls to school and also getting things ready for Charles before he left for work, a fact that made Mikayla's stomach lurch now. Charles wasn't one to forget things. He might not say something at the moment, but Mikayla knew he'd bring it up at some point and it wouldn't be easy. The combination of the call and antic-

ipation of what mood Charles might be in left Mikayla
sick. She pulled over twice to dry heave, which cost her
even more time getting back home. All she could do was
pray that Charles would be gone and that he'd work late.

"Why? Why would God do this right now?" Mikayla
mumbled to herself as all sorts of thoughts ran through
her mind. Damian said he was getting released from pris-
on. Mikayla had been sending money for his appeals, but
she never thought it would work. She'd only snuck and
sent the money to keep up her end of their bargain. Damian being released meant that Mikayla's secret would
be walking and talking in front of her every day. All she
wanted was to move on with her life cleanly. No attach-
ments to the past. She thought she'd made it out, and
because she hadn't looked back, she felt safe in her new
life, no matter how unpredictable things in her life could
be on most days.

The phone call had brought back memories Mikayla
had worked hard to suppress. Mikayla couldn't help
but have flashbacks of what she'd been through. The
thoughts made her stomach cramp harder than child-
birth labor pains. Mikayla actually felt sick again, but she
knew pulling over again wasn't an option. She looked at
the dashboard clock, and her heart rate sped up.

Finally pulling up to her house, Mikayla scrambled out
of the car and rushed up the driveway. She didn't feel like
fighting. Not today. As she fumbled through her pocketbook for her keys, her eyes darted around nervously.
Charles's car was missing from the driveway, a good sign.
That meant Mikayla could be alone with her thoughts.
Letting out a deep, relieved breath, Mikayla finally lo-
cated her keys. Still uneasy from the phone call, Mikayla
looked over her shoulder once more and rushed through
her front door.

As soon as she stepped inside, something hit her. A
bolt of lightning flashed behind Mikayla's eyes, and a

force beyond her control had taken hold of her. Her mind immediately went to the past. To the attack back then. To what she had done back then. That was impossible though. The phone call had just come today. No one could arrive on her doorstep that fast. Or could they?

With a scream stuck in the back of her throat choking her, and a brutal force pulling her down, Mikayla scrambled on the hardwood floor of the foyer. The motion caused her pocketbook strap to twist, making a tourniquet on her arm, cutting off her circulation. Another blow caused an unbearable pain in her head.

"Ahhh!" She was finally able to let out a bloodcurdling scream. She could hear a man's animalistic breathing. Instinctively, Mikayla placed her hands up in defense, but it was to no avail. Another blow to the top of her head caused the images again. Mikayla saw herself stumbling backward.

"You just can't do the right thing," Charles growled.

Mikayla felt a burst of heat in her chest. It wasn't an attacker. It wasn't a shadowy figure from her past. It was her husband. He was in one of those moods. He had promised never to do it again after the last set of broken bones and bruised body parts. Once again, he had lied.

"Charles, no!" Mikayla finally managed to scream.

"You can't fucking be a good wife to save your gotdamn life!" Charles growled as he wound her ponytail around his hands for a better grip. "All I ask for is loyalty! That's it! I give you everything you need! You give me nothing! You lie about everything!"

Mikayla let her body go limp. She knew the results of fighting against Charles. She'd done this dangerous encounter many times since they'd been together. It started off with a slap, then a few more slaps and punches, and then this—a full-on beating that wouldn't stop until he was exhausted.

"Where have you been?" he screamed, reaching under Mikayla's bowed head and slamming his balled fist into her face. "It don't take that long to drop off no kids. Who was you with? You didn't buy any fucking cupcakes. I checked every account! You're a liar!"

Blood sprayed from Mikayla's face like a lawn sprinkler, sending a fine dark red mist onto Charles's pants. Blood from her nose dripped into the back of her throat as he yanked her head back to look into her eyes. She could hardly breathe.

"Who is it? Who you fucking, bitch? Who you using my money to court with?"

"Charles, please! Don't, please!" Mikayla gasped, pleading as he dragged her across the floor farther into the house. She could feel the skin on her knees splitting. An open-handed slap landed on her cheek. Mikayla saw small, squirming flashes of light out of the sides of her eyes. Now she knew what people meant when they said they'd seen stars.

She was praying Charles didn't kick her or full-on body slam her this time. Mikayla was sure her ribs hadn't fully healed from the last time, and she feared that another kick or blow would surely send bone fragments into her heart or lungs and kill her instantly. The pain pulsing through her head became so unbearable that she placed her hand on top of the hand Charles had embedded in her hair.

"You keep making me do this shit, Kay! You keep on pushing me to this!" Charles roared, continuing his assault. He had to convince himself and her that he was justified in doing this. Mikayla was used to that too.

Mikayla knew that he would beat her until the demon that she was sure lived inside of him had finally had enough. He would reach down to the crumpled pile that was left of her and help her up off the floor. He would force her to have sex. Then he would be nice to her . . . for a while at least.

Charles dragged Mikayla toward the stairs. When she fought not to be taken upstairs, he punched her in the back, causing her to involuntarily emit a loud cough. He'd literally knocked the wind out of her. Urine ran down her legs. As she drifted to a place between consciousness and hell, she thought about her kids and silently thanked God they weren't there to see this.

When he was finally finished, Charles stood Mikayla up and helped her to the stairs, throwing her limp, injured arm around his neck and bearing her weight on his shoulders. His switch had been flipped. He was her husband now. The loving, caring one.

"I'm sorry. I just love you so much, Kay. I can't even think about you with another man. When I didn't find you here, it . . . it . . ." he whispered as he placed Mikayla on the floor of the bathroom so he could clean her up.

Mikayla struggled to breathe because every breath hurt. She felt like all of her ribs were broken. Her knees burned from the friction burns she had suffered from being dragged. As bad as she wanted to scream out or even moan, Mikayla did not want to take a chance on making him angry again. She'd just let him do whatever it was that made him feel better about what he'd done to her.

"Come here, let me help you clean up," Charles consoled in a low, soft voice, a complete contradiction of the man who had just attacked her. Mikayla kept her eyes closed. She lay in a fetal position, every inch of her body aching.

Charles went into the linen closet and got a hand towel. Mikayla could hear the water running. Then she felt warm rag against her battered skin.

"Ssss." She winced, shrinking away from his touch.

"I am so sorry," he said, wiping more blood from her face and neck. "You hear me, Kay? I said I'm sorry. It's just because I love you so much. I just lose it sometimes," he said, his voice quivering with the tears Mikayla expected. This wasn't at all new to her. If she didn't say something, he might turn on her again.

"I know you are. I forgive you," Mikayla whispered because it was all she knew how to do.

After she was cleaned up, Charles undressed her and put her in the bed. When he said he would stay home with her and take care of her, Mikayla knew what that meant. He was staying home to make sure she didn't call the police or her friends and tell them what happened. Mikayla was used to all of this. It wasn't ideal, but it was better than living like she had as a child. It was better to take those beatings than for her kids to live without like she had as a kid. What other choice did she have? Mikayla didn't see many options.

"I'll go get you something for the pain," Charles said like an angel.

Mikayla managed a halfhearted smile. What else could she do? If she acted ungrateful, it might set him off again. When Charles returned with the pills, Mikayla was happy to swallow them. Now she'd be able to escape into a drug-filled sleep.

Within fifteen minutes, Mikayla was thrust into a fitful sleep. The phone call still lingered in her subconscious, and her sleep took her to another place. It was a place she hated to revisit, even in her dreams.

"Ow! No! Mommy, please!" Mikayla screamed, curling her wet body into a fetal position, her back and the tops of her hands still exposed. The punches landed on her back with so much force she urinated on herself.

"Where is it?" her mother screamed. "Bitch. You better give it to me now!"

"I don't know! I don't have it! I swear!" Mikayla bawled as more painful blows rained down on her back.

"You got my money, and I need it! Now!" her mother hollered. She punched until she was too tired to continue. Mikayla sobbed. Her body throbbed. Her mother ranted and ranted, but Mikayla wasn't giving in this time. She needed to feed herself and her brother, and she didn't care anymore.

"Bitch! I said give me the money!" her mother screamed, ready to hit Mikayla again.

"I'm not giving you shit!" Mikayla screamed, finally getting the strength to stand up for herself. Mikayla had practiced for this moment. The last time her mother took all of the food stamps and welfare money and left her and her brother starving, Mikayla had decided she would fight back the next time. She was going to stand up for herself and her brother.

"What, you little bitch? Get the fuck dressed! Either that or your ass will be in the gotdamn streets!" her mother yelled back, pointing her finger in Mikayla's face, trying to leverage the same threat of homelessness against Mikayla that she always used.

"I don't care! Me and Damian have to eat! The money you get from the city is for us!" Mikayla ranted, sticking out her chest. She was tired of her mother's shit.

"You think you bad? Bitch, that's my money!" her mother spat, hitting her hand up against her chest for emphasis. "I'm the bitch who gave birth to y'all with no thanks or help from ya no-good daddies. And yours, that motherfucker lives right around the corner with his new family, and he knows who you are but ain't never give a fuck about you! He ain't proud you his! And I ain't either! Now give me my fucking money!"

Mikayla's chest heaved up and down. She had never met her father. Her mother had told her that he'd died in a car accident right after she was born. She didn't want to believe what she was saying.

"This ain't your money!" Mikayla screamed.

Her mother wasn't backing down. "I knew I should've had an abortion with you! From the time I was pregnant, I hated you! You ain't shit, and you ain't never gonna be shit!" her mother spat, the words dropping around Mikayla like small bombs, exploding in her ears.

That was it. Mikayla snapped. She pulled her fist back and punched her mother in the face. As frail and dope sick as she was, her mother didn't have time to react before Mikayla hit her again. Getting her bearings, her mother shook her head slightly and dug her fingers, nails first, into Mikayla's face like an attack cat.

"Aggh!" Mikayla belted out, but she kept fighting, grabbing her mother's hair and yanking her down toward the floor. They both fell. Her mother hit her head on the floor, and Mikayla's knees slammed in to the hard floor tiles. Mikayla swung wildly, throwing a bevy of wild punches. Her mother's mouth was bleeding as she struggled under Mikayla's weight.

"I hate you!" Mikayla screamed, going crazy, taking out years of frustration on her mother.

"Get the fuck off me!" her mother hollered as she thrashed, trying to break free. Suddenly, she bucked her body upward, throwing Mikayla forward. She was able to slip from under Mikayla. Scrambling up off the floor, her mother raced to the kitchen, where she grabbed a knife from the counter.

"You think you bad? Huh? You think you did something?" her mother asked as she charged at Mikayla with the knife. "You gon' die, bitch!" her mother growled, her eyes bugged out of the sockets.

Mikayla ran toward the front door, fumbling with the locks to get out as her crazed mother charged at her.

Mikayla felt the door slam behind her as she raced toward the stairwell. Mikayla took the stairs two at a time down to the first floor. When she made it outside, she noticed her belongings scattered on the patch of grass outside her building. Then Mikayla heard her mother's voice. She was at the window, cursing and throwing out all of Mikayla's clothes and personal belongings.

Mikayla stood there shivering and crying. Reality had hit her harder than her mother could ever have. Mikayla didn't know what she would do.

She ran across the street to the corner store and got a couple of plastic bags. After using her sleeve to wipe the snot and blood off her face, she hunched down and picked up as many of her few clothes and belongings as would fit in the bags. She didn't know where she would go, but one thing remained true: she still had the money. Her mother hadn't won. Mikayla had no idea where she was headed, but she boarded the bus toward downtown Baltimore. Mikayla told herself she had to get her little brother somehow and that after they were together, she would never live like that again. Ever.

Mikayla awoke from her nightmare with a start. Charles was standing over her, smiling. Mikayla's heart throttled up in her chest.

"I made you something to eat," he said sweetly.

Mikayla smiled painfully. She pointed to her swollen jaw and shook her head.

"You can eat it. That's just a little bruise," Charles said. He put the food down on the nightstand. "Eat up."

Mikayla struggled into a sitting position and sat on the side of the bed. Forcing herself, she took a spoonful of the soup.

"That's a good girl," Charles said in a low whisper. "You can be good when you want to be, Kay," he said.

Mikayla took another slurp from the spoon and realized that the pain in her mouth could never match the pain in her heart.

Chapter 4

Charlie, Emerson, Mikayla

Mikayla sat at her kitchen table, staring out of the large glass doors that led to her deck and backyard. It was the same place she'd been the day she'd gotten the call that had since put her life on the ledge. It had been almost two weeks since that call and everything that followed with Charles. Mikayla was mostly healed, except for the stubborn green and purple ring under her right eye and a healing gash on the bridge of her nose. She imagined that boxers probably stayed secluded after a fight to heal and get back to normal, just like she had. No calls, no going out in public, no looking in the mirror unless she had to.

In the days since his attack, Charles had been taking the kids to school before he left for work. Of course he did. He couldn't chance one of the teachers at school noticing anything different about Mikayla. School administrators and teachers were nosy motherfuckers. That was what Charles always preached.

Mikayla was jolted out of her thoughts by her doorbell ringing five times in succession and then a loud pounding on the door. Mikayla jumped, and it took her mind a few moments to recover before she jumped up from her seat and rushed toward the door.

"What the hell?" she grumbled. Her eyes darted toward the cable box clock. She wasn't expecting anyone at that time of morning. In fact, Mikayla rarely had company, since she knew Charles had secretly put in Nest home cameras that he could access from his cell phone to see everything going on inside the house while he wasn't there.

The doorbell rang again, and more pounding resounded through the house before Mikayla could make it to the door. She sucked her teeth and thought about cursing out whoever it was, even it was the police with some emergency. Everyone who knew Mikayla knew she hated when people popped up at her house unannounced.

"Are you fucking kidding me?" Mikayla hissed when another round of banging reverberated through the house just as she touched the doorknob. "This better be a gotdamn emergency," she grumbled. "Somebody's ass better be on fire. Who the fu . . ." She started as she tugged on the doorknob and yanked her front door open. Her words went tumbling back down her throat like she'd swallowed a handful of hard marbles. Her eyes bulged. Immediately her heart began galloping in her chest.

"Didn't expect to see us, huh, Mikayla?" Emerson spat with one hand on her hip and her head cocked to the side. Charlie didn't say anything, but the expression on her face—pursed lips, both eyebrows raised—didn't exactly read, "Hey, girl, we missed you."

"Ladies! What a surprise," Mikayla sang, her voice going three octaves higher than normal, the phoniness ringing loud and clear. She used her hand to try to sweep any little piece of hair over her bruised eye since she hadn't had time or even thought to grab sunglasses to cover it. The scab on her nose was still a dead giveaway that something had gone down.

"Come in. Come in," Mikalya said nervously, barely keeping her composure. Not only was she caught off guard by a visit from her two best friends, but she was nervous about them being in the house and Charles looking and listening in on their conversations. Mikayla wished they hadn't barged in like this, but they were really the only people in the world aside from Damian who Mikayla felt loved her sincerely. There was no way she could turn them away now, not with the look Emerson was wearing on her face.

"I'm so happy to see y'all," Mikayla lied in a phony, singsong voice.

"Oh, now all of a sudden you're happy to see us?" Emerson sassed as she rushed inside. "Are you crazy not calling us or answering our calls in two weeks, Mikayla? You missed our monthly lunch. You missed Charlie's birthday dinner, and did you forget you said you'd let me take the girls to my assistant's daughter's birthday party last week? Two weeks? Are you damn crazy?" Emerson off-loaded in a mini rant.

"Stop it. You're being crazy. It was nothing like that. I was going to get with you ladies today or tomorrow. I just had a lot of stuff around here to take care before the girls' camping trip, and Charles, you know, he is still using me to help out with club business every now and then. I love y'all the same, just had so much going on." Mikayla copped a plea. "What about my hugs?" she chuckled nervously, still a little thrown off by the intrusion.

"Now it's all hugs," Emerson said, still slightly chastising Mikayla. She exchanged a quick, dry embrace with Mikayla. "I forgive you. Although you're lying like shit about not ignoring us. You were definitely ignoring us," Emerson grumbled playfully.

Charlie and Mikayla's embrace was a bit longer and felt slightly more sincere. "I was so worried about you," Charlie said as they moved apart.

"Oh, I'm fine. Nothing to worry about at all. Just working, working, working. Trying to take care of the club's

business and keep these kids together," Mikayla replied,
ushering the ladies farther into her house. She used her
hand to make sure her hair was still swept forward over
her eye. An abrupt flashback of Charles's attack flashed
through Mikayla's mind and caused her to pause for a
second.

Mikayla blinked away the memory as she watched Emerson and Charlie take a seat on her plush leather sofa,
which sat in front of her expansive bay window. Mikayla
sat across from them in one of the plush, high-back arm-
chairs.

Emerson crossed her legs and crossed her arms over
her chest. She eyed Mikayla suspiciously. She'd known
Mikayla long enough to know when something was amiss.

Charlie sat on the edge of the couch with her back perfectly and painfully straight, looking down at the floor.
The house all of a sudden seemed tiny as it filled with
waves of tension. The minutes of awkward silence didn't
help either.

"Okay, KayKay, we know something is up. What's going
on?" Emerson asked, finally breaking the uncomfortable
silence.

Mikayla jumped up from her seat like a jack-in-the-
box, her nerves giving her a bit too much spring in her
step. "Where are my manners? Do you ladies want something to drink? I have iced tea. Charles has some Coronas
in there," Mikayla said a bit too cheerfully.

Emerson and Charlie looked at each other knowingly.
They were both thinking the same thing: *there is definitely something wrong!*

Mikayla returned with bottles of water and two Corona
beers. She set the tray on the table and sat back down.
Emerson cracked open a beer and took the longneck bottle straight to the head like she needed it to survive this
weird meeting.

"Listen. We've all been friends too long to do this phony shit," Charlie began, finally relaxing back against the chair.

"You're right, Charlie. I have just been feeling down lately, and I didn't want you ladies to know. I like to be upbeat when I'm around you all. I mean, I feel bad about you . . . your . . ." Mikayla said, losing her words.

"My what? Impending divorce?" Emerson cut in. "What's there to feel bad about? Things didn't work out," Emerson snapped kind of indignantly.

"Well, I just didn't know how you'd be. And, you," Mikayla continued, turning toward Charlie. "I did listen to your message about Jace and the woman who called you. It's just that day I had so much going on, and then I forgot to call you back."

Charlie put up her hand. "No need for the excuses. I mean, if we can't get in touch with one, we always have the other, right?" she said, looking over at Emerson. "It's just that, honestly, KayKay, we don't believe you. We think something more is going on with you," Charlie said flatly, making a point to look at Mikayla's right eye and healing face.

Mikayla's face paled. She looked up into the corner of the room at the cameras Charles had installed. They were tiny, but once you knew they were there, you just knew.

"I see it," Emerson said, pointing to her own right eye instead of pointing right at Mikayla's healing black eye.

Mikayla sighed loudly. "It's so crazy how things happen. Was at Zuri's soccer game and, wham, right in my damn face with a ball. Blacked both my eyes, cut my nose and lip. I was embarrassed to even come out of the house. There was no way I could've come to any events like that. I mean, everyone always thinks the worst when a wife shows up with a bruise or black eye, much less a whole face looking smashed," Mikayla said.

"Embarrassed? Embarrassed about what? If you really got hit with a damn soccer ball, why not just say that? Since when did you think we'd start judging you? Even if you really didn't get hit with a 'ball,' we wouldn't judge. No, we'd be here for you," Emerson said, using air quotes when she said the word "ball."

"For real, KayKay. We are a sisterhood, remember? We were worried about you. You thought not returning our calls and avoiding us was going to work?" Charlie asked, genuinely hurt.

Mikayla's eyes dropped to the floor. She ran her hand through her hair and sighed loudly.

"No damn way it was going to work," Emerson said, taking a swig of her Corona. "Mikayla Chantel King, don't you ever play yourself again. Bitch, as much as you sometimes got on my nerves and for as many times as I wanted to tell you to shut the hell up and mind your damn business, I still consider you a sister. We deal with problems together. Remember that time we handled that situation for Charlie when that big-Bertha-ass chick was trying to hurt her? It was you who got that little revolver with the mother-of-pearl handle and ran that bitch away. And what about that female officer, Broadbent, when she was trying to move in on Mason? We went down to that station and turned it out. Girl, what the hell makes you think we wouldn't have your back when you are going through difficult times?" Emerson preached.

"I know but—" Mikayla started. She wanted so badly to pour out her soul and tell them all about Charles. She wanted them to rush upstairs with her and pack all of her and her girls' shit so she could run as far away from him as possible. And what about the phone call from a few weeks ago? Mikayla still hadn't settled that in her mind. What if things from her past just popped up into her life now?

"No excuse. You can't get rid of us that easily, Mikayla," Emerson interrupted.

Mikayla shook her head in shame. "You have no idea how hard this has been. I missed y'all."

"We missed you too, but I'm telling you now, it's time for you to come clean," Emerson continued.

"I know that's right," Charlie added supportively.

"I'm so happy that you ladies still have my back. It says a lot about you both. It means a lot to me," Mikayla said sincerely.

Charlie tilted her head. "Why you acting like this hasn't always been us? We are always here," Charlie said. "You know we love you even if you're crazy." Charlie laughed.

"Oh, my God. You chicks are going to make me cry," Mikayla joked, dabbing at fake tears. They all started laughing.

"I was coming here to cuss you out, and then your ass would've really been crying. Had me calling you like a madwoman. I could've put out an APB on you for real," Emerson proclaimed. "I still might have a little pull down at the BPD."

"Girl, I was not going to anywhere. You know my life story. Where the hell am I going with two kids in tow?" Mikayla said.

"So the eye, what really happened?" Charlie blurted. It was still bothering her.

Emerson and Mikayla both raised their brows and shot Charlie a surprised look. Charlie wasn't usually as vocal and straightforward as Emerson.

"I mean, I just don't believe you got hit by no ball, KayKay," Charlie said, quickly realizing she had let her emotions get the best of her for a minute.

"I told you," Mikayla said, looking up at the camera. "I admit that I ignored your calls. I said I was sorry. But don't come in my house and go there, Charlie. I don't say anything when you're in these situationships you always seem to get into. Why? Because that's your business," Mikayla said defensively.

"Whoa, whoa," Emerson said, putting both of her hands up. "We did not come here to argue, bitches. We came here to make sure this one's ass was in one piece and that's it. We will get around to serious shit later. Y'all bitches is fucking up my little beer buzz with all this serious talk," Emerson scolded. "And if anyone needs a beer buzz, it's me. Shit, I'll be divorced in a few days, and my mother is staying with me. Nary a one of y'all lucky bitches better complain about diddly squat right now," she continued.

All three women busted out laughing. It was like old times again. Mikayla hadn't realized how much she'd missed her besties. Suddenly, everything she was going through with Charles seemed to fall away.

"Speaking of your mother—" Mikayla started.

Emerson quickly cut her off. "Tuh! Please do not get me started. I get that she's worried sometimes because she thinks without Mason I'll be fragile but, Lawd, she drives me crazy. She's always been a helicopter mom, which is why I think I rushed to get married to Mason in the first place. I mean, we were kids. We didn't know any better. We damn sure didn't know what we wanted for our lives at nineteen years old," Emerson relayed.

Charlie shifted uncomfortably in her seat. "So you feel good getting a divorce from someone you've been with half your life?" she asked. In her head, Charlie was thinking that Emerson ran Mason away. She secretly felt Emerson was ungrateful because from what Charlie could tell, Mason had always been a good, hardworking, and faithful man to Emerson.

Mikayla raised her eyebrow at Emerson as if to say, "Answer the question."

"It doesn't feel good, but honestly it doesn't feel bad. Mason wanted to control things. He didn't want me to have my own life. He wanted me to be some stay-at-home wife with 2.5 kids and a picket fence. He couldn't understand what woman wouldn't want that for herself. He couldn't get that I wanted a career, some independence . . . shit, my own money," Emerson said with feeling.

Charlie sighed loudly. "I guess some of us want what you thought was ridiculous," she grumbled.

Emerson and Mikayla both shot her a look.

"What?" Charlie said, eyes wide. "I'm just saying that if I ever found a good man, I would cherish him, and marriage is my whole entire life goal. You both have that, and I just want to experience it before I'm too old and gray," Charlie continued.

"Just make sure it is what you want," Mikayla said cryptically.

"Yup, I agree. Make sure you know for sure it is what you want," Emerson agreed. "I think we all want what we think we are missing when really what we need to do sometimes is focus on ourselves first."

"Well, you seem like you just gave up," Charlie replied, rolling her eyes after.

Emerson looked over at Charlie through wide eyes. "You can't be serious."

"Um, Charlie, maybe this is not the, um, time," Mikayla stammered, noticing the look on Emerson's face.

Emerson turned her whole body toward Charlie. Emerson's jaw had gone square, and her shoulders went back. "I didn't give up on it. Mason ruined it. We had such a perfect love. Or so I thought. I can't believe he would be so closed-minded. He would not budge. He would not support me. And then he badgered me about having children. He made me feel like less than a woman every single day. That

is so disgusting. And to add insult to injury, he blamed me
for everything. Every miscarriage was my fault. When he
didn't get promoted right away, it was my fault. Any differences we had. It was all my fault that we didn't work out.
That he couldn't find it in his heart to love me, his wife, for
who I am. He had a picture of who he wanted me to be, and
he never let it go. I dealt with a lot from Mr. Mason Dayle,
some things too personal to share, but I didn't just give up.
So don't you ever fix your lips again to accuse me of just
giving up. Besides, since when do we take the men's side
over our friend's side?" Emerson said with feeling.

Mikayla and Charlie watched intently, hanging on her
every word. Charlie opened her mouth, but she didn't get
a chance to say anything.

"Never. That's the answer. We never take the men's
side over the friend's side. Part of the code, remember?"
Emerson continued, her voice breaking off. Everyone
was quiet for a few minutes, each of them thinking about
what was said.

"I'm sorry," Charlie said, breaking the silence. "It's just
that I hate to see marriages end. I want to be married so
badly. Y'all know that. I didn't mean anything by it. I'm
in my own damn feelings. I really loved you guys together. The perfect couple in my eyes." She had to clean it up
real quick.

"I get it," Emerson sighed. "This is the hardest thing I've
ever had to do. I still love Mason. But it's just not right
anymore. So I've hired an attorney. She's a good friend of
mine from school days and the best in the industry. She
is known to get women everything they deserve. Not that
I'm looking for anything from Mason. I just want it to be
fast and painless," Emerson said.

"Good luck with that. Down at the kids' school, I've
heard so many divorce nightmare stories about women
not getting what they deserve," Mikayla said pessimisti-

cally. She shivered a little bit. "I can't even imagine life if Charles and I ever . . ." Mikayla said, her voice trailing off as if she believed saying the words would make something happen.

"Well, anyway, enough about the bad shit," Charlie said, clapping her hands together.

"Hell yeah, I agree," Emerson said loudly for emphasis.

Mikayla shook her head in agreement. "Yes. Positive vibes only."

They talked and talked, catching each other up on the positive things that had happened in their lives over the past couple of weeks. Then Mikayla said, "I have to hear about this funny story you have to tell, Charlie."

"Chiiiiiilllle," Charlie sang. "Y'all don't even want to know this bullshit."

"Yes, the hell we do!" Emerson pressed.

"Yes, the hell we do!" Mikayla repeated.

Charlie stood up. "I got to stand up for this one," she said, clapping her hands and rubbing them together. "So I'm in the damn house. All decked the fuck out in lingerie. Fucking fifty-course meal of brunch and breakfast on the table. Candles and all, bitches," Charlie went on.

Mikayla and Emerson chuckled.

"Not the candles," Emerson said to make a point.

"Yes, bitch. The candles!" Charlie said, clapping between each syllable. "Let me just finish. So my phone rings, and this nigga Jace's boo tag comes up on my screen. Immediately my pussy pulses, and I'm ready to hear the nigga say he downstairs, outside my building . . . something. Tuh! It's a bitch on the line," Charlie relayed, her body moving animatedly.

"No!" Mikayla said, throwing her hand up to her chest, clutching her invisible pearls.

"Oh, no, the fuck," Emerson said. "Why didn't you call us right away?"

"Let me finish. Let my ass finish!" Charlie went on, stomping her foot playfully. "So the bitch commences telling me she is with Jace and she's his women and yada, yada. Of course I'm hot all over at that point. No-ass control over my feelings, so I curse the bitch out and promise to beat her ass. She is bold, telling me to come on down and shit. That was all the invitation I needed, bitches," Charlie said, bouncing on her feet like a boxer. "I got dressed in my fighting gear so fucking fast. I ain't have no Vaseline to put on my face, but I smeared a lot of shea butter on my shit."

Mikayla and Emerson busted out laughing. They laughed so hard even Charlie had to laugh at herself.

"I know, right? What kind of gangsta bitch am I if I don't keep the fighting Vaseline ready? I guess you can call me a bougie gangsta bitch. Shea butter it was," Charlie said, barely able to stay serious.

"So you get all ready and then?" Emerson asked with high anticipation in her voice of what was coming next.

"And I get in my car, and fucking traffic in downtown Baltimore was a monkey's ass!" Charlie blurted, slapping her hands together. "My ass is in the traffic, cursing and slamming my fists on my steering wheel. All along my phone's blowing up with calls from this bitch. I was screaming, 'Uh-uh, bitch, don't have second thoughts now. I'm on my fucking way!' I was so mad I swerved the car and hit another fucking car!" Charlie exclaimed, using her hands to indicate a big explosion.

"Oh, shit!" Mikayla said loudly. "No, you didn't."

"Yes! But that wasn't even the half of it! A big dude-looking chick and her little fem bitch got out of the car I hit. They dragged my ass out of my car and was about to jump me and fuck me up!" Charlie yelled so that her story would have more feeling.

"No, the hell they didn't," Emerson said, her mouth agape. "Not the whole jumping someone like they were in high school!"

"Yup! I was ready to fight both of those bitches, too," Charlie replied, her voice suddenly calmer. Charlie shook her head as she recalled the whole ordeal.

"So what happened after that?" Mikayla asked. "Did they hit you? Did you hit them? Girl, what?"

"Nope. The shit just died down. Police arrived and broke that shit up," Charlie said anticlimactically, flopping back down on Mikayla's couch to signal the finality of her crazy story. When she finished, she lowered her eyes toward the floor. She was scared to say too much and give herself away about what actually happened at the end of that scene. Her mind quickly raced to that day.

"Join the club," Mason said. "Listen, let's go grab some lunch so I can make sure you don't go get yourself arrested," he said in a brotherly way.

Charlie stared at Mason, contemplating his innocent invitation. Nobody had really ever cared about her, especially a dude. She had to admit Mason's concern made her feel good inside. She knew she was supposed to regard Mason as public enemy number one because of his differences with Emerson, but she couldn't help but feel good in that moment.

Charlie had never really looked at Mason long enough to see that he was handsome. When they were kids, Charlie thought he was the ugliest boy Emerson could've chosen. But in that moment, Mason reminded her a bit of a cross between Idris Elba and Lance Gross. She had to blink a few times. She was having a hard time getting her focus back. Gorgeous or not, he was her best friend's soon-to-be ex-husband.

"This day couldn't get any worse when that bitch pulled me out of the car. I mean, what was God thinking

today?" Charlie said as she and Mason walked toward
a small café up the street from the body shop he'd taken
her battered car to.

"Everything for a reason. I had just left the gym, and I
surely wasn't thinking about being a cop while I was off
duty. I couldn't even believe my eyes when I looked good
and noticed that it was you, damn near my sister, about
to be beat up by two chicks. I was like, 'All right, universe, what tricks do you have up your sleeve today?'"
Mason said, laughing after.

"For real, that shit is not even funny. I didn't know
what to do next," Charlie said, shaking her head as they
sat at their table.

"I knew you were a feisty one, but you know, since we
were kids I haven't really . . ." Mason trailed off.

"I know, right. You expect everybody to be different
by the time they're our age. Not me," Charlie admitted,
waving her hands in front of her goofily.

"Well, let's just say you are one of a kind. I don't think
I've ever met a woman so beautiful yet so unrefined.
You're an original, that's for sure," Mason said, still
chuckling.

Charlie paused for a few seconds. She wasn't sure if
she'd heard him correctly. Had he just called her beautiful? She wasn't sure if she wanted to hear him correctly.
She blew out a windstorm of breath. "It's not easy being
a girl," she said meekly. It was the best she could come
up with. She was struggling to hide her shock at what
Mason had said to her.

"Look, at least I saved you from God knows what,"
Mason said. "How you going to be a gangsta and tell the
person you coming to their spot? That girl could've had
anything waiting for you. I think it was your lucky day."

"You right. You right," Charlie agreed, blushing. She
was agreeing to it being her lucky day in a lot of ways.

"Lesson learned?" he asked, extending his hand toward her for a friendly shake.

"Lesson learned," Charlie repeated, taking his hand into hers. In that moment when she touched him, she had felt something. It was as close to being electrocuted as she thought she'd ever come. She let out an exasperated breath and nervously ran her fingers through her curly hair.

As Mason turned away to call over their waitress, Charlie's shoulders slumped. She would be the one to feel some sort of spark with a man who would forever be off-limits to her. Charlie knew she was wrong for having a second thought about Mason. She was wrong for even being in his company, seeing that he wasn't on speaking terms with Emerson. The thought of Emerson finding out Charlie had broken even a tiny piece of bread with Mason made Charlie shudder. That was how cruel the universe always was to Charlie. She'd think she found the one, but there was always something keeping her from true happiness.

"My entire body aches," Charlie said, holding the side of her neck and moving her head gingerly.

"Let me see if you might've torn something," Mason said. He got up and came around to her side of the table and touched her shoulder, sending a cool chill down her back. She shrugged away from him and pretended it was from pain and not that she was uneasy because of the feelings boiling up in her.

"Yeah, you'll need to see a doctor. You'll feel worse tomorrow. Get a massage, too, while you're at it," Mason told her, taking his seat again.

Charlie knew right then, somewhere in her mind, she had already crossed the line.

"Hello? Earth to Charlie," Emerson called and snapped her fingers.

Charlie snapped out of her little daze. "Oh, sorry. Just thinking about it all. It was just crazy," Charlie said, remembering where she was at the moment. She never told her friends that Mason was the police officer who saved her that day. In that moment, Charlie didn't know why she left it out. That moment between her and Mason was private, although it was innocent. Charlie knew better than to speak on it and risk any glimpse of emotion showing in front of Emerson and Mikayla, especially after she'd already shown a bit of favoritism for Mason earlier by accident. Charlie didn't say anything about the rest of her story or the rest of that day.

Emerson's and Mikayla's eyebrows shot up at the same time. They glanced at one another, and then in seemingly synchronized movements, they turned their eyes to back to Charlie. "And?" they said almost in unison.

"That's it. I got her insurance information, and I have to go tomorrow and pick up the police report," Charlie said like nothing.

Emerson let out a long sigh. "Bitch, did you ever finish driving to Jace's and fuck up the girl? I mean, shit, where's the rest of the story? Did you just get in your car and go back home after the fight? I mean, you were dressed to fuck someone up."

"Right! What happened with that?" Mikayla asked, not even realizing she was on the edge of her seat.

Charlie knew she wasn't a good liar in front of her best friends. They'd all been friends since they were thirteen. They'd know right away. She had to think fast. Mikayla and Emerson were waiting and prepared to hang on Charlie's every word.

"Naw, after that close call something told me to just chill. Seeing the police kind of took the wind out of my sails for the violence I was about to go dish out. I figured a girl like me from West Baltimore who made it out better not go waste that shit getting arrested behind some lowlife who wasn't worth my damn time in the first place. I just knew in that moment I was too good to be out there doing that shit," Charlie said, repeating some of the things Mason had said to her that day to convince her that she had too much going on for herself to go risk it on someone who didn't care about her at all.

Emerson raised one eyebrow suspiciously. She held her hand up at Charlie. "Hold on. Hold on," Emerson said, using her "flag on the play" hand signal.

Charlie immediately realized that she might've come off as guilty. "What?" Charlie asked, faking.

"So you telling me the bitch we've known twenty-two years, the one who stays ready to fight, the one who will kill a next bitch over a man, suddenly got some sense knocked into her by a car accident?" Emerson asked on the verge of laughter.

Charlie realized Emerson was joking and relaxed a little. She smiled, playing along. "I've evolved, bitch," Charlie replied, tilting her right pinky finger toward the ceiling like the proper English people do when they have tea.

"Yeah, okay," Emerson said. All three of them started laughing.

Mikayla finally felt slightly relaxed. She knew she'd have to deal with Charles once he saw them on the cameras. But knowing Charles, he would've called a dozen times by then. Mikayla looked at her cell phone. An hour had already passed with no call from him. She shrugged lightly and thought he must've gotten busy at the club. Maybe some vendor was there trying to sell a new brand of liquor. Either way, Mikayla was welcoming the bit of peace that came with him being gone and with her girls showing up.

"A'ight, KayKay, you're up. Emerson is dealing with her mother and a divorce. I almost had to beat a bitch up and broke up with the fake man of my dreams. Aside from getting hit by a ball, what's good? No stories to tell?" Charlie said. She was not going to let the ball thing die down. It didn't sit right with her at all.

"Me?" Mikayla seemed shocked by the question. She chuckled. "My life is boring. Everything in my world is great lately. I take care of the house. Charles takes care of the business and everything else. My girls are wonderful. I really can't complain," Mikayla bragged.

"But with shit being so perfect, just why the hell haven't we heard from you?" Charlie pressed.

"Oh, well, there is one thing that happened. My mother called. My brother . . . he's getting out early," Mikayla said, almost whispering.

Emerson and Charlie sucked in their breath.

"Oh, shit," Emerson finally managed.

"Will they stay away?" Charlie asked, her hand on her chest. "They . . . they bring out the worst in you, KayKay."

"I don't know. It's been a while since the call and nothing so far. I don't even know when," Mikayla said. "I stopped being on pins and needles. I can't live like that. I'll just deal with it when it comes."

"Do you think he will, you know, tell that story to anyone?" Emerson asked flatly.

Emerson's words exploded like small bombs in Mikayla's ears. She instantly felt nauseous. Within seconds, her entire face and neck turned a deep shade of red. Mikayla flattened her lips into a straight line and her eyes hooded over.

"I don't know, but I am prepared to do again what I need to do. I have the girls now, and I will not let them grow up like I did. I know my family, and they're probably trying to figure out how to take me down, but I will not go down without a fight," Mikayla said with feeling. "I'm sure he is a changed person, angrier than back then. Angry at me. Angry at the whole world."

"We are here for you. Whatever you need," Charlie said softly.

Mikayla chewed on her bottom lip and tapped her foot on the floor. Talking about her family was a very sensitive topic for Mikayla, and she had no desire to discuss it. Mikayla was really holding her tongue because she wanted to tell her friends that she was scared to death of what might happen if her mother and brother showed up at her doorstep.

Charles didn't know much about her past, except that she grew up in foster care after a certain age and that she'd met her two best friends in middle school. Mikayla didn't like to revisit life before Emerson and Charlie. She didn't like to revisit where she'd come from, which resulted in the nightmare that had haunted her for years since. It was her past, and it could destroy everything she had now. If she could, she would pack up, take her kids, and run. But she didn't work or have her own money, so that was impossible.

Mikayla let out a long sigh. Now wasn't the time to go over all of the worst aspects of her life. She shook her head a little bit to erase the thoughts.

"I know that's right," Emerson chimed in. "We will do whatever needs to be done to help you. And we mean whatever."

"Listen, all of this talking got me hungry. I'm starving." Charlie changed the subject, trying to ease some of the tension that had suddenly returned to the room.

"I'm kind of hungry myself," Emerson agreed.

"Yeah, I haven't eaten since dinner last night," Mikayla agreed.

"Okay, then get your ass dressed so we can go get some food and some drinks. I feel like we all need one, two, or fifty," Emerson joked.

"It's damn early for drinks," Charlie said.

"It's never damn early for drinks. Even breakfast comes with mimosas," Emerson corrected her.

"True, true," Charlie agreed, then laughed.

Mikayla jumped up excitedly. "Just give me a few minutes," she laughed. It had been a long while since she'd shared a fun time out with her girls. She would be home before Charles got in, and since he hadn't called her, she took that as a good sign that he was too distracted to worry about her. Mikayla was feeling good . . . for now.

Chapter 5

Charlie, Emerson, Mikayla

"You know what? I just realized I haven't been to our spot in a minute," Mikayla said as she, Emerson, and Charlie entered Miss Shirley's Cafe—a well-known brunch spot in Baltimore. Just like they expected, it was packed. But they knew they didn't have to wait. They had connections. Emerson walked up to the hostess podium and murmured something to the young woman there. She turned around and signaled to someone else, and within minutes they'd found a table for Charlie, Emerson, and Mikayla.

"I love them in here. Always the royal treatment," Charlie said.

"That's what happens when they're one of your biggest clients and they want some free advertising on your page now," Emerson whispered. She felt good about using her influencer status to get perks. There was a time when she'd depended solely on Mason's police perks to get freebies and VIP treatment around town. Emerson felt powerful in that moment. She wasn't going to lie about that. If she wasn't sure before about her decision to stand up and be on her own, she was certainly sure now.

"Right this way," the young hostess said, ushering the ladies farther into the quaint restaurant.

Emerson led the pack. She could see quite a few people recognizing her from Instagram and Twitter as the
social media celebrity she was. She tried to act noncha-
lant about it, but inside she was jumping for joy. Emerson didn't know how she could have ever thought the
simple life as a cop's wife was enough for her. That was
crazy talk now that she thought about it. She was glad
she'd never been able to carry a pregnancy to term, or
she would've been tethered to Mason forever.

Emerson, Charlie, and Mikayla were seated at Emerson's favorite table. She always said the table was in the
perfect spot—not too far from the door so she could see
the comings and goings. She had to keep her finger
on the pulse of everything Baltimore in order to keep her
image as a homegrown celebrity authentic.

"So what y'all thinking for today?" Mikayla asked as she
scanned her menu like she didn't know every single thing
on it already. The scent of Miss Shirley's famous monkey
bread wafted around and made Mikayla's stomach growl.
She'd been trying to watch her weight, especially with
Charles's criticisms always at the forefront of her mind.
But today Mikayla decided she wanted to let her hair
down without judgment. She'd forgotten to even check
her phone to see if Charles had called. It was nice not to
be worried all the time. That's exactly what Charlie and
Emerson did for Mikayla: made her days better.

"I like everything. I think I've tried just about everything on this menu," Emerson replied without looking
up from her menu. "Today I'm going for something with
seafood in it. You know us black folks get tired of chick-
en."

All of the ladies laughed.

Charlie nodded her agreement. "Seafood sounds good
to me."

"Good morn . . ." the cute little young waiter started,
then after taking a quick look at his watch said, "I mean

afternoon. My name is Randall, and I'll be serving you this early afternoon."

"Mmm, cute," Charlie said, raising both eyebrows at the handsome young man. "You must be new." She eyed him up and down.

Emerson and Mikayla giggled. The young man blushed.

"Leave him alone, you damn cougar," Emerson scolded. They all laughed again.

"I'll start with two mimosas but with pineapple juice and heavy on the adult stuff," Emerson ordered first.

Mikayla went next. "Coffee for me for now."

"For me, whatever you have back there that's dark and stormy like me." Charlie winked, continuing to flirt shamelessly. The young man nodded, smiled politely, and rushed from the table.

"You're really trying to find you a man, huh? You changing it up? Starting off younger this time?" Emerson said, then chuckled.

"Hey." Charlie threw her hands up. "Maybe I'll have better luck with the young ones. Mold them," she replied, using her hand like she was forming something out of invisible modeling clay. More laughter.

After their drinks came, they placed their orders and just enjoyed each other's company as they waited for their food. "Ugh, with work and my mother, I forgot how much fun we have when we are not all about adulting and shit," Emerson said.

"I know, right. Lucky you two don't have to throw kids into the mix. Your life becomes totally about little people once you have them," Mikayla said.

Charlie's eyebrows arched and she squinted at Mikayla. Emerson caught it too.

"Girl, please. KayKay can talk about her babies. I'm perfectly fine with the station God has placed me in my life. Yes, I tried a lot and couldn't bear the fruit, but I would never begrudge anyone else talking about their babies. Besides, maybe God knew that motherhood just wasn't for me," Emerson said, slightly defensive in her tone.

"I hear you. I just want—" Charlie started.

"Oh, shit," Emerson whispered, abruptly cutting Charlie off. Emerson stared past Charlie, her eyes suddenly trained in on something or someone at another table. Charlie snapped her lips shut and turned slightly to see what had Emerson so caught up.

"That's Charles," Charlie huffed, seemingly blown away. Mikayla looked over and immediately averted her eyes.

"That is your damn husband," Emerson said like it was not common knowledge.

"For sure," Charlie followed up, suddenly pushing back slightly from the table.

"Sit," Mikayla commanded.

"But you're not moving. It's like you're in shock or some shit. I'll go over there and break that shit all the way up," Charlie said like she was ready to put in some work and all of her earlier talk about having everything to lose had dissipated.

"I'll go. It's probably a quick business brunch. He has them all the time. Nothing to be alarmed about," Mikayla said softly and with a smile while keeping her eyes glued to Charles and his table guest. Her heart banged against her chest wall so hard she thought she'd lose her ability to breathe. The pressure from her friends was mounting, but her fear of Charles was lingering, too.

"I'll go over and introduce myself," Mikayla said, pulling her cloth napkin from her lap and throwing it onto her place setting. "I'm sure it's nothing."

"Um, introduce yourself? More like break up whatever is happening. Girlfriend is touching and smiling a bit too much for that to be a business meeting," Charlie declared, pushing the issue.

"Just let her take care of it. We can't afford a scene. Not in public where people recognize me. I didn't build my brand all the way up for it to be dragged down by someone else's shit," Emerson said selfishly, shaking her head. "As I see it, this is between husband and wife. No need for a big, loud scene."

"You would say that," Charlie retorted, disgusted. "Okay, Mikayla, you do as you want while protecting someone else's brand. But I'm just telling you now, if I were married and out with my girls and saw my husband cozying up with a bitch, your image be damned. I would be tearing up this place," Charlie proclaimed. Then she picked up her drink and swallowed all of it.

"I got this. I'm fine. There won't be a need for a scene, I'm sure," Mikayla said. Emerson and Charlie nodded their approval. Mikayla smiled weakly. It was phony, but she was used to being phony. Inside, her body felt like it was disintegrating. How dare Charles! While Mikayla walked around with a recovering black eye, he was out with, from what Mikayla could see, a beautiful woman who Mikayla clearly paled in comparison to.

"I'm sure everything will be fine. Shoot, we might even get our whole bill paid. You know how Charles is, a real man's man," Mikayla said before she set off toward the table on wobbly legs at best. She took a deep breath, used her hands to iron out the wrinkles in her blazer and jeans, fluffed her hair to make sure her black eye was only partially showing, and started tentatively toward the table.

Just go right up to him and ask what is going on, Mikayla. You are not the wrong one here. It doesn't matter if he tries to flip it around. Stand your ground. He can't hurt you in here with all of these people. You have to save face in front of your friends. Don't back down.

"Well, good afternoon, Mr. King." Mikayla walked right up to Charles's table with the confidence of a wife with a need to know.

Charles unlatched himself from the woman's clutches and cleared his throat.

"Mrs. Charles King." Mikayla boldly stuck out her hand in front of the woman for a shake. The woman furrowed her brows, her eyes scanning Mikayla as if she had spoken a completely different language or like she was intruding on a private moment.

"That's right, Mikayla King, Mrs. Charles King. His wife," Mikayla said for clarification, letting her dangling hand drop to her side. "You mean to tell me Charles didn't tell you he was married? Well, maybe that's because he was going to tell me that you are a business associate here for a business meeting. Right, Charles?" Mikayla smiled, but it certainly contradicted what was running through her mind. The creases in Charles's forehead and his tapping foot spelled out his guilt straight away.

"He didn't say he was married at all," the woman said, jerking away from Charles like he had a disease.

"Listen, this is business," Charles said to Mikayla. Then he turned his attention back to the woman. "Stay. Let's finish this, and I'll handle everything else later," he said to her, seemingly unfazed by his wife standing over them. He shot Mikayla a look that said he'd handle her later. Mikayla's heart sank. She figured, based on the look on Charles's face, that this meeting would garner her an ass whooping later. If that was the case, she wasn't going to back down. Either way, in that moment, she felt like she was losing everything.

I can't believe him!

Mikayla fiddled with a stray string hanging from the bottom of her blazer. She took a deep breath. "I suggest you leave, miss. You look like a classy woman, and I'm sure you don't want a scene in here." Mikayla beamed, being fake, ignoring Charles's menacing glares at her.

"That's a good idea. The one thing I don't do is drama," the classy woman said, snatching up her expensive bag.

Charles couldn't do anything. Stuck between his wife and his whatever she was, he sat there defeated. Mikayla watched his jaw rock, and she knew that if he could, he would've grabbed her around the neck and taken her down right on the spot. She also knew she had the upper hand right then.

"Was out with my girls, saw you, and figured at first it was business," Mikayla said levelly, trying to stave off her nerves and, most of all, her hurt.

Charles's shoulders went up and down as he chortled. "So that's where you got the courage to come over here? Your friends," he said like he didn't believe in her. "You think your friends know anything about me and what I have going on? You think your friends will feed you and the kids like I do if you decided to show off for them? Don't do something you'll regret, Mikayla."

"Ah. There he goes," Mikayla replied snidely, somehow mustering up a courage she hadn't had in years. "There goes my husband, the man who uses words and fists to keep me down. The man who holds money, and our home, and our life over my head every single day of my life. I was waiting for him to show up," Mikayla said through gritted teeth, her voice going slightly louder. She felt emboldened even if was only for that brief moment.

Charles tapped his hand on the table impatiently. "Sit down. Do not make a scene or it'll be one you can't finish," Charles instructed, pointing at the seat recently vacated by his bimbo. "Maybe you need to eat. Maybe that's why you're not thinking rationally right now," he said.

"I'm not going to sit with you, Charles. Not behind your . . . your date. You didn't invite me here. In fact, I don't know the last time you took me out. I'm here with my friends," Mikayla said, turning around to peek at

Emerson and Charlie. They didn't disappoint, because they were staring right at her.

Charlie tilted her head as if to say, "Do you need us?"

"Is this how you want to handle this, Mikayla? You want to make something that was nothing into something. You won't sit with me and discuss it so I can explain? Is that your final answer?" Charles asked, his jaw stiff and his fists balled. Totally different from the soft, canoodling lovebird he had been a few minutes earlier.

Mikayla shook her head. "I'm here with my friends," she said, standing her ground although she was scared to death inside. Her body trembled, but she fought like hell not to show it. Mikayla didn't know what hell she would pay later.

Charles tossed his cloth napkin on the table and stood up. He got close to her. Her heart jerked painfully in her chest. She stepped back a few steps. She immediately picked up the scent of Jazz Club—her favorite cologne that Charles usually wore when he was going to work at the club at night. It was also how he'd smelled a couple of weeks ago when he had beat her ass like she was his worst enemy. A wave of nausea followed. Mikayla swallowed hard and shifted her weight from one foot to the other.

"I guess we will discuss this in the privacy of our own home," Charles said dismissively. He turned toward Emerson and Charlie and waved as if to say, "Nothing to see here."

Mikayla watched as Charles stalked away from her like she didn't even matter. Her entire body was alive with nerves—scared ones and angry ones. But mostly relieved ones.

Motherfucker! Bastard!

Mikayla's stomach fluttered as she stood there stunned, watching Charles leave the restaurant as if she hadn't just busted him with another woman. What was she going to say to her friends? What was she going to do when she got home?

After a few minutes, she gathered herself. She noticed that not just her friends were starting to watch the scene, but other restaurant patrons had started to whisper their speculations about what was happening. Mikayla tugged on the lapels of her blazer and shifted on her feet again. She knew this wasn't over. She knew there'd be much more to deal with, but for now, she had to at least look like she had tried to handle things.

Mikayla's face was flushed as she headed back in the direction of her friends.

"Well?" Charlie asked before Mikayla could sit down.

"Just like I said. Business," Mikayla said evenly, keeping her emotions at bay.

"What? From here it looked like you was about to set it off on ol' girl and she stormed out like she had just found out that nigga was married," Charlie relayed as she leaned back in her chair, scrutinizing Mikayla.

Mikayla waved her off. "Men will be men, even in business," Mikayla defended.

Emerson twisted her lips. "Please don't let me hear you say that shit ever again. You sound like my mother. That's some old-school bullshit if I ever heard of any. It's the reason everyone would have me stay with Mason although he never supported anything I wanted to do in life. You can be straight with us. If the nigga got busted, he got busted."

Before Mikayla could even dignify Emerson with an answer, she saw their waiter approaching. Charlie let out a tiny breath. Mikayla smiled and clapped her hands lightly.

"Ahh, our food. The whole reason we came here today," Mikayla sang. "Right on time."

"Right on time, all right, with your cute self." Charlie smiled, winking at the waiter. The mood quickly shifted. "Your food looks delish," Charlie crooned, looking over at Emerson's plate.

"Don't it though," Emerson played along.

"Okay, okay. I'm sorry. It's just that I don't know what to think with that situation, and Charles didn't want to discuss it here," Mikayla said, shaking her head.

Charlie widened her eyes and stuffed a huge piece of waffle in her mouth as if to indicate she had nothing to say.

"Don't be like that. It's difficult being married," Mikayla said.

Charlie arched her eyebrows and blinked a few times.

"Here is what I'll say, Mikayla. I don't get in between marriages, but if Charles's version of a discussion is going to have you getting hit with any more soccer balls, then we're going to have a problem," Emerson interjected.

"Yes!" Charlie blurted a little too loudly. Emerson and Mikayla shot Charlie a look. "I'm sorry, it's just I couldn't hold it in anymore like we don't know what really happened and shit," Charlie clarified.

"So let us know what we have to do," Emerson followed up, picking up on what Charlie was implying.

"Well, y'all can start with letting us have a peaceful brunch before I have to pick up the girls," Mikayla replied, reaching for her fork.

"All right then, but just know we won't stand by and see too many more of those, Mikayla," Emerson said, pointing at Mikayla's healing bruises.

"Too many more? No, we won't see no more of those," Charlie said, folding her arms in front of her chest.

Mikayla blanched. "I love y'all," she replied, although her stomach was in knots anticipating how things might go in her life.

Chapter 6

Charlie

Charlie was kind of paranoid. She like felt all eyes were on her as she sauntered up the walkway leading to the front doors of the Baltimore Police Department's western district station. She was confident that she looked good as hell, thanks to the professional makeup she'd had done earlier. Charlie felt kind of silly now. Had she really gone to Sephora to get her makeup done to meet up with Mason for ten seconds for a stupid accident report? Yup, she definitely had done that. Was it all to impress Mason? A man who was off-limits to her?

Charlie shook off any second thoughts. She was there now, looking like she was about to walk a damn runway in a fitted dress that hugged all of her brick-house curves. Charlie blew out a breath, held her head high, smiled, and greeted the police officers and detectives passing her as she made her way to the door. Charlie could see and feel a million eyes on her. She probably looked out of place, or maybe she just looked that damn good. She could only imagine how many fine-ass men worked in the police station. Charlie couldn't even say why she'd never met any of Mason's cop friends instead of hooking up with all the unlucky bums she'd been saddled with over the years.

"Good morning, I'm here to see Officer Dayle," Charlie told the receptionist that sat right inside of the doors.

"Officer Dayle?" the woman asked, face crinkled. "You mean Detective Lieutenant Dayle? Mason Dayle?" the receptionist corrected her and then smiled warmly. She was eyeing Charlie like she knew some kind of secret that Charlie wasn't privy to.

Charlie opened her eyes a little wider. She wasn't able to hide her surprise at another thing Mason and Emerson had hidden from their friends. When the hell did Mason get promoted to lieutenant of the detectives? Charlie cleared her throat. "Yes, yes. That's him," Charlie clarified, trying to play it cool, although she could feel heat rising into her cheeks. Charlie thought about slowly backing out of the police station and just going back home. Maybe she was there for the wrong reason. Maybe she was way out of her league and stepping into something she had no business in. Maybe she was a horrible fucking friend.

"He will be right down," the receptionist said as she hung up her phone.

Charlie shook her head and took a deep breath, deciding to just stay put. She was there now. Running away would just make her look crazier than she already looked with a full face of perfectly beat makeup, heels, and a dress fit for a hot date.

You're only here for the report, Charlie. There is nothing wrong with that. You didn't come for any other reason. Just the accident report, she reminded herself. The constant pep talks with herself had helped Charlie stop feeling guilty about her thoughts over the past few weeks. Those feelings were also why she'd taken so long to come get the report from Mason.

"Charli Baltimore," Mason sang as he approached, referring to the spitfire female rapper from the nineties. Charlie blushed. People often told her she resembled Charli Baltimore.

Lawd, this man is fine! How didn't I know he was so fine before! Stop it, Charlie! More pep talking.

"Mr. Man Mason," Charlie replied with a nickname of her own. She didn't even know how she'd come up with that so fast. Her entire body was jittery around Mason now. She wasn't looking at him like a brother anymore, and that was clear. "Why didn't I ever know you were the big man on campus around here?" Charlie asked.

"I guess that's something you'd have to ask yourself or your friend. It was like after I married her no one, none of you, wanted to get to know me anymore," Mason said.

"Well, more like she kept you away from us," Charlie replied, rolling her eyes a little bit. "I mean, except for the events that you had to be at with her. I never knew what was up with that. It's not like we didn't know you were her boyfriend from fifteen years old and our friend too before you became her husband. I mean, we all from the same hood, right?"

Mason shrugged. "I guess that's neither here nor there now, right? What they say, water under the bridge?" Mason said, parting a handsome smile.

Charlie looked away. "Well, I came for the report like we agreed. Or did you forget I was coming today? I know I'm mad late coming for it, but you know how life is."

"Forget? Ha! How can I forget the girl who almost got me beat up while I was off duty?" Mason joked. "C'mon, I'll take you up to my office. I have the report there. It's been there waiting for your late ass," he said jokingly as he stepped in front of her to lead the way.

Charlie followed him, half wobbling on her Christian Louboutin heels. She had really gotten fancy to come to the damn police station. She felt so stupid now. Jeans and sneakers would've definitely done the job. Now she'd have to lie and say she had somewhere to be since she was all dressed up. Charlie followed Mason past rows of desk and lots of ogling eyes.

"Nothing to see here, hounds," Mason yelled at the hungry-eyed group of detectives who had stopped dead in their tracks to watch Charlie walk by.

"Right this way," Mason said, opening a door to an office that looked like it used to be a cubicle that someone put a fake wall in front of. The wall didn't even go all the way up to the ceiling.

Charlie stepped inside slowly, and Mason closed the door behind her. Once inside the fake-wall office, Charlie could still hear all of the buzz from the guys on the floor talking about her. Charlie looked around suspiciously like she expected Emerson or someone they knew to materialize through the walls.

Charlie let her oversized Gucci bag slip from her hand onto the floor, and she sat down. The scene in the office was eerily familiar, like déjà vu. It had been happening for a few weeks now. Charlie would picture herself with Mason alone in different places, but they were always being friendly and nothing more.

Mason stepped behind his desk and shuffled through some papers while Charlie tried to look around and appear unaffected.

"I had the damn thing here for so long. Now I can't find it in all this mess," Mason mumbled.

Charlie stood back up. She decided she wouldn't waste a good outfit sitting down. She walked over to a mahogany bookshelf that contained rows of awards and plaques Mason had earned over his years at the BPD. Then she looked at his windowsill and noticed a huge bouquet of roses. She shook her head slightly.

"You always keep gorgeous flowers in your office?" she asked, touching a few of the soft petals, feeling confused and conflicted. There had to be at least two dozen fully opened roses in all colors—pink, red, lavender, white, and orange—arranged so beautifully they were breathtaking. *What man keeps flowers in his office? This gets weirder by the minute. What the fuck are you doing here, Charlie?*

"Ah, my roses. Long story," Mason said, shaking his head.

Charlie tilted her head, silently saying, "I have time today."

"I had started this flower subscription when I would send my wife flowers every Friday. It would've cost me more money to cancel the shit than to just have them bring the flowers to me here instead of the house," he explained.

Charlie felt tears welling up in the backs of her eyes. She didn't know what was coming over her.

"You all right?" Mason asked, noticing. He walked closer to her.

"Don't worry about me," Charlie said, fanning her hands in front of her face to try to dry up her tears before they fell.

"What did I say?" he asked, his eyebrows dipping on his face.

Charlie shook her head. "Do you know what I would give for a man to send me flowers every Friday? For a man to send me flowers any day?" she confessed, finally letting her tears fall.

Mason sighed and shook his head. "That's the crazy thing with life. Something one person takes for granted another person would give anything to have. That's how cruel life is," Mason lamented.

He walked over to the rose bouquet and picked them up. "I think every woman deserves to receive flowers. Not just for special occasions, but just because," Mason said, holding the flowers out in front of him for Charlie to take them.

Charlie stepped back a few paces. She shook her head. "No, I . . . I can't. They were for . . . I can't," she stammered, feeling like she was in over her head now. She shouldn't have even come there, and if she did, she should've just arranged for Mason to leave the report at reception.

"Listen, don't feel a way. They weren't for Emerson anymore. She stopped loving flowers years ago. She told me as much. She said if she never saw another rose from me it would be too soon," Mason relayed, pushing the flowers forward again.

"Really?" Charlie asked, confused. She couldn't understand what woman wouldn't want her man to give her flowers as a gesture of love and respect. Charlie had never received flowers from a man, and she'd dated many. She certainly would've appreciated flowers over the years.

Charlie flopped down into a chair and put her face in her hands for a few seconds. If she could scream at the top of her lungs without alarming the entire office, she would have. Frustration was a mild word to describe how she was feeling in that moment. It was surreal to her that she was there, in that moment, feeling like she was falling for her best friend's future ex-husband. If Charlie wasn't sure before, she was damn sure now. She blew out a long, exasperated breath, lifted her head, and looked at the flowers again. She shook her head and fought back angry tears.

"Why is life so cruel like this?" Charlie asked, her voice quivering.

Mason set the flowers on the edge of his desk. He didn't have to ask her what she meant. Clearly he was feeling the same way she was feeling, and it wasn't the first time either.

"We can't say what fate will do. God has a plan for everyone. Your life was already laid out before you were born. Sometimes one person is the anchor you need to get where God wanted you to be in the first place," Mason said cryptically.

Charlie understood what he was saying, but she didn't accept it. There was no way Emerson's divorce, such a painful thing, could be Charlie's key to unlocking love. No way!

"No. That's wrong. Your friend's misfortune can't be the anchor to you finding your soul mate," Charlie cried. She choked on her tears. She grabbed a few Kleenex from a box on Mason's desk and attempted to clean up her face. Charlie didn't think she would ever find a man who she felt like this about, but why did it have to be like this? She caught a chill just thinking about it and shivered.

Mason moved closer to her and embraced her. "Listen. We haven't done anything wrong, Charlie. We had lunch. What's the harm in that? You're here to get your report. Nothing more," he said, pulling her to him.

"But the feeling . . . I know what I'm feeling, Mason," she said through tears.

"Me too, but I won't ever do anything you are not comfortable with. I'll leave you alone. I understand how you're feeling. I get it," he said.

"I don't know if I want you to leave me alone, that's the thing. That's the fucked-up thing," she said, lifting her head out of his embrace to look at him squarely. Taking in an eyeful of his beautiful face wasn't the smartest thing to do. She shook her head and brought herself back to reality.

"No. Mason. No. We have a girlfriend code, and I have to live by it. No," Charlie said, standing up abruptly and grabbing her bag.

Eager for a distraction, Mason rushed around his desk and retrieved her report. Charlie tapped her foot nervously. "Okay, here it is," Mason said, holding the report out for her.

Charlie reached for it, and her hand brushed his. She felt that electric pulse again. She took a deep breath. "So what do I do with it?" she asked, finally clearing away the tears and the brain cobwebs that had overtaken her for a minute.

"You just need it for your insurance companies. The insurance companies will duke it out about who was at fault and decide who will pay the damage bills. You probably won't have to worry about anything until you get your new insurance contract and see that your bill went up," Mason explained.

"Shit, I need that like I need another Incredible Hulk pulling me out of my damn car," Charlie joked, lightening the tension that had enveloped them a few minutes earlier.

"Don't worry, all you have to do is call me. Mr. Man Mason, if anyone tries you again," he joked back.

Charlie lowered her eyes. She was feeling a tornado of emotions in that moment. She was torn between "go for it, girl" and "bitch, are you crazy?" Charlie knew she had to get her ass out of there before she lost her mind.

"I'm sorry for getting emotional on you," she said, her voice low. "You must think I'm some love-crazy chick with no life who goes around fighting dudes' girlfriends," she said, shaking her head in disgust.

"Nah. I don't think that at all. But you must think I'm a dirty dog for still being married and feeling something for my future ex-wife's best friend," he said flatly.

"It's my fault. I put you in this position with my dumb stuff," she apologized. Mason put his pointer finger on her lips. Charlie didn't fight it.

"Shh," he hissed.

Charlie looked up into his gorgeous eyes, and there went that feeling again. He leaned down and kissed her. Charlie parted her lips and allowed his tongue into her mouth. She felt her entire body come alive with electricity. It was a few seconds before they both realized what they'd done. Charlie pulled away first.

"Oh, my God," she whispered harshly, putting her fingers up to her lips like she couldn't believe what had just happened.

"Charlie, listen, I'm . . . I didn't mean to—" Mason stumbled over his words.

"I wanted to," Charlie said softly. "I wanted that."

Mason shoved his hands down into his pockets like he was on punishment for a bad act.

"It's not your fault," Charlie assured him. "It's me. I'm like some desperate chick out here on the prowl. I knew better, and I let it happen. I'm the fucked-up one. She's my friend. She's just your ex now."

"This is not the place to discuss things," he said. "Let's do dinner. No strings attached. Just to talk. Just to sort things out. I promise I won't cross the line ever again," Mason said, his hands up in surrender.

"Okay. I'd like that," she agreed. She started toward the door in a flourish.

"Charlie," Mason called.

Charlie closed her eyes for a few seconds and then turned around slowly.

"These belong to you," he said. He was holding the flowers out toward her again.

"Oh, shit. The flowers," Charlie huffed, embarrassed. She rushed back to him. Her hands trembled as she took the flowers from him. "Wow," she gasped, holding the flowers close to her face. She closed her eyes and inhaled the scent of the roses. Was this what everyone meant when they said to stop and smell the roses?

"Thank you, Mason," Charlie said sincerely. "For everything. No matter what shakes out, I'm grateful for every moment. And I'm especially grateful for you being the first man to ever give me flowers."

"Thank you too, Charlie. You know, for a man going through what I'm going through right now, it is not easy to believe in fate and all that good stuff anymore. But something changed for me over these past few weeks since your accident," he admitted.

Charlie smiled. With that, she turned the doorknob to his office and walked out into the hound's den. She garnered even more looks and double the amount of hushed murmurs passed among the staff as she walked through, carrying that huge bouquet of flowers.

Charlie rushed to her rental car like her legs were on fire. Her feet ached in her heels, and her heart thrummed so fast she thought it would jump loose from her chest. She rushed inside the car, locked the door, and screamed so loud she was sure someone would come busting out the windows thinking she was being attacked.

"Oh, my God!" she hollered. "Charlie! What the fuck are you doing? You can't! You're such a dumb bitch! Always!" Charlie cursed at herself, mad that she'd lost all sense and sensibility when it came to Mason. Charlie massaged the sides of her head. Her mind raced. If she had a blunt, she would smoke it down to the nub, and she hadn't had weed since her college days.

Charlie needed to talk to someone. She couldn't hold this in. She certainly couldn't talk to Emerson. She took a deep breath and courageously hit call under Mikayla's name. She closed her eyes and waited for Mikayla to answer. Charlie held her breath when she heard Mikayla's voice filter through the phone.

"KayKay? Ugh," Charlie grumbled when she realized it was Mikayla's voicemail. She hung up.

"Maybe that's God saving me. What was I thinking anyway? I can't tell anyone about this. I was bugging for a minute. Even Mikayla will think I'm crazy and fucked up for this," Charlie spoke out loud to herself.

Suddenly her phone rang in her hand. Charlie almost jumped out of her skin. She looked at the screen and saw Officer appear on her screen. It was Mason.

"Hello," she answered quickly.

"Hey," he replied. "Making sure you made it out of the stationhouse in one piece since there was a bunch of dudes drooling. I was sure you'd get eaten up before you could make it out."

If smiles had a sound, Mason would've surely been able to hear hers. "Hah! Nope, I made it out of there in one piece, and so did these beautiful-ass flowers," Charlie replied, looking over at her flowers. "Thank you again, Mason."

"Ah, no thanks needed. You brightened everyone's day around here. Obviously mine," he said.

Charlie didn't know what to say. And she was never one to run out of words. No man had ever been like this with her.

"So we said dinner, but we were a little thrown off. We never made a real plan," Mason said, filling in the silence.

Charlie's heart jerked in her chest again. She thought he was just talking to smooth things over in the office when he'd asked her to dinner. But obviously he was serious. Dating a girlfriend's future ex-husband was a big no-no, but Charlie couldn't bring herself to refuse Mason.

"Drinks and dinner sound good, so long as we keep our shit together and don't cross any lines. Mason, I don't know if we should be doing all of this," Charlie said honestly.

"Totally understandable. Let's start out slow. Strictly platonic," Mason replied. "Remember what I said earlier: we can't always fight what God has planned for us. That's just the real of it, Charlie."

Charlie smiled so wide every single one of her teeth were showing. *I like that. I like that a lot.* He was right! Who was she to fight what God had planned, especially after all of the failed and straight fucked-up relationships she'd had in the past? Not that she wanted a relationship with Mason. *It's just all in good fun,* she told herself.

"You're right. I like the idea of platonic. All in good fun," Charlie replied.

"How about this evening?" Mason blurted.

"Uh, sure," Charlie answered, feeling like a high school girl being asked on her first date. Her evenings were actually wide open nowadays since she had written off men after the Jace debacle.

"I'll come by your building and grab you around eight," Mason told her.

"Friendly, platonic dinner at eight," Charlie said, giggling coquettishly.

"Friendly, platonic dinner at eight," Mason repeated with a hint of joy in his tone.

"Thanks again for the flowers," Charlie said. "I'll see you later."

"Can't wait. And stop thanking me for the flowers. You deserve them."

Charlie didn't realize how wide she was smiling until her moment was interrupted by a knock on her rental car door. Her mouth quickly flattened into a straight line. Charlie smoothed her hands over her hair to put it back in place. She had been unconsciously twirling strands of her hair between her fingers while she was speaking to Mason.

"Yes?" Charlie piped up, her face stoic and serious as she rolled down the window.

"Are you coming out?" a man asked.

"What?" Charlie asked, a bit thrown off.

"The parking spot. Can I get your spot?"

Charlie's shoulders relaxed. "Oh, yes. I'm coming out." She rolled up her window and smiled. "I'm coming out in all kinds of ways, and I am going to say it is all God's plan. Matter of fact, I want to hear that song," Charlie spoke to herself as she scrolled through her phone and found Drake's song "God's Plan."

"'God's plan . . . God's plan,'" Charlie sang along, smiling from ear to ear like she'd just won the biggest prize of her life.

Chapter 7

Emerson

Emerson used her right hand to swipe two loose, dangling faux locks away from her face. She massaged her throbbing left temple. Her head was bent over the desk as she scanned the stack of papers in front of her for what seemed like the millionth time. She let out a long, exasperated sigh. This was going to be harder than she thought.

"I know it's a lot, Eme, but in most of these cases, the women don't have as much as you do," her attorney and friend, Macy Markowitz, told her. "At least you still have your career intact. Some wives walk away with nothing after years of sacrificing for their husbands. And I do mean with nothing."

Emerson sucked in her bottom lip and bit down on it. "I guess you're right. I just never thought it would come to this. I pictured myself being with this man forever. We've been together since we were literally kids. Ten years old, serious at fifteen, married right after college," Emerson lamented, her voice cracking.

"We didn't have things all figured out in the beginning. Things were kind of pure, you know? We still had sort of a friendship in its purest form. And we thought along the way we had figured life out. He got his career and he was happy, but I wasn't. He didn't want me to be me. I

couldn't feel caged in anymore. I feel bad now, like all of
this is my fault. I still love him, but I don't know if we can
ever like each other again. Love is an obligation. Liking
someone has to be from the heart," Emerson said. She
dropped the pen on top of the stack of papers and fanned
her hands in front of her eyes.

"Whew. I'm sorry," she whispered, trying to keep the
tears from falling and her makeup from running. "This
crying bullshit is so not me. I'm the tough one, you know?
I promised myself while you were on your way here that I
was not going to shed one damn tear, and look at me now.
A wreck."

Although Emerson had prepared herself for months
for this very moment, seeing it there in black and white
in front of her had finally cracked the shell of her usually "cool under pressure" composure. Emerson had tried
everything to move on, but she couldn't fully let go of the
hurt she'd suffered. She'd had a few dates with the hopes
that she could get Mason out of her mind. None of it had
worked.

Emerson pulled three sheets of Kleenex from the box
sitting on the end of her home office desk. She dabbed at
her eyes with the tissues. She took a deep breath, swallowed hard, and picked up the pen again.

"Can you believe that I am such a mess over a man?
Look at me. And I was the one who asked for this divorce,
not him. Some of my older friends and colleagues said
getting a divorce made you feel brand new, like you can
have any man you want out there, so why do I feel like my
life is over?" Emerson said.

Inside, Emerson knew she was no longer the four-eyed,
rail-thin, anxiety-filled girl who latched on to the first
boy who'd smiled at her. But that was exactly how she
felt now—desperate, wanting acceptance, and afraid to
be alone.

Macy gave Emerson the once-over and had to agree that she could have any man she wanted. Emerson was a beautiful woman. Her high cheekbones, full lips, and blemish-free mocha skin were what a lot of women paid high-dollar plastic surgeons to look like. Her body was flawless—flat abs, toned legs, perky tits, and a tight, round backside. She definitely could have any man she wanted. Yet her failed marriage to Mason still dominated her thoughts. Emerson hated to fail at anything. She also hated the thought of being alone. Loveless. Worthless. But she'd never admit it. Her claim to fame was that she was happy to be independent. It was a facade that she'd grown wary of for a few weeks now, especially because her friends seemed to be enmeshed in their romantic worlds. Charlie must've been courting yet another new prospect they'd hadn't met yet, because she'd been scarce. Mikayla was always entrenched in her marriage and life so deeply they'd often have to go dig her out.

Before Emerson signed, Macy reached across the desk and placed her hand on top of Emerson's. "Trust me, hon, you can definitely have any man, or woman for that matter, you want. And once all of this is over, I'm encouraging you, just like all of my clients, to go out there and live. Try new things. Be who you really are inside," Macy comforted her with a reassuring squeeze and a warm smile.

Emerson got goose bumps from Macy's touch, and she drew her hand back fast, not understanding the sudden feeling.

Macy caught herself as well and straightened up. "But like I said earlier, I think if you look at the other women, you are in a great place. You could be sitting in front of me right now, desperate to walk away with nothing but hurt feelings. I think things are going as planned," Macy reassured her.

Emerson lowered her eyes back to the paperwork. "Divorce" and "irreconcilable differences" were just a few of the terms swimming around on the paper and in her mind.

Emerson's head pounded now with the same dizziness she had after Mason had grabbed her roughly and almost beat her down. She remembered how her chest had tightened and how she'd lost her mind and control. Just like now, the same hot tears had run down her face in streams.

"Son of a bitch! Son of a bitch!" Emerson had screamed that night, right before she'd worked herself up so badly she'd missed her event, and her mother ended up putting her in the mental hospital the next day. She felt like screaming those words again now.

Emerson shivered at the thought. She couldn't risk that happening again or anyone finding out, ever.

"Emerson?" Macy called out. "Are you all right?"

Emerson blinked a few times. She cleared her throat and her mind.

"I feel like I lost you there for a moment," Macy joked.

"Yes, um, I'm fine," Emerson rasped.

"Are you sure you're ready?" Macy asked, her forehead creased.

"As I'll ever be," Emerson answered. Gripping the pen, she finally courageously scribbled her name on each page of the divorce papers wherever it asked for the petitioner's signature. She fought back her tears with every pen stroke.

"There. All done," Emerson said bravely as the tension in her muscles eased. "I am almost single and ready to mingle." She sniffled and gave a nervous chuckle.

"Look, Emerson, about what I said earlier, I . . . I didn't mean anything," Macy said, stumbling over her words. "I just meant you're a beautiful woman who should have no trouble finding love again."

"Honestly, I haven't ever had anyone be as caring and attentive as you have been in these past few weeks, Macy. I appreciate everything, especially your advice. And trust me, I am not closing my heart to love again, no matter who it might come from," Emerson confided.

Macy shook her head up and down and smiled. "That's a brave way to look at things," she said. She stood up. "Everything in your own time. Sometimes what we think is best for us turns out to be the opposite. Just be sure next time, whatever it is, it is really want you want. Oh, and just in case, you have forty-eight hours to change your mind," Macy told Emerson, nodding at the divorce papers on the desk.

Emerson sighed. She stood and smoothed the wrinkles out of her clothes. "I don't think I'll change my mind. Thanks for everything, Macy," Emerson said as they exchanged air kisses.

"These papers will be served within two weeks, so expect to hear from Mason," Macy advised. Emerson nodded and started for the door for Macy to follow her.

"Oh, Emerson?" Macy stopped walking behind her.

Emerson stopped and looked at Macy quizzically.

"Be safe. I've seen these things get ugly," Macy said.

"I'm not worried. Mason would never do anything to jeopardize his precious career," Emerson said and continued to walk Macy out.

As she watched Macy get into her car, Emerson turned back into the house and thought about what Macy had said. Emerson had seen quite a few divorces take a turn for the worse, but it wasn't always the husband who was the aggressor in those situations.

Emerson rushed back inside the house. The day had drained her. She needed to take her medication because she felt herself slipping, and God knows she couldn't afford another stint on the psych ward. If one ounce of that information got out to the public, it would derail her entire career. And that would simply destroy her.

It was only two hours after Macy left that she had to return. Emerson had mixed her psych medicine and alcohol. It was enough for her to be officially intoxicated, something she hadn't been since her days in college. She'd called Macy, crying, and Macy had rushed right back over. When Emerson pulled open the door, she practically fell into Macy's arms, sobbing.

"Shh," Macy comforted her, holding on to Emerson like she'd just been injured.

"I . . . I can't believe it's done. I know that's what I said I wanted, but . . ." Emerson blubbered through her tears.

"You don't have to explain," Macy whispered, stroking Emerson's hair.

Emerson pulled away and looked at Macy's face. There was something unspoken that passed between them. Macy took her signal and pulled Emerson into her and kissed her. Emerson started to resist, but that didn't last too long. They kissed passionately, almost animalistically. Macy's hands worked feverishly over Emerson's body. Emerson's head spun, but the heat of passion was burning away the deep loneliness that had consumed her life for months. Emerson didn't think about anything else in that moment but the feeling of being wanted. She didn't even know how they'd ended up in her bedroom, but once they were there, she was all in.

"Lie down," Emerson instructed, licking her lips seductively. She loved being in control. Tonight she would take the dominant role, a fantasy she had harbored for some time. Macy was excited. She obeyed. "On your stomach," Emerson commanded.

Macy stretched out and spread her arms up above her head. Breathing hard, Emerson opened her thick legs and straddled Macy from behind, letting her neatly trimmed triangle and wet labia kiss Macy's ass cheeks. Moving sensually, Emerson began kneading Macy's shoulders gently. Then she leaned down and spread her naked body over Macy's, pressing her firm C-cup breasts into Macy's back. Wetting her lips and extending her long tongue, Emerson started with the back of Macy's neck and licked her way down her spine, grinding her swollen clitoris up against Macy's ass as she made her way down.

"Wow," Macy grunted. Her throbbing body pressed into the mattress until it hurt. Without warning, she flipped over and swiftly changed positions with Emerson. Emerson seemed shocked, but she was too intoxicated to fight it. She felt like she wasn't in command of her brain, her body, or her life for that matter.

Macy inched down until she was on all fours. She worked until she found her destination. She let her tongue dance down Emerson's body. She wasn't sure how Emerson would react to this new situation, so she hesitated a minute. She stopped to watch Emerson arch slightly. That simple movement was Macy's invitation. Emerson moaned loudly. The excitement of what was to come made her hot box even more soaking wet. Macy put her face into Emerson's love box. Emerson grabbed a handful of the bedsheets in response. She had never done this, but it felt so right. Starting at the top, Macy licked her way down until she found Emerson's treasure button. Then she blew on it gently.

"Ahhh," Emerson cried out. She felt a little tingling sensation all over her body. Macy licked at Emerson roughly, moving her head from side to side. She grew more excited as she ravished Emerson with her tongue, in and out, in and out. Emerson began involuntarily pumping her body toward Macy's tongue. Emerson didn't know what had come over her, but it was as close to ecstasy as she'd been in a long time. Macy gladly obliged. She bent farther and flicked her tongue from Emerson's clit all the way down toward her ass.

"Oh, shit!" Emerson screamed out, feeling her juices welling up. Macy abruptly stopped, smiling slyly, making Emerson whimper and beg for it.

"Please give it to me. Don't stop," she begged.

"Gladly." Macy smirked. "You ready for more?" she whispered.

Emerson was in another world. She couldn't answer.

"I guess that means yes," Macy said as she slipped her middle finger inside, penetrating Emerson ever so slightly, in and out.

Emerson punched the bed. She felt violated, but it felt so good she wouldn't dare tell Macy to stop. Macy used her other hand to reach up and pinch Emerson's left nipple. She could feel them hard and rigid.

"You want to me stop?" Macy asked.

"No, please," Emerson said. Her inner thighs were soaked with her own juices. Macy moved her head and licked the sensitive area between the vagina and the anus. This drove Emerson even crazier.

"Urgh," she screamed. She couldn't take it. She loved every minute of it. The more she screamed, the further Macy went. The next thing she knew, Emerson was panting, "Huh, huh, huh." Then her eyes rolled back into her head. Her face was red, and a large green vein throbbed at her temple. "Ooh," she screamed as she came, erupting like a volcano.

"Mmmm," Macy moaned as she lapped up Emerson's creamy surprise.

That was the hardest Emerson had ever cum. Her body relaxed, and her head lolled to the side. She was exhausted. Macy smiled. It was her turn.

Chapter 8

Mikayla

It would've been a usual day in the neighborhood for Mikayla. Just like any other day, she would've woken up a dedicated wife and mother, going about making sure Charles and the girls had all of her time and attention. She would've jumped out of bed and started out her day like any other, making breakfast, washing and dressing her girls for school, preparing Charles's clothes for work, and doing all of the mundane things housewives do for everyone else but themselves. That would've been her life, but instead, today Mikayla sat up in her bed unable to get her day started at all. She'd tossed and turned all night, as she had for a couple of weeks now. Her hair was wild, her body was funky, and she hadn't slept. In fact, Mikayla hadn't gotten more than two or three hours of sleep at a time in two weeks or so since the incident with Charles in the restaurant and the aftermath that had followed.

Until then, things with Charles had stopped affecting Mikayla this deeply. She'd taught herself how to pretend it was all great at home. But this time had been different. It seemed like Charles had taken his cruelty to a new level. Honestly, she'd have rather he beat her down and treat her good after than what he'd done this time. There was something more cruel about mental abuse than physical abuse in Mikayla's assessment.

Mikayla couldn't help but feel like she only deserved to suffer. *Maybe it's karma*, she told herself. Maybe this was the kind of life she deserved.

Mikayla couldn't stop replaying in her mind what had happened when she got home that afternoon from Miss Shirley's.

Mikayla made sure to have the kids with her when she got home. She'd picked up her girls, Kai and Zuri, from school, and they were blabbing on and on about something or other as Mikayla unloaded them from the car and brought them inside the house. Mikayla wasn't scared of Charles attacking her right then, because she was confident that he wouldn't do it in front of the girls. He might've been a monster to Mikayla, but he was a good father to their girls.

Mikayla moved through the house like the hired help. She hung up jackets. She facilitated bathroom runs. She washed hands and set out homework. She went to the refrigerator and retrieved the dinner she'd prepped the day before and set about cooking it. She did everything a wife should do. She wanted to stop thinking about Charles, the other woman, and the bold way she'd stood up to him that might come back to literally destroy her. Mikayla wanted to pretend it was a normal day.

When she heard her front door open and close, she was brimming inside with nerves. Charles entered the house. Mikayla was so nervous, she dropped a glass in the sink and broke it.

"Daddy! Daddy!" Kai and Zuri bounded out of their chairs and barreled into Charles's arms. A chill shot down Mikayla's spine. This was why she sacrificed so much to be with him for the rest of her life. Giving up her aspirations to be a lawyer when she met and fell in love with Charles was all for her kids now. Mikayla questioned lately whether it was worth it, but each time

she did, she thought about her girls. She couldn't give them the life they had now. Not alone, without Charles and his money.

Tears fell down her cheeks as she thought about the trap that had become her life. She was tired of being dependent, but there was no plan to become independent.

Mikayla listened to the girls ramble on to Charles. "Daddy, I did this," said Kai. "No, Daddy, I did mine better," Zuri rebutted.

Mikayla swiped her tears away, took a deep breath, and headed out of the kitchen to greet her husband. She had to act like nothing had happened or else he might not. Mikayla said a silent prayer as she walked toward him.

"Hello," Mikayla rasped. When she got no response, she smiled down at her children. "C'mon, little ladies, let Daddy change his clothes, and you all get back to those assignments," she said. She ushered her girls back to the table.

Not one word came from Charles. He barely even looked in her direction.

That wasn't a good sign. When he was like that, Mikayla knew he could be unpredictable if she didn't try to smooth things over. She'd already practiced a thousand ways to say sorry for standing up for herself in the restaurant, although she still felt justified in what she did. He had been there with another woman, for God's sake!

Sweat beads lined up on her forehead, threatening to ruin her weave as she contemplated what to do. Mikayla settled her girls and then steeled herself to go speak to her husband. She took a few deep breaths and climbed the stairs. She walked the long hallway to their bedroom. Mikayla's heart sank as soon as she stepped inside of their bedroom.

She almost tripped over the bags. She groaned loudly, because the packed bags could mean one of two things. Charles was traveling, and she'd be alone with the girls for days or even weeks, or Charles was going to threaten to leave again and watch her fall apart. Mikayla looked around. Charles had luggage packed and lined up across the floor. There was no way he had time to do this that fast. These bags were already packed and hiding in the house, *Mikayla thought, exasperated and disappointed all at once. She eyed the bags good, and that was when she noticed that it wasn't just his usual traveling bags by the door. There was much more this time. Mikayla swallowed hard. It looked to her like he was packing and never coming back.*

"Charles?" Mikayla called softly, trying to keep her voice steady as an uneasy feeling crept up on her. The sound of her own voice reverberating off the walls made her feel even more dreadful inside. Instinctively, Mikayla felt something just wasn't right.

"Charles?" she called out as she walked slowly into their closet. "Charles, I came to talk," she called again, growing more frantic. Finally, Charles appeared from the back of the closet. He smirked, and Mikayla's eyes went wide as dinner plates. She'd seen that look many times, but that day it was slightly different. She swallowed hard. It was something more evil than she'd ever seen. Charles's look was more like the devil himself was dancing in his eyes.

"What are you doing?" she said, flashing a fake smile. It was all she could do to keep from screaming and scaring her girls. She was trying real hard to stamp down the sick feeling in her gut. Charles looked at her steely eyed and stone-faced.

"I . . . I'm sorry for earlier," she stammered. His glare just had Mikayla feeling uneasy. She couldn't stand it

anymore. She needed to know what the hell was up. If it was a beating she was going to take, she wanted to get it over with. They stared at each other for at least thirty long seconds. "Charles?" she said, breaking the eerie silence. "Why do you look like that? The bags?" she said, her voice cracking.

"Look, Mikayla. Don't act like you don't know what this is," he said, lowering his eyes away from hers. His voice was even, stern. "You knew better and—"

"What? I don't know." Mikayla started shaking. What was he talking about? He couldn't even look her in the eyes. That wasn't like him. He had always been the one to command everything in their lives. Charles not being able to keep eye contact was a bad fucking sign. Mikayla could feel her heart squeezing tight inside of her chest, but she couldn't speak.

"I'm leaving. I'm having all my things moved out today," Charles said with not one ounce of emotion behind his words. Mikayla didn't see one shred of remorse in his words nor in his face. She felt like a bell had gone off in her head. There was loud ringing, and she felt off-kilter. Her legs shook. She actually felt like he'd punched her again. She felt like the wind had been knocked out of her.

At first, when she opened her mouth to say something, nothing came out. "Why?" she finally whispered breathlessly.

"Don't make this harder than it has to be, Mikayla. We will talk about the girls after I'm settled in a new place and you've figured yourself out," Charles said coldly, another punch to the gut. He couldn't be serious. He knew there was nothing for Mikayla to figure out. He'd figured her life out for her for the past twelve years she'd been married to him. He'd told her what to eat, what to wear, where to go most of the time. How could he expect her to figure out herself now? He knew she didn't know how.

"*Charles, are you mad because I went out with my friends?*" *she asked, tears rimming her eyes.* "*I didn't mean the stuff I said in the restaurant. I was just thrown off by . . .*" *Mikayla's heart was hammering so hard she felt nauseous. She was scared to death. She'd have rather taken a million beatings than lose her husband and have her girls suffer. He had to be playing a cruel joke on her, she reasoned.*

"*It doesn't even matter. I'm leaving. It's over, Mikayla. It's been over,*" *he replied dryly.*

"*No! No!*" *she screamed as she threw herself into him. She couldn't care in that moment.* "*Stop saying that. Touch me,*" *Mikayla cried, trying to put his limp arms around her.*

"*It's final, Mikayla. I don't love you anymore,*" *Charles said, turning his back on her.* "*And after today, I see that you don't love and respect me anymore either.*"

"*No! That's not true! Stop it!*" *Mikayla huffed and puffed, and something snapped inside of her. Charles pulled away from her and started walking out of the closet. She ran after him as he walked away dismissively. She felt the need to be face-to-face so he could look her in the eyes and tell her why he was doing this to her. She didn't care how dangerous that could turn out for her given Charles's penchant for violence against her. Mikayla's desperation drove her forward.*

"*After everything, Charles, don't you turn your back on me!*"

He whirled around, and his large barrel chest was heaving up and down like he was about to pummel Mikayla. That gave her pause, and she backed away a few steps.

"*Charles, why are you doing this to me again? Leaving? What about the girls? What about everything we have built?*" *she cried as she searched his cold eyes for answers. Mikayla was actually begging for her abuser to stay. She didn't realize just how sick she was in that moment. She didn't realize how far down Charles had taken her life. It was probably lower than she'd ever lived, except this time she had material things and wasn't as poor as before.*

Still she begged him to stay. She got on her knees in front of him and actually begged him to stay with her. "Please," she cried. "I'll be good. I'll do anything. I won't ever do something like that again," she pleaded, all dignity gone. All of the bravado she'd had earlier that day was a complete contradiction to that moment.

"There's nothing you can do this time," Charles snapped.

Mikayla felt weak. "What are you talking about? I did everything for you! I'll do anything for you!" she cried. "I could give up my friends! I'll just stay here and take care of you and the girls. I swear. I'll be everything you want me to be, Charles," she groveled. Her dignity lay at his feet, and Mikayla could see the satisfaction playing across his face. It was a cruel act of mental abuse he was inflicting on her. It was like training a dog, and Charles knew just what whistle to blow.

"You know what to do then," Charles said, giving in to her pleas.

Mikayla shook her head up and down like an obedient pet. Still on her knees, she unzipped his pants. Mikayla reached up and grabbed his throbbing penis. Seeing her beg for her life had actually turned her husband on, just like beating her up and taking care of her after did, and he was rock hard. Mikayla went about the work she knew she had to do to keep her life intact. It wasn't like she hadn't been used to this all of her life. Mikayla had done a lot of things to survive, then and now.

Now Mikayla's doorbell ringing incessantly was what finally snapped her out of reliving her last nightmare, the one that had taken her down to the shell of a person she was right now. Her first instinct was to ignore the doorbell. She couldn't stomach another pop-up visit from Emerson and Charlie at the moment.

In the two weeks since Charles had threatened to leave Mikayla and then treated her like a dirty whore and made her beg him to stay, she'd cried and cried until she made herself so sick she had started throwing up nothing but her stomach acids. Mikayla didn't even have enough energy to get the girls to school the first day after. She had slept curled up in a fetal position for days. It wasn't until a few days later that she was able to even drag herself out of bed. Her emotions ran the gamut from sorrowful to all-out, full-on rage.

But today, after weeks of a mentally debilitating roller coaster, an unnerving calm suddenly came over her like a warm blanket. Mikayla didn't know what it was, but she bolted up in the bed. Suddenly, she had mustered enough strength to pull herself out of bed. She wrapped herself in her robe and went downstairs to answer the doorbell.

Mikayla pulled open the door. God had to be playing a cruel joke on her. The day she'd been dreading had finally come. After everything she'd been through as a child, everything she'd been through at the hands of her husband, now this. Mikayla blinked a few times, and suddenly her world went black.

Chapter 9

Charlie, Emerson, Mikayla

"C'mon, Damian. We have to go inside," Mikayla said to her brother, annoyed that he'd totally stopped walking.

"I don't want to," Damian said forcefully. "I don't like it here. I don't want to go in there. We need to go home."

"It's going to be better than home. If you won't go in with me, we won't be together," Mikayla said, trying again to get her brother moving. Even though she was twelve and her brother was eight, she had always been like his mother. Mikayla had been the one who made sure he ate, bathed, and was safe. Their mother was too busy on a mission to get high every single day to bother with taking care of them. On many occasions, until Mikayla got old enough to care for them both, their mother had left them hungry and dirty.

"But it's not our house," Damian said, nearly in tears.

"Let's go. I'm not going to hold my door open much longer!"

Mikayla and her brother both almost jumped out of their skin. They stood at the entrance of the strange house with their eyes stretched wide. Damian latched on to Mikayla so tight she could feel his heart beating against her hip.

"Well?" the old woman shouted at them. Then a man stepped from behind her. He was tall, ugly, and looked up to no good.

Mikayla and Damian had stayed in that foster home for three years, and it was hell. But one day, they'd had enough and things turned.

"I'm gonna ask you again, what happened to my orange juice?" their evil foster mother growled, her long, yellow, corroded pointer fingernail stabbing at Damian's forehead.

Mikayla and Damian stood in front of the refrigerator and noticed that the lock that was usually on it had been broken off. Mikayla shook her head no. "We . . . we didn't drink it," Mikayla said firmly, moving on her legs like she had to pee.

"We can't even get in there," Damian followed up. "So how we gonna drink your stupid orange juice?"

Mikayla and Damian both knew it was a setup. They hadn't had food or drink without strict permission in years. But the old woman always wanted a reason to discipline them. She would find reasons or make shit up.

"Neither one of us drank it," Mikayla said, her voice quivering.

"Gotdamn liars!" the woman roared. Then she pulled her thick black leather belt from its usual place.

"You can't hit us. We didn't drink it," Damian said, his eyes squinted into dashes.

"Oh, yeah? You think you can steal out of my fridge and then talk to me like this?" the old woman spat. "Well, I got something for no-good kids like y'all," she hissed.

"Please, don't," Mikayla pleaded through tears. Damian stepped in front of Mikayla. Although he was younger, he was hell-bent on protecting her.

"We said we ain't drink it," he said again through gritted teeth, sticking out his little chest. "And you ain't gonna hit me or my sister with that belt."

"Oh, yeah? We gon' see about that," the old woman said through her teeth. Without further warning, she swung her belt, and it caught Damian right across his face.

"Ouch!" he shrieked, crumpling to the floor and holding his face.

"Don't hit my brother!" Mikayla screamed. Without warning, she rushed into the old woman with the force of a big black wrecking ball. Caught off guard, the old woman fell back and landed with a thud on her back. It sounded like something at the base of the old woman's skull cracked. Mikayla jumped up like she was surprised by her own strength. She looked at Damian, who was still holding his face. They both knew the situation had just gone from bad to worse.

Mikayla and Damian looked at one another. Mikayla was crying, but Damian didn't shed a tear. Even with the thick purple welt that had cropped up on his face, he never buckled. Mikayla knew then that it wouldn't be the first time they'd have to take someone down to survive.

Mikayla jumped out of her sleep and whipped her head around frantically. Her chest pumped up and down so fast she had to cough to catch her breath. When her eyes came into focus and landed Charlie's face, she leaned over and gagged.

"Hey. Hey. You were dreaming," Charlie said softly, concern creasing her face.

"Oh, my God," Mikayla gasped, placing her hand on her chest. "What happened? How did . . ." She looked around the hospital room strangely.

"I don't know exactly, but you fainted and hit your head really badly. They said some old injury or old concussion might've caused you to be blacked out so long. I'm just thankful you're up now," Charlie said, touching Mikayla's hand gently.

"My girls . . . Charles . . ." Mikayla struggled to speak against the oxygen mask.

"They're fine," Charlie said, stopping short of saying that Mikayla's mother and brother had arrived. Charlie didn't want Mikayla upset again. The doctor who had come earlier told Charlie that the best thing for a head injury like Mikayla's was pain medication and lots of rest. "You know those girls love their daddy," Charlie said, twisting her lips. She couldn't help but think that this was all because of Charles. Charlie knew damn well Mikayla wasn't getting hit by soccer balls or falling or running into walls. It was always an excuse. The old head injury the doctor found was a dead giveaway.

Mikayla finally relaxed against the pillows on her hospital bed again. Charlie was right. Charles would never let anything happen to their girls. She'd always said that he might've been rough to tolerate as a husband, but he had always been a good father.

"I'm happy you're here, Charlie. I guess I'm lucky," Mikayla said, parting a weak smile.

"I'm happy to be with you, but not happy to be here. Somebody going to have some 'splaining to do before this is all said and done," Charlie half joked.

Mikayla let out a halfhearted chuckle, but deep down inside she knew that Charlie was serious. She would probably be confronting Charles if she hadn't already. Charlie was a loyal friend to the end.

"Where's Eme?" Mikayla asked, looking over at the door.

"She should be on her way," Charlie replied. "I kind of found out about this first and then I called her," Charlie said, then caught herself. How was she going to explain to Mikayla and Emerson that she'd gotten the call from Mason about Mikayla? Charlie hadn't even bothered to ask Mason any details when he'd called and said an emergency had been called in at Mikayla's house and that a female adult, most likely Mikayla, had been rushed to the hospital unconscious.

At the time, Charlie had practically hung up on Mason as she raced out of her apartment, forgetting that she didn't have her car. Charlie had gotten an Uber and raced to the hospital. She'd remembered to call Emerson after she was already there. Charlie thought about that now and knew that Emerson would be ready to kill her when she realized Charlie had been there long before her. Emerson was controlling like that.

"What do you remember about what happened?" Charlie asked Mikayla, trying to see if Mikayla would tell her exactly what happened. Charlie always had her suspicions whenever Mikayla would turn up with some old bruise or new ones too, but being admitted to the hospital had taken things to a new level for Charlie.

"I . . . I don't remember much. I don't know if I was dreaming or what, but I think the last thing I remember was seeing my brother in front of me," Mikayla replied, closing her eyes from the pain in her head.

"You think you were dreaming?" Charlie asked. "I know you said your mother called a few weeks ago and said he was getting out, but that could've just been her wanting to fuck with you like always."

Mikayla turned her face away. She didn't know if she was dreaming when she'd seen Damian. She knew in her heart that she loved him but that he was probably also very angry at her. If she was having nightmares about what had happened to them, Mikayla was sure he probably suffered from memories all those years locked up too.

"I need pain medicine," she rasped. "I can't take the pain in my head."

Within a second, Charlie was on her feet. "Okay, *chica*. Let me go get somebody to help you. I'm going to send them in and then go check and see where Emerson is, okay?" Charlie said.

Mikayla nodded her approval. Charlie raced out of the room to get the nurse.

Emerson rushed down the long hospital corridor, terror etched on her face. Her friend Macy was hot on her heels after insisting that she tag along for moral support. Macy had become a great support for Emerson in the weeks since she'd signed her divorce papers.

"Room 211, that's what Charlie said over the phone," Emerson huffed, her heels ringing off like gunshots against the hard, tiled hospital floors.

"Right here." Macy pointed, stopping abruptly in front of the door.

Emerson sucked in her breath and whirled around when she found the empty bed inside.

"Where . . ." Macy started.

Emerson pushed her out of the way and rushed back into the hallway. She raced down to the nurses' station. "The patient who's supposed to be in room 211, what happened? Where is she?" Emerson demanded.

The nurses behind the counter all looked up at the same time.

"Hello? She's speaking English here," Macy snapped before anyone could speak.

"Ma'am, who are you looking for? That room has been empty since this morning," a short, Hispanic nurse answered looking straight at Emerson.

"Um, Kay . . . I mean, Mikayla King," Emerson stuttered, her nerves on edge.

"Are you related to the patient?" the nurse asked a little too suspiciously for Emerson's liking.

"Her sister. She's her sister," Macy filled in before Emerson could snap at the nurse.

Emerson shook her head and pinched the bridge of her nose. Her mind was so scattered. She'd been out to lunch having wine with Macy when she'd gotten the call from Charlie. Emerson hadn't even heard Charlie all the way out. All Emerson heard was "emergency," "hospital," and "Mikayla." She ran straight to the hospital, Macy in tow.

"I just need to see my sister. I was told room 211, and it is unnerving coming here to find an empty room," Emerson snapped, her foot tapping against the floor expectantly.

"Okay, ma'am. It's okay. Your sister was moved to room 222," the nurse placated her in a soft voice.

"Thank you," Emerson huffed. "Do you know if anyone else has been here with her?" Emerson asked.

"Yes, her husband and another sister arrived early this morning a few hours after she was brought in by ambulance," the nurse reported.

Emerson's shoulders slumped with relief. At least Charles had stepped up. She knew the other sister the nurse referred to had to be Charlie.

Emerson and Macy headed toward the room number the nurse had given them. Macy was talking and offering constant support, but the chatter was starting to grate on Emerson's nerves.

"Shhh. Please, just for a minute. I have to gather my thoughts just in case she is in worse condition than I can imagine right now," Emerson snapped, holding up her finger. Macy stopped talking. She folded her arms across her chest and squinted her eyes, but she didn't say anything else.

Before Emerson could walk into Mikayla's room, she heard her name coming from the left. It was Charlie. It had been two weeks since their last meet up, and Emerson had been so busy she hadn't had time to even check in with Charlie or Mikayla. She felt terrible, but she had to admit, Charlie looked great. She was glowing, which always meant that Charlie had found a new love, even if it always did turn out to be temporary. Emerson stood waiting before she entered the room. She knew Charlie probably knew just what the hell was going on.

"Hey." Emerson greeted Charlie with a short hug. "Thank goodness you got here so fast," Emerson huffed. Although it had crossed her mind that she lived closer to the hospital than Charlie, she didn't ask any questions. As long as one of them had gotten there right away.

"Girl, she looks terrible. She was completely out of it when I first got here. Then she woke up panting and stuff like she was having a nightmare. The doctors said she had some old head injury, like she's been concussed a few times or something, and then when she passed out, it made it worse because she hit her head. I really think this nigga Charles is beating on her. I swear to God if I find out, Emerson, I swear . . ." Charlie rambled.

Emerson's eyes were wide. She couldn't keep up with how much information Charlie had thrown at her in a matter of seconds. "Oh, my God," Emerson replied. She touched her chest because she felt like her heart was breaking into tiny pieces. She wasn't one to normally lose her cool in public, but Mikayla was one of her best friends, and to hear that she had many old injuries just broke Emerson's heart.

"I think she needs to leave him," Charlie told Emerson.

"We have to see if she'll tell us what's going on. Without knowing for sure, we won't be able to convince her, and we won't be able to help her take action either," Emerson replied, still kind of shocked.

"They just gave her something for the pain, and she's sleeping," Charlie said, "so just go in for a quick second, and then let's go get something to eat."

Emerson agreed, but she wasn't hungry. She was in and out of Mikayla's room in minutes. Tears danced down her face as she rushed out of the room.

Macy moved to her side and grabbed her hand. Emerson yanked it away roughly. "Not now. Not here," Emerson whispered roughly through her tears.

Charlie watched the exchange with furrowed brows, but she didn't say a word. They all walked in silence to the hospital's cafeteria.

"Charles!" Emerson called out as soon as she spotted Mikayla's husband. Charles turned around slowly, like he was expecting to see his worst enemy. Emerson stopped dead in her tracks, and her mouth fell open when she saw Mikayla's mother, Jewel, and Damian stand up from the table where Charles was sitting.

"What the fuck are they doing here?" Emerson gasped. "This can't fucking be good."

"Oh, my God. She wasn't dreaming," Charlie whispered, her mouth also hanging open slightly. "She told me she thought she dreamt they had showed up at her door. It was no damn dream."

"You know this can't be good for KayKay, right? That woman brings out the absolute worst in her," Emerson said, her head moving like it was on a swivel from Charles to Mikayla's mother and brother and back again.

"Oh, my God," Charlie said again, still not able to find the words. "You think that she came to fuck up KayKay's life for real? After all this time and everything she did to her in the past?" Charlie whispered harshly as she and Emerson moved in slow motion.

"Yes. The bitch is evil, and so is that bastard. I always knew that's why his name is Damian, like that devil boy from that movie, just spelled differently," Emerson answered. "And look at them, smiling like somebody really is happy to see them."

Emerson's eyes stayed wide as they approached Charles, Jewel, and Damian.

"Hello," Emerson said tentatively, looking at Jewel suspiciously. Emerson hadn't had any encounters with Jewel, but she'd seen pictures. By the time she'd met Mikayla, she knew enough about Mikayla's birth mother to formulate her own opinions about the woman. Over the years, Emerson would witness Jewel drop in and out of Mikayla's life, and each time Jewel would leave Mikayla's life in emotional shambles. Emerson, and later on Charlie, had been the ones who'd always helped Mikayla dig out of the mess her mother would always leave her in.

"Her friends," Charles said, his form of an introduction.

Charlie's right foot tapped anxiously on the floor. "Correction, we are her sisters," Charlie snapped.

"Well, I am her mother, and this is her brother," Jewel said with a comeback of her own.

"Damn, let me find out my sister got some hot-ass friends," Damian said, stepping forward and rubbing his chin like a hungry wolf.

Emerson exhaled a windstorm of breath. Macy stepped closer to her. Emerson was not in a good mental space at that moment. She wanted to spit on Jewel and Damian and tell them to take their sorry asses right back to wherever they came from because Mikayla had been living just fine without them for years now. Emerson knew some things Mikayla had shared with her about her so-called family, and none of it had been positive.

"Fuck all these stupid introductions that don't matter," Charlie snapped. "So what happened to her, Charles? Huh?" Charlie asked pointedly. She didn't care about anyone's feelings, and in her assessment, this wasn't the time or place to be walking on eggshells.

"That's a good question," Charles replied snidely. "You're her sister. You tell me. Doesn't she tell you everything?"

"Wait one damn minute. I know you not going to act like you don't know how she got so many old injuries and how she ended up knocked the fuck out today," Charlie snapped, rearing her balled fist.

Emerson stepped between Charlie and Charles. "No, we are not doing this here, now. Not in public. We will talk about all of that after Mikayla is better," Emerson said, pushing Charlie back. Emerson wasn't for making rowdy scenes.

Charles chuckled at Charlie's aggression. "It's good to know she has sisters who will fight for her," he said with more snide sarcasm in his words.

"Well, it's not good to know that she has a man who beats the shit out of her," Charlie snapped back, yelling over her shoulder as Emerson dragged her away.

"Enough!" Emerson scolded Charlie. Emerson and Macy pulled Charlie away. "If we do this, he will get us restricted from the hospital, and then we won't know shit about what's going on with her. Is that what you want?" Emerson said.

"It's just not right, Eme. I know it was him. I know KayKay been lying to us about that shit for years," Charlie hiccupped through a sob. She quickly covered her mouth with a shaky hand. "I can't even talk about it. Out of everybody, she don't deserve to be treated like that. Not her."

"I know, but we have to be smart about this. You know how abusers are. He'll isolate her from us if we press too much. We have to go at this slowly," Emerson lectured.

"He is a fucking piece of shit as a man, Emerson," Charlie said through gritted teeth. "He fucking cheated on her right in her face and acted like she didn't have a right to say shit to his ass. She's fucking scared of him. I feel that shit in my bones every time I'm around her. You believed her when she said she got hit with a soccer ball? No! That shit was a perfect punch in the fucking eye. And it wasn't the first time we saw her with bruises after she went ghost for a week or more, so imagine how she must've looked if we would've stormed her house the day after," Charlie cried, her hands trembling just thinking about it all.

"Shh, I know. I know. We are going to get to the bottom of it," Emerson comforted her, holding on to Charlie and patting her shoulder.

"I'm telling you, he is totally abusive. He probably beats her ass and then after tells her it was her fault. I can't sit by and watch this shit. You know this is exactly what my mother went through with her boyfriends, and it's the same reason she couldn't stand her kids. She never knew what love was, and she didn't know how to find it either. One ass whooping after the last. That's all I saw growing up, and it's exactly why I can't trust these motherfucking men," Charlie said, pouring her heart out. This whole thing had done something to her emotionally. She wasn't blind to domestic abuse. In fact, she was an expert on it by now.

"I will kick his ass, Eme. I know people who will put hands on that motherfucker so fast he won't know what hit him," Charlie growled. "I will find a gun, and I will blow that bastard away if he even tries anything. We need to save her. I'm so scared for her. I know we've taken it lightly all this time, but this shit, this hospital shit, it's a wake-up call." Charlie was breathing fire like a dragon. She had no patience for abusers.

"Shh. Keep your voice down. We don't want everyone to hear you talking like this, Charlie," Emerson whispered.

"I know damn well you are not considering letting him get away with this bullshit, Eme. We have to stand by Mikayla and make her start standing up for herself. Every time he does it, there is a chance she won't make it out. Do you know how serious blacking out is?" Charlie wouldn't stop. It was like something had come over her.

"It's not up to me to let him get away with anything, Charlie. It's also not up to you. All we can do is be there for Mikayla when she is ready to change things," Emerson informed her sadly.

"This shit just burns me the fuck up," Charlie said, clenching her fists. "He is not going to keep doing this. I won't keep acting like I don't see it," she promised, shaking her head and swiping angrily at the tears streaming down her face.

"I hear you. I support you and Mikayla through thick and thin, you know that. We are all in this together, but right now, making a scene is not the answer. Charles will get what is coming to him if what we suspect is true," Emerson replied. "You know that what goes around comes around, and every single dog has his day. He can't keep doing things and not think that karma will eventually catch his ass red-handed. Karma is real, Charlie. Karma is very fucking real, and I believe in karma so deeply that I simply don't worry about when people do me wrong. They will get theirs," Emerson said with feeling. "You just never know. I'm telling you, with karma on your side, life can change in an instant. We can't control these sorts of things. The only thing we can control is out reaction to them. We can't be out here reacting like we are still kids in the streets of Baltimore," Emerson said.

Suddenly, Emerson's eyes darted over Charlie's shoulder. Her eyebrows shot up in surprise. "Is that . . ." Emerson squinted.

Charlie turned around, and all of the color drained from her face. "Mason," Charlie whispered so low only she heard it.

"What is he doing here?" Emerson grumbled. Her friend Macy moved to her side like a protector.

Charlie stood stock still, shocked into immobility. She was screaming in her head to play it cool, but she couldn't seem to control what was happening to her.

"Ladies," Mason greeted them after finally getting across the expansive cafeteria to where they were standing. He was smiling, which instantly pissed Emerson off. She didn't know why, but seeing him look so happy just did something to her inside.

"What are you doing here?" Emerson asked, getting right to the point.

"I'm a cop. You forgot?" he answered, his smile fading. "It was officers from my station who responded to the call. It's not like I haven't know Mikayla as long as I've known you. I came to see about her. Is that all right with you?" he answered, annoyed by Emerson's audacity.

Charlie hung her head and shook it. Suddenly she felt like she was standing barefoot on a block of ice. She closed her eyes and said a quick, silent prayer that her guilt wasn't playing out all over her face

"Charlie, long time no see. How you been?" Mason said all in one breath, his voice a bit too cheerful for Charlie's liking.

Charlie swallowed and cracked a fake smile. "Hey, um, hey, Mason. Yeah, long time no see. I'm fine. I'm just fine," Charlie answered robotically. She just couldn't lie to save her life.

"Well, I guess I'll go on up and see her," Mason announced. They all stood there in different stages of awkwardness.

"Um, I'll walk with you and show you where," Charlie blurted, suddenly able to move. There was no way she was going to stand there with Emerson and her guard dog Macy and risk showing any signs of guilt.

"Thanks for saving me, Charlie," Emerson said, then rolled her eyes.

"Or saving me, whichever way you want to look at things," Mason came back, then smiled.

Charlie could see that there was definitely no love left between those two. She felt slightly happy inside, but she was too scared to recognize the feelings coursing through her body as happiness.

"What are you doing? Are you crazy?" Charlie asked, speaking low through her teeth as soon as she and Mason were out of Emerson's and Macy's earshot.

"I came to see about you under the false pretense that I was checking on Mikayla," Mason replied in the same way Charlie had spoken to him, through the teeth. "I mean, not that I don't care what happened to her. But I care much more how you are doing."

Charlie shook her head and smiled. "You're too much, you know that?"

They stepped onto the elevator together, and it was empty. Mason wasted no time moving closer to Charlie.

"You're the one who's too much, and that's exactly why I can't stop thinking about you and wanting to see you and be wherever you are," he said, pulling her in for a kiss.

Charlie didn't fight it. She'd stopped doing that days ago. She was in love with Mason Dayle, the ex-husband of her best friend.

When the elevator doors opened, Charlie and Mason pulled apart, but not before they came face-to-face with Anna, Emerson's mother.

"Charlie? Mason?" Anna said, her eyes darting from one to the other.

"Ms. Leighton," Charlie sang, shocked as hell. "What are you—"

"I'm here visiting a friend of mine," Emerson's mother cut Charlie off. "And you two?" she asked, eyeing Mason suspiciously.

"Mikayla, she's been admitted for a head injury," Mason answered before Charlie could gather her thoughts.

"Yes, and Mason heard about it at work and came over to see if Mikayla and Emerson were okay after everything, you know?" Charlie said nervously, looking at Emerson's mother and then over at Mason.

"Oh," Emerson's mother huffed. "Speaking of Emerson, does she know you two are here . . . together?"

"Yup. Yeah. I mean, yes. She was . . . we were downstairs when Mason came, and then Emerson asked me to walk him up and show him to Mikayla's room because she didn't want to, and she is here with Macy, and she—" Charlie prattled nervously.

"Macy? Her again?" Emerson's mother snorted. "Anyway, please send Mikayla my well wishes. I am late for an appointment as it is. It was good seeing you, Charlie," she said. Then she glared at Mason. "Mason," she droned, then walked onto the elevator in a huff.

"Oh, my God," Charlie gasped, holding her chest like she was about to have a heart attack. "What the fuck are we doing?"

"She didn't see anything. I'm sure," Mason said.

"How do you know that?" Charlie snapped. "Did you see the way she looked at us? I'm telling you, she was suspicious, and she will do anything to make sure her precious Emerson never has to deal with shit. She is on to us," Charlie said, walking in circles now.

"Stop," Mason commanded. "Look at me," he said. "She doesn't know anything. That woman would've been all over my ass if she even suspected anything. She was just shocked to see people she knew, just like we were shocked to see her old ass."

"You're wrong. I'm telling you. I sensed it," Charlie huffed, moving on her feet again.

"Don't be silly. She is not Miss Cleo. She does not have a crystal ball. Besides, that kiss was over way before those doors opened," Mason said, even though he wasn't sure.

Charlie swallowed hard and managed a halfhearted smile, which looked like a terrified frown. "I damn sure hope you're right," she mumbled.

"Now come on and let's do this visit before your other BFF and her wo-man friend come up here and start their shit," Mason said.

"Wo-man. Okay, I get it. I definitely get it," Charlie replied.

They both started laughing.

"Ohhh, I'm just thinking about something," Charlie said like a light bulb had gone off in her head.

Mason raised a brow at her.

"I hope you didn't drive her to the other side of the fence," Charlie said jokingly.

"I'd like to drive you somewhere," he whispered, then touched Charlie's butt just as they approached Mikayla's hospital room door. They didn't have a care in the world about who might be watching them.

Chapter 10

Mikayla

"Mommy! Mommy! Mommy!" Zuri and Kai screamed and barreled into Mikayla as soon as she entered her house. Mikayla stumbled backward a few steps before catching her balance. She embraced her daughters, and her heart filled with joy. She'd missed them, and it was obvious they'd missed her.

"Hey, baby girls. I've missed you two so much," Mikayla said sweetly, wrapping her arms around her girls as tight as she could. "You both look so big. I wasn't even gone that long."

"I was sad when you were gone a long time," Zuri mumbled into the skin of Mikayla's neck.

"Yeah, don't leave for a long time and 'pend the night outside," Kai followed up with her own complaint.

"I know. I'm so sorry. Mommy had to get better or the doctors wouldn't let me come back home," Mikayla said soothingly.

"I hate when Daddy cooks," Zuri groaned.

"And that lady said she's our grandma, and she doesn't look nice. And that guy said he is our uncle, and he's scary." Zuri whined complaints, holding on like she didn't believe Mikayla was staying.

"Shh," Mikayla comforted them, stroking her daughters' heads. "I am back, and I won't ever, never, ever leave

you both again. I promise, okay?" Mikayla freed herself
from her daughters' tight grips. "I tell you what. As soon
as Mommy is finished taking a hot shower and changing
clothes, we can go get ice cream and get a new toy. Deal?"
Mikayla said, bartering with her girls out of guilt.

"Yes! Deal!" they cheered. "Hurry up, Mommy!"

Mikayla watched her daughters race up the staircase
toward their room.

"Ahem," Jewel cleared her throat.

Mikayla turned around to find her mother standing
with her arms folded across her chest, regarding Mikayla
expectantly. Mikayla shifted her weight from one foot to
the other. She realized she must've appeared like she was
so unhappy to see her mother that there was nothing she
could do at that point to hide it.

"I thought you'd be gone by now," Mikayla said, breaking eye contact with her mother.

"I told you on the phone we were coming and thinking
about getting someplace close for me and Damian," her
mother said. Her voice alone made Mikayla's skin crawl.
She'd hated her then, and just because her mother had
been drug free for a few years didn't mean that Mikayla didn't hate her now. The ship on being mother and
daughter had sailed many years ago, and Mikayla had no
desire to board the boat again or even try.

"Look, just name your price, Jewel. I know you're not
interested in being here for me or the girls. Since I've
known you, which is all of my life, you've never done
something for nothing," Mikayla said flatly.

Her mother laughed. "My daughter. My beautiful
daughter. Always thought the worst of me. Now, why
can't I be here to finally settle in my mind that I am a
grandmother? Huh? Why can't that be the reason?"

Mikayla squinted her eyes into dashes. She hated that
her mother mentioned her girls or being anything to

them. She jutted an accusing finger in her mother's direction. "Don't talk about them or being anything to them. You don't give one hot damn about them. You waited until Damian got out and you brought him here so that you can hang what happened over my head. I know you," Mikayla rasped.

"I know you too, Mikayla," her mother hissed. "I know that you like to pretend me and Damian don't exist in your little perfect white-picket-fence world. But we exist, and we are here, and whatever we ask for, you will provide it. I was glad to meet my new son-in-law," her mother said.

"Shut up, Jewel," Mikayla whispered harshly. "Don't—"

"What? He seems like a very nice man. I had a few conversations with him, and it seems like he doesn't know much about you growing up," her mother said, smirking knowingly.

Mikayla advanced on her like a cheetah on the prowl. Her mother backed up until her back was against a wall. Mikayla got close to her face.

"You better not try to ruin my fucking life any more than you have. You better keep your mouth shut or else," Mikayla said, her breath hot on her mother's face.

"Or else what, Mikayla? I think I'm the one who has the upper hand this time," her mother said facetiously.

"Hey, what's going on?" Charles asked.

Mikayla jumped. She hadn't heard him come into the house or the living room. She backed away from her mother and parted a phony, nervous smile. "Nothing. Just catching up," Mikayla lied.

Her mother chuckled. "And, boy, do we have a lot of catching up to do," she said, raising her eyebrows at Mikayla.

"I brought in some takeout," Charles announced. "Everybody is probably hungry."

"I'm starved," Mikayla's mother replied. "Just starved."

Mikayla turned to start toward her steps and was suddenly halted when she saw Damian. He'd been to see her at the hospital, but having him in her house was just different. It was more of a reality check.

"You a'ight, sis?"

Mikayla recognized that slight snide sarcasm in his question. He was no longer her little brother. Damian had grown into a huge hulk of a man. His face had hardened after years of being locked up. And his menacing eyes always signaled to Mikayla that their secret was always right at the tip of his tongue for anyone who would listen. Mikayla sucked in her breath and blew out a long breath.

"I will be," she said with just as much shade as Damian. She knew he could tell that he and their mother weren't welcome in Mikayla's home. Not by her anyway.

"We all will be soon, very soon," her mother stepped over and said, smiling like an evil villain.

"C'mon, let's eat. Our new family has welcomed us with open arms," Damian said with a grin. "Yeah, me and my new brother-in-law had a good, long talk. Was telling him about how I got locked up so young for something I didn't even know. You know, took the fall for someone I loved and then felt like they turned their back on me," Damian said.

"Nobody ever turned their back on anyone that I can recall," Mikayla responded defensively.

"Oh, yeah. Seems like everybody got a different recollection," Damian said.

"Everything all right here?" Charles asked, returning from the kitchen. "You all need to come eat."

"I was just telling my sister about our talk," Damian said, smiling. "Told her that I was thinking about maybe sticking around for the long run. You know, try to make up for some of the years I lost," he said.

"All of that is in due time. For now, let's enjoy a meal," Charles said. He connected a look with Mikayla that seemed contradictory to the smile on his face. Mikayla knew Charles could turn his charm on and off. She also knew she would be the one on the receiving end of whatever he was really thinking.

"I just love this house. I could see myself living in something like this, you know. It would be a leg up in life like I never had before," Mikayla's mother was saying as she walked away with Charles.

"A leg up. That's all a nigga looking for, sis," Damian said. Then he turned around and followed his mother and Charles into the kitchen.

Mikayla's insides were ablaze. Once her mother, her brother, and Charles were gone from sight, Mikayla closed her eyes and exhaled. Immediately, being home felt like she had walked into hell. It was times like these that if it weren't for her girls, Mikayla thought she would end it all. She'd tried suicide several times over her lifetime but had never succeeded.

Mikayla knew that nothing good could come of her mother and brother being there. It was like having a heavy metal chain weighed down with lead hanging from her neck having them around. Mikayla had suffered so many things at her mother's hands, and she'd been through a lot with Damian over the years, too. Mikayla slowly climbed the stairs toward her bedroom, but she couldn't quiet the voices in her head now. *You were a terrible daughter. You were a terrible big sister. You were a terrible best friend. You are a terrible wife. You are an even worse mother.*

With her hands shaking, Mikayla opened her purse and looked inside. The tension in her muscles eased when she spotted what she was looking for. Suddenly, as if someone had plugged a newly charged battery into her back, Mikayla hurried into the master bathroom and locked the door. Her chest pumped up and down as she dumped the contents of her purse onto the floor by the door. Mikayla picked out the pill bottle and clutched it tightly in her hand. Painkillers were for more than just physical pain, she reasoned. Mikayla knew all about it. This wasn't her first foray. She knew when she'd gotten admitted that she should've told the doctors, but she didn't want to. She needed relief.

Mikayla rushed to her sink. She yanked opened one of the small cabinet drawers and retrieved her handheld mirror. Mikayla placed the mirror faceup on the sink. She anxiously retrieved a red and yellow two-toned capsule out of the pill bottle. Eyeing it closely first, Mikayla held the capsule between her thumb and pointer finger and brought it to her mouth. She didn't swallow it. Instead, she used her front teeth to gently squeeze the small capsule until the top half dented in just enough to allow her to pull it apart from the bottom half. Mikayla's mouth salivated as she dumped the contents of the capsule onto the mirror. Mikayla couldn't wait to get home from the hospital to take the pills this way. She'd had to swallow them or get the drugs through the IV while she was there. Mikayla didn't have time to swallow the pills and wait for them to work. She needed to shake these horrible feelings that being back in her home and having her mother around evoked.

"Look at how ugly you are. You lucky I want you. Nobody else will."

Mikayla shook off the sound of Charles's voice in her head. She used her left pointer nail to separate the pill contents into three tiny, uneven mountains.

Mikayla used the same finger to hold down her left nostril. Then she lowered her face within inches of the mirror and inhaled with her right nostril, immediately vacuuming up the first pile.

"Ah." Mikayla jolted, her back bolting upright. Her head lolled back, and she squeezed her eyes shut. She pinched her nose close and danced around for a few quick seconds. When she had done this back before she had kids, Mikayla had gone down a rough road. She'd done things she wasn't proud of. She'd hidden stuff from Charlie and Emerson. Mikayla knew the consequences of getting high and had vowed back then that if she ever got clean, she would never do it again. But here she was, needing an escape from her reality.

"Hah," she breathed out noisily. She felt calmer already. Mikayla returned to the mirror. This time, she used her right pointer finger to hold down her right nostril, lowered her face to the mirror, and inhaled with her left nostril, leaving only residue behind.

"Whew," she blew out, shimmying her shoulders. "That's what I needed. Feeling human again. Fuck all of them. Him, her, him, them."

Mikayla used her nose to suck up the last line. She felt powerful now, like she could conquer the world.

"Taking my babies shopping. Not worrying about shit," Mikayla sang, prancing over to the shower doors. She slid the doors apart, reached inside, and turned on the shower. Mikayla undressed, modeling in front of the mirror. She shrugged. "You don't have to look how you did when you were twenty. You're a mother," she spoke to herself. She said only kind things to herself when she was high. Most of the time, she spoke negatively about herself thanks to years of mental abuse from her mother and then from her husband.

"Screw you, Charles. Screw you, Jewel. Screw all of y'all. Screw everyone who knows me," Mikayla chuckled, sticking out her tongue like a little kid. She hadn't felt this good at home or about herself in forever.

Still dancing euphorically, Mikayla stepped through the glass shower doors. Once inside, she stood directly under the huge rainfall showerhead in the center of the shower's ceiling. Mikayla closed her eyes, raised her face toward the ceiling, and let the downpour rain over her sensitive skin. It felt like tiny needles were pricking her all over. All of her senses were heightened, and it hurt so good. After all, she had learned early in life that pain was just weakness coming out.

Mikayla spun around in the water and moved backward toward one of the wall spigots. She stopped to let the hard spray from the spigot beat down on her head and back. Mikayla winced. The water setting was set so that the water sprayed out with the most force. Mikayla closed her eyes. The water pelted her so hard she flattened her palms against the opposite wall to brace herself. Pain. It was all she knew. She closed her eyes.

"Ow! No! Mommy, please!" Mikayla screamed. The black leather belt landed on Mikayla's back with so much force she urinated on herself. She bawled as more painful blows rained down on her back. She didn't understand why every time her mother got high she became a target. Mikayla sobbed. Her body throbbed. When her mother finally collapsed to the floor exhausted, Mikayla uncurled her aching body.

"Mommy? Mommy, I'm sorry," Mikayla cried, although she knew she hadn't done anything wrong. "Mommy? Do you forgive me? I'm sorry."

This was the routine between Mikayla and her mother—her mother would viciously attack her, and Mikayla would end up apologizing and trying to make things right.

"Mommy? Mommy? Please talk to me," Mikayla *cried out. "Mommy! Mommy!" she screamed louder, shaking her mother. "Mommy! Mommy! Mommy!"*

"Mommy! Mommy!" Zuri and Kai shouted, frantically twisting the doorknob to Mikayla's bathroom. "Mommy! Mommy!" they hollered louder, more hysterically.

Mikayla was jarred back to reality. She lifted her head slowly, realizing she was on the floor of her shower, knees to chest, rocking. "Oh, my God," she whispered, touching her face, her arms, and her legs, making sure she was not a 10-year-old girl anymore. She scrambled up off the shower floor and slid the glass doors open.

"Mommy!" Her girls were crying now. Mikayla could tell.

"Um, yes. I . . . I was in the shower," Mikayla called from the other side of the door, stumbling over her words. Mikayla whirled around, trying to find a towel. In her haste, she noticed the mirror still on the sink with the white residue on it. Mikayla rushed over, picked the mirror up, and licked up the last of the drug's residue from the glass surface. She quickly opened the cabinet drawer and tossed the mirror back into it. With her heart pounding, Mikayla wrapped a towel around her naked, dripping-wet body and rushed to the door. She took in a deep breath and exhaled before she opened the door.

"Mommy!" Kai wailed, her face red from crying.

"Baby girl, I'm fine. Just needed to take a hot shower," Mikayla chimed, plastering on a fake smile.

"I thought you were gone again," Zuri sobbed.

"No, baby girl. I'm right here. I was just taking a shower," Mikayla grabbed them and closed her eyes. "I'm here. I'm always going to be here," Mikayla whispered until they felt safe, a feeling Mikayla had never experienced as a child. In that moment, Mikayla knew she'd have to do everything she could to keep her family together for the sake of her girls.

The first thing she would have to do was find a way to get rid of her mother and brother.

Chapter 11

Charlie

Charlie let out a soft moan and a puff of hot breath. Mason had taken in a mouthful of her left nipple, and he ran his tongue over it with gentle passion. Charlie's stomach fluttered, and her head spun like she was on a merry-go-round. Whose life was this she'd been living?

She breathed hard, longing for him to enter her. Longing to feel him deep inside of her. Charlie didn't remember ever feeling her thighs and entire body trembling with anticipation like it was in that moment. There was something different about this experience with Mason. There was something different about all of the experiences with Mason so far. The way he spoke to her. The way he listened to her. The way he cared about the things she cared about. Charlie felt deep down inside that it wasn't all an act. She somehow felt that everything Mason said and did was genuine.

"You ready for me?" Mason whispered in her ear.

Charlie sucked in her breath and let out a breathy, "I'm so ready."

Mason leaned up and slid her fire red lace panties down over her hips and thighs, past her knees, and off. He put them up to his nose and sniffed deeply.

"Damn, your pussy smells so good," he said. That turned him and Charlie on at the same time. Her mouth salivated as she waited to be fed.

Her body was on fire. The heat of lust coursing through her made Charlie want to scream. She reached up and pulled Mason down on top of her. Enough was enough. She couldn't take the waiting anymore. It was too much.

"I need you," Charlie gasped. "Please. Don't tease me. I need you. I need you now."

"Me? You sure you want me? Tell me exactly what you want." Mason ignored her pleas, and he teased her anyway. He flashed his gorgeous smile.

Charlie's facial expression became serious. She didn't want to be teased in that moment. The longing was too strong. The desire filling her loins had her feeling like she would bust. She could feel her clitoris throbbing, waiting for some relief.

"Don't tease me. I want to feel you so bad," she groaned, reaching down and pinching her own nipples.

"I won't make you wait any longer. Here I am," Mason said, falling down and wedging his muscular body between her legs.

Charlie felt his thick dick again her thigh, and she gasped. Mason eased himself into her warm, gushy center.

"Yes," she hissed, feeling his long, thick dick filling up her insides. "Yes!" Charlie screamed out. She wanted more. She lifted her waist from the bed and returned Mason's careful, steady thrusts one for one. She wasn't usually one to fuck back, but this dick was too good. She wanted more and more. It was awkward at first, but soon Charlie and Mason were matching each other thrust for thrust. It was a dance, and Charlie heard music in her ears although none was playing. This had to be love. This was what she'd been missing all her life.

"Yeah, fuck me back. I like that," Mason grunted. "I like a woman who knows what she wants," he panted. He picked up his speed. Charlie twisted her hips in circular motions and picked up speed too until she was the one in command.

"Oh, shit," he gasped, bucking his waist. "I can't, uh, I can't take that shit right there," Mason stammered.

Charlie giggled. She loved how powerful she felt knowing she'd made him lose it. Charlie felt things in places that hadn't been alive on her body in years. She ground harder and harder into Mason. She was working for the dick. It was pain and pleasure. It was love and lust. It was combustible. And it was forbidden. Charlie hadn't forgotten that either.

"Shit!" Mason called out gruffly. He buried his face in Charlie's neck as he pumped, and she swirled until the sensations were too much to take. She saw fireworks behind her closed eyes. The feeling was right there. It was so intense Charlie's thighs trembled hard, and every nerve in her body was sensitive to every touch and move.

"I'm about to cum. I can't take it. Oh God," Charlie yelled out. That gave Mason more motivation. He moved in and out of her harder and faster. Charlie winced. It hurt so good.

"Aggh," she finally belted out. "I'm coming!" she screamed.

"Me tooo!" Mason growled, crushing his mouth over Charlie's just as he busted his nut. Both of their bodies seemed to ease at the same time.

Mason collapsed on top of Charlie and lay between her legs, both of them out of breath.

"I love you, Charlie," Mason panted.

Charlie froze. She didn't know what to say or how to respond. Most of her experiences weren't like this. Saying "I love you" meant you were trying to trap the man, so even if she thought she had felt it with one of those dudes, she would've never said it. She lay in silence, stuck on stupid.

***

Two hours and three orgasms later, Mason stood in front of the wall-length mirror in Charlie's bedroom, getting into his suit for work. Charlie watched him, amused and smitten.

"Is this what life with a very important person is like?" Charlie asked, letting the sheet drop so her breast was exposed to entice Mason.

"When you find a very important person, you ask him. In the meantime, this is what life with a man newly in love is like," Mason replied.

Charlie sighed. She knew it had bothered him when she didn't say "I love you" back. She sat up in bed, and this time she wrapped herself in the bedsheet, suddenly uncomfortable with being naked physically and emotionally.

"Listen, Mason. I'm sorry," she said, lowering her eyes so that she was no longer holding eye contact with him through the mirror. "All of this is new to me. Do you know I was actually taught that if you said 'I love you' to a man too soon you'd scare him off?" she confessed.

Mason shook his head. "Hood love manual 101, huh?"

"Right. So when you said it, it wasn't that I wasn't feeling it too, it's just I'm so scared. Also, I just feel like, what are we doing here? I feel like I'm setting myself up for another downfall. We can't be seen out together. We can't let anyone know. Hell, I can't even tell my two best friends in the world that I'm in love," Charlie lamented, still hanging her head.

Mason walked over to her and used his pointer finger to lift her chin so that she was forced to look at him. "I understand. I didn't say I love you to have you say it back. I said it because it is how I feel, Charlie. And in my own hood defense, I grew up with the same notion. It took me years to say it to Emerson, and honestly, I don't think we were ever in love. I think that because we were best friends as kids and we thought everyone expected us to get married one day, we loved each other as friends but were never in this kind of love. The kind of love I feel for you is 'woman and man' love, not 'obligated friend' love," Mason said truthfully.

Charlie's heart raced. She couldn't believe what he was saying, but she also wanted him to keep going. She wanted to feel that she was good enough or just as good as Emerson and Mikayla, because she'd always felt like she wasn't good enough to have a man fall in love with her and treat her good.

"Thank you for saying that, Mason," Charlie said. She stood up and let the sheet fall away. She hugged him tight. "I do love you, Mr. Man Mason."

"You're trying to make me lose my job though," he huffed as he felt heat from Charlie's body against his chest.

"You're already about to make me lose everything, so all is fair in love and war. I'd go to war for this love," Charlie joked. Her words were so powerful, like beautiful music to Mason's ears.

"That might be the nicest thing anyone has ever said to me," he whispered hoarsely.

"I've watched you for the past three months. I see a man who tries so hard to please everyone around him. But be true to yourself, Mason. You deserve the best, and even if that doesn't mean me, you deserve someone who can love you the way you deserve to be loved," Charlie said, her words raw and honest.

Mason pulled back and looked her in the face. She could see slight confusion, or maybe it was confliction, playing across his face. He seemed stunned by how perceptive Charlie was at reading him.

"You really are the fucking best thing that has happened to me in forever," Mason said softly. Charlie closed her eyes and held on to Mason like he was the last man on earth. She sobbed so hard her entire body rocked. Charlie hadn't realized just how much she needed a good cry. It was refreshing. A new start. Baptized with her own tears.

"I love you, Mr. Man Mason Dayle," Charlie said, her heart pounding against his chest. Charlie promised herself that she would take her time before she ever said those words to a man, and in that moment, she knew she'd taken all the time she needed.

"And I love you, Charli Baltimore," Mason said lovingly.

Charlie melted against him and cracked a smile. This man had turned her world on its axis. But sometimes, depending on perspective, up was down and down was up.

Chapter 12

Emerson

Emerson wasn't expecting company when she pulled back her door and found Macy standing on the other side. Macy's eyes bugged out, and her skin looked pale.

"Macy? What are you doing here?" Emerson asked, surprised by the unannounced visit. Emerson knew for sure they hadn't discussed meeting up. In fact, Emerson was scheduled to be at a podcast interview in the morning, and she'd purposely put her cell phone on do not disturb to keep the calls and texts from distracting her.

Macy didn't say a word. Instead, she rushed into Emerson's arms and crushed her mouth over Emerson's in a hasty fit of passion.

"Mmmm, wait. What . . ." Emerson mumbled, stumbling backward. "Wait," Emerson groaned, trying her best to push Macy off of her so she could find out what was going on. Macy wouldn't let up. Her hands were up Emerson's shirt within seconds.

"Oh, my goodness. What has gotten into you?" Emerson gasped for breath, still trying to fight off Macy's aggressive advances.

"I need you," Macy huffed. "Now."

"Wait, this is so . . ." Emerson stammered, totally caught off guard. She tried to push Macy away and get an explanation for her barging in. Usually they had to

set their meetings up in advance so that they could secretly meet on the down low, which was usually in the
very late evenings. Emerson couldn't chance her mother
coming by or one of her friends seeing Macy there too
much. Emerson had to keep up her divorced "damsel in
distress" image for the new direction—women's empowerment—she was taking her social media platform. It was
paying off lucratively, too. She had even been fielding
different deals for a book about rebounding from divorce,
rebuilding after sacrificing for your spouse, and all of the
married feminist tropes she could think of.

Emerson hadn't talked to Macy for several days on
purpose. And now here she was, acting wild and out of
control. It scared Emerson to her core. It wasn't like her
either.

"I said I need you," Macy mumbled. "You can't start
something and just throw me away, Emerson. That's not
how this love thing works."

"Macy, wait," Emerson said, putting up her hands.

"I fucking need you. I need you now," Macy rasped, her
eyes filling up.

"What is this about?" Emerson asked. "You're scaring
me. I mean, we have our agreement, and we have separate lives, right?"

Within seconds, Macy was sobbing like a baby, and her
entire body vibrated with grief. Emerson sat down and
pulled Macy down next to her. Emerson was still confused, but she hated to see her friend and, as of late, her
lover broken down.

"What is going on with you, Macy?" Emerson whispered.

"I broke up with her for you," Macy cried into Emerson's chest. "She was who I thought I'd be with. But then
things happened with us. It . . . it was so fast, and now I
can't live without you. I love you, Emerson. I'm in love
with you. I don't want her anymore."

"Who?" Emerson whispered, just to confirm.

"My girlfriend," Macy replied. "I told her I was in love with you," she croaked.

Emerson gasped. Suddenly she didn't know how to feel. Granted, she'd been having sex and hanging out off and on with Macy for the past three months, but it was all in fun. It was all to stave down the loneliness she felt from the divorce. Emerson didn't consider herself a lesbian. She'd enjoyed the sex, but she didn't love Macy other than as a friend. But now, with Macy crying at against her chest, the reality hit Emerson like a brick falling out of the sky. If Macy was in love with her, she would have to break it off. There was no way she could lead her on any further. Emerson knew this relationship with Macy would affect her relationship with her mother and, even worse, threaten her career.

"Did you hear what I said? I said that I love you. I've left her to be with you. I don't care," Macy said, pulling away so that she could look at Emerson's face.

"You can't do that, Macy," Emerson rasped, her voice cracking. Macy looked at her lover incredulously.

"I can't be with you. It's not . . . it's not the right time," Emerson stammered, confused and kind of distraught.

Macy stood up, her chest rising and falling until it was heaving like a prizefighter. She looked at Emerson with pain etched into every crease of her face. She knew exactly what Emerson was about to say.

"Go back to her and try to fix it. Go and make it work. This is a scandal that you and I both can't afford. Just because you love someone doesn't mean you're always meant to be with them," Emerson said with finality.

Macy squinted her eyes into dashes and stumbled backward. "I gave up a lot for you, you selfish bitch," she spat. Her mood changed so quickly that Emerson balked.

"See, this is what I wanted to avoid," Emerson said, shaking her head.

"Oh, you weren't saying that when we made love, that you wanted to avoid me," Macy said.

"Macy, don't make this hard. Please just leave," Emerson said, walking to her front door.

"This is not over, Emerson. You can't just come into people's lives and walk out when you want like you did to Mason," Macy spat.

Emerson blinked like Macy had just spit in her face. Those words hurt. "Just go," Emerson said through her teeth. She didn't want to say anything more. She'd suffered enough loss.

Macy stormed past her. "You haven't seen the last of me, Emerson. You can't just discard me like last week's trash."

"Don't threaten me, Macy," Emerson said, her nostrils flaring. She was terrified in that moment. Macy looked completely deranged.

Emerson slammed the door, put her back against it, and slid down to the floor. She couldn't control the sobs that overtook her. Maybe she did love Macy. They'd shared some special moments and extremely good sex. Emerson dug the balls of her hands into her eyes, and as she sobbed, she thought back.

Macy put her pointer and middle fingers in her mouth and sucked them sexily. She wet them with her saliva and then pulled them out of her mouth slowly. She reached down and fingered her intended target with her soaked fingers. Her fingers got even more soaked. Moans of pleasure and approval filled the air. Macy held Emerson's thighs and opened them up gently. Macy looked down at Emerson's pretty, pink pussy. It was nice and lubricated now.

"You ready to feel me?" Macy whispered, her breath husky with lust. She was so excited her breaths came out in jagged puffs.

"Yes," Emerson cooed. Her mind was on cloud nine, and she felt like she was having an out-of-body experience. Emerson still didn't know how she'd gotten to this with Macy.

Macy used her hands to open Emerson's flower, and then she gently thrust her tongue into the center. More excited coos filled the air. Emerson's legs trembled with pleasure.

Macy licked and lapped and used the tip of her tongue to go up and down Emerson's clitoris.

"Oh, my God," Emerson rasped, wiggling so that Macy would hit the right spot.

"That's right, show me what you want," Macy said.

"Ahhh," Emerson screamed out, inching forward toward Macy's tongue.

Macy finally fully obliged, thrusting the tip of her tongue deep into Emerson's tight center. Immediately, Macy felt the tight grip of Emerson's inside muscles holding on to her tongue.

Emerson couldn't explain the sensation. It was so different from the feeling she got when she had made love to Mason all those years. It was much more intense and satisfying. Emerson didn't understand how things had changed for her so suddenly. This new desire had come out of the blue, but it felt so right. So natural. In that moment, Emerson believed this is where she belonged. Emerson panted heavily. Macy's tongue work sent a burst of pleasure through Emerson's body, which threatened to make her scream in pleasure. She pushed as if to say, "Give it all to me."

"So good," Emerson panted, grabbing two handfuls of the bedsheets. "That's so fucking good."

"You like it?" Macy growled hoarsely before she let go of all her inhibitions. She moved a little bit and dug her knees into the bed for leverage. She urged Emerson to turn over and get on her knees. Shaking all over, Emerson complied. Macy positioned herself behind Emerson, spread Emerson's ass checks, and licked up and down with just enough force to make Emerson scream.

"Oww! Yes!" Emerson squealed. *"Yes! You bitch!"*

The dirty talk was driving Macy wild. The more Emerson talked, the harder and faster Macy licked and slurped. Macy loved to be told what to do in bed.

Emerson let out a guttural sound as Macy's skillfully licked her and used her fingers in tandem with her tongue. Emerson could feel the ecstasy building in her loins. She moaned like an animal in heat. Her body was covered in sweat now, and her legs trembled.

"Wait. Don't cum," Macy commanded. Emerson's eyes shot open. She didn't think she could hold back. Not with how hot and passionate she was feeling at that moment. She felt like a volcano was about to erupt out of her pussy.

"I . . . I can't," she started. Suddenly that sensation that was pleasuring her stopped.

"What are you doing?" Emerson huffed, slightly annoyed.

"This," Macy whispered. Macy moved around and positioned herself in front of Emerson. She pushed her back on the bed and forced Emerson's legs wide.

"I'm about to . . ." Emerson whispered harshly, grabbing on to Macy's head.

"Do it. Right here," Macy instructed. With that, she lowered her mouth over Emerson's pussy.

Emerson looked down with wide, stretched eyes. That was all she could take.

"Shit!" Emerson growled. Her body buckled and her legs quaked as she released her love juices all over Macy's face, mouth, and tongue.

"Mmmm. I love to taste you. So sweet," Macy cooed, lapping up every bit of Emerson's juices.

"Shit! I can't fuck with you. It's too fucking good. Never in my life," Emerson panted. "I could easily become addicted to that."

Macy curled up under Emerson and ran a hand over her breasts and down her stomach. "We can do this every night if you want."

"Imagine that," Emerson replied.

"I can imagine it. I can definitely imagine it. You'd be much happier than you were with him," Macy said, leaning up on her elbow to look at Emerson.

Emerson closed her eyes as Macy continued to stroke her gently. Although she felt conflicted, Emerson couldn't help feeling hot for Macy all over again.

"Listen, Emerson. Don't lie to yourself. Don't you think it's time to be happy?"

"It's complicated," Emerson answered. She didn't want to say that she would never go public with a lesbian relationship.

"Well, it doesn't have to be," Macy replied, moving her hand down to Emerson's throbbing clit.

"I think you know you have feelings for me," Macy said. "Just don't wait too long to tell me."

Emerson closed her eyes. She didn't want to think about anything other than that moment.

Emerson snapped out of her memory to her doorbell ringing. She scrambled up off the floor and pulled the door back.

"Mom," Emerson huffed. "You're back."

"I certainly am," her mother said, pushing her way inside. "And from the look on your face, it seems like you need me here."

Chapter 13

Charlie, Emerson, Mikayla

"I mean, come on, Eme, why do we have to wait like we are not important or some shit? She does this all the time," Charlie complained, picking up her glass of Moscato, sipping slowly. She wasn't one to usually complain, but lately, her patience with her friends was wearing thin. "Enough is enough with Mikayla and this shit. We either go there and grab her by the hair and drag her away from all those crazies, or we just stop acting like we care," Charlie continued, tilting her head at Emerson for emphasis.

Emerson picked up her glass of wine and took a big gulp. "Well, Charlie," Emerson said, slamming her glass down, "what do you want me to say? Mikayla said she'd be here. I can't just make her ass appear out of thin air. It's like she has just gone off the grid or something. But I get it. She's probably off trying to repair what is broken in her life. Everyone has their own shit they're dealing with in real life. These are all things that are out of my and your control. We can wait a little while longer, and if you want to leave, then we'll leave. But at least let's give her a chance. She is dealing with way more than you and me," Emerson said, her tone more like a parent's than a friend's.

Looking past Charlie, Emerson shifted her head and stared down the bustling sidewalk to see if she noticed Mikayla coming. The air was thick with tension. Emerson couldn't place it. She didn't know if it was Charlie's attitude or the situations she was dealing with in her personal life. Either way, the day was already starting off with the wrong energy.

"I know you're right. It's just that I hate that she won't wake the hell up. Charles may provide for her, but he is no Prince damn Charming. And her mother, whew, that lady makes my skin crawl. She looks like the damn Crypt-Keeper and acts like it, too. I feel sorry for the brother. I mean, he did just get out of being locked up most of his adult life," Charlie replied, changing her tone. She even had a hint of sadness in her voice. "I just wish Mikayla could be as strong as you and—"

"I think that's her," Emerson said, cutting Charlie off midsentence. Emerson squinted and craned her neck to see if that was, in fact, Mikayla walking in the direction of the restaurant. Charlie turned around and looked over her shoulder.

Emerson and Charlie watched as Mikayla came into full focus. She looked horrible, and they could see that even from a distance.

"Is she fucking staggering?" Emerson whispered without taking her eyes off of Mikayla.

Charlie turned back around, shaking her head. "And she looks like she literally just rolled the fuck out of bed. This shit stops today," Charlie said, drinking more of her wine.

Emerson's cell phone buzzed on the table. "Hello?" she answered. She stood up.

"Here, we're right here, KayKay." Emerson fake smiled as she spoke into her cell phone, waving. "Yes, just go inside and tell them you're with us. It's under my last name, Dayle. We're in outdoor seating. I've already told them to expect you," Emerson instructed. She tapped her cell phone screen to disconnect the call and flopped back down in the chair across from Charlie.

Charlie shifted uncomfortably in her chair when she heard Emerson still refer to her last name as Dayle, her married name.

"You were right, she looks kind of crazy," Emerson leaned in and whispered to Charlie. "I actually think she's high. And that's saying a lot from a distance. I guess we will find out what's going on in a few seconds."

"Well, you know me. I like to get straight to the point of shit. Ain't no need in pussyfooting around shit. She either admits that Charles is abusing her and lets us help her get out of that shit, or I'm officially done trying," Charlie said, twisting her lips, making reference to Mikayla's sloppy appearance that they could see even from a distance.

Mikayla came through the restaurant, and the hostess escorted her to the outdoor seating area where Emerson and Charlie had a corner table that could fit four.

"KayKay!" Emerson sang, extending her arms toward Mikayla for a hug.

"Eme," Mikayla answered with a jovial smile, embracing Emerson.

"Nice of you to finally show up," Emerson said, following it with a chuckle to make it seem like she was joking. "We've been anxiously awaiting your arrival, Queen," Emerson joked some more, smiling down at Charlie. Mikayla wore the same beaming fake smile as she extended her arms toward Charlie.

"You're not going to hug me?"

Charlie nodded and, without standing up, blew Mikayla a weak kiss. "Hey," she droned dryly.

"Sit. Sit," Emerson said. "We haven't ordered anything but drinks while we waited for you. I'm starving, and obviously, this one is hangry."

"I'm sorry I'm late. Between the girls and Charles and those other two being in the house, it's a wonder I'm not locked in a loony bin," Mikayla sighed, moving her hands across her hair to try to neaten it. She could see the questions dancing in her friends' eyes.

"Girl, say no more. I totally get it. Divorce final. My mother won't go the hell home, always lingering. Business picking up and has me running crazy. It's a wonder I'm not in a damn straitjacket right now myself," Emerson replied, chuckling. With that, both women looked over at Charlie.

"So what's new with you, lady?" Mikayla asked, smiling.

"Just waiting for you for over an hour, that's it," Charlie answered, parting a halfhearted smile.

Emerson raised an eyebrow at Charlie and mouthed the words, "Be nice."

Charlie crinkled her brows and opened her hands as if to ask, "What?" Mikayla seemed to miss the exchange, or at least she pretended that she did.

The waitress came over, smiling, with her tiny notepad in her hand. The women ordered their entrees and drinks.

"You look different," Mikayla said to Charlie.

Charlie tilted her head quizzically. "Different how? Ain't nothing changed but the weather," she lied.

"I don't know, it's like a glow or something. Kind of how women look when they're pregnant. But I guess we'd have to know about a new boo if that were going to be the case," Mikayla joked.

Charlie didn't smile or laugh at the joke. She'd actually been feeling a little funny lately and had thought about it, but she had immediately put pregnancy out of her mind. Mikayla saying that instantly made Charlie uneasy, and her stomach became even queasier than it had been. She pushed her wine glass away, just in case. Charlie glanced at Emerson to gauge her reaction to what Mikayla had just said. Emerson was looking right back at her suspiciously.

"Nope. No pregnancies here. Maybe just the good facials I've been treating myself to as part of my new self-care routine," Charlie said, raising a brow and putting emphasis on the words "self" and "care." It was immediately apparent she was sending a dig about Mikayla's appearance.

Mikayla's facial features shuttered close. She picked up her water and took a gulp.

Touché. Charlie. Touché.

"Nothing wrong with a little self-care," Emerson interjected, giggling nervously to try to break up the tension between her friends. She shot Charlie a look that a mother would give a child who was acting up in public.

Mikayla shifted in her chair. She was thinking she should have cancelled.

"Well, how about we catch up. It's been what? Two months?" Emerson inhaled, clapping her hands together and exhaling her words. "What is new in everyone's worlds?" Emerson asked, trying to start a new conversation. "I'll start. I am fielding a few book deals, and it looks promising. I have been feeling really good about my career, and I was on the morning news yesterday promoting my new 'life after divorce' platform," Emerson bragged.

Mikayla sniffed. She picked up a napkin to wipe her suddenly dripping nose. She needed a hit. "Nothing new for me, except having my mother around reminds me just how much I can't stand her and of what . . ." Mikayla paused, her eyes darting around.

"Happened back then," Emerson filled in, leaning closer to the table. "You think he will tell anyone about it? Do they bring it up when Charles is not around?" Emerson asked, glancing from Mikayla to Charlie and back again. "I've been worried about that."

Mikayla lowered her gaze to the table. Emerson and Charlie could see tears rimming Mikayla's eyes.

Charlie finally softened. She touched Mikayla's shoulder. "Don't let those motherfuckers do this to you. I mean it, KayKay. They don't get to come back into your life and fuck it up for you, Zuri, and Kai. Let us know how we can help you get rid of them. I still got connects on the west side who would disappear those two in a hot minute," Charlie said, surprising herself at how easily she'd become empathetic toward Mikayla after being mad with her. That was the extent of their friendship bond. They never really let outside things get between them.

"Charlie is right. We definitely have each other's backs," Emerson agreed.

"Shit, we can do what we have to do, and then I'll have my team of attorneys to get us out of it. You name it and I will do it. And it feels damn good to be in the position of independence for the first time in my life," Emerson announced, sitting up proudly. "Mason just don't know what the fuck he's missing."

Charlie swallowed hard and looked down at her nails. *He ain't missing you at all.* Then she shook her head just slightly enough for her friends not to notice. She needed to stop. She needed to remember that she would always be seen as the one in the wrong if the truth got out.

Mikayla sniffled again and wiped her running nose. Charlie and Emerson both looked at her suspiciously. They remembered Mikayla's little crash with addiction when they were younger. They'd been the ones to get her into a ninety-day detox and help her over it back then.

"Here, I got this for you," Charlie said, sliding a small booklet toward Mikayla. "It's from the job. About domestic violence and family violence. Before you get all defensive, KayKay, I work with this every day. There is no judgment on my part, just concern, pure concern. And if you don't think about yourself, please think about my nieces. Even if you won't take help from us, there are tons of resources out there." Charlie reached over and flipped through the pages until she found what she was looking for. "Tons of good resources and assistance sources." She tapped on the page. "I just want the very best for you and the girls. I sometimes toss and turn thinking about y'all. I can't just act like I don't know or I don't see anymore, Mikayla."

"It's true, Mikayla. There are so many ways to get out of bad situations these days," Emerson concurred.

Mikayla examined the words in front of her carefully as Charlie pointed out this or that. She remained silent, but in her mind, she was screaming, *how fucking dare they ambush me like this!*

"So don't take it the wrong way. We just want you to be safe," Emerson said, pushing the issue.

"And alive," Charlie interjected, her tone serious. "Seeing you in that hospital was a wake-up call for us. We can pretend all the other times were just you being clumsy, but you blacking out was not a joke. I know you later said it was because your mother and brother showed up and you just fainted, but I was there when that doctor said you had old . . . he said old head injuries that hadn't properly healed," Charlie went on, looking at the booklet like it might save all of them from this uneasy conversation. "So don't discount anything. Just think very long and hard about it," Charlie finished up.

"Okay, so I was invited here to be ambushed?" Mikayla asked, her legs swinging in and out under the table. "That's what we are doing now? Making me take time away from my kids to come here and be accused of shit y'all don't really know anything about? That's it?" she pressed angrily, using the back of her hand to wipe her leaky nose. All decorum had been lost at that point.

"It is definitely not an ambush," Emerson replied, holding her hands in front of her like she was calming a beast. "Why can't you see anything from a positive light? Why does this have to be seen as negative? We love you. We want what is best for you. That's all."

"Meeting up with my friends for a good time only to find out they wanted to make my life the spectacle of lunch should be seen as positive?" Mikayla retorted. "I've been with Charles for years. He is my husband, and no, sometimes it hasn't been easy. But no one gets to accuse him of things they don't have proof of, not even you two. When I'm all alone, and me and my girls are left with nothing, where will the both of you be? Huh? You off being a new celebrity and you off loving whomever you're clearly loving right now. Where does that leave me?" Mikayla's voice hitched. Her head immediately started pounding. She wanted to jump up and run to the bathroom for a hit. This was all too much.

"Right here, with us," Charlie filled in. "That's where it leaves you. Where you were before you met him is where you'll be after he's gone. Ain't shit change but you."

Mikayla lowered her eyes toward her lap. She knew that Charlie and Emerson just wanted what was best for her, but she also knew that her girls deserved more than she had growing up, especially a mother and a father together. She wasn't going to go back on the promises she made to them when they were born. She would sacrifice her own life to protect them from any hurt and pain.

"Like I said before, you have no idea what you're talking about. You may think you know my life, but you have no idea," Mikayla said harshly, ignoring the sense in her mind that told her it was all out of love and concern.

Emerson's creased forehead eased. "Okay, Mikayla. Have it your way. We will drop the subject if that's what you want."

"Oh, we will? Just like that?" Charlie asked, her left eyebrow moving up. "It's not that cut-and-dried for me. For real."

"Honestly, I just want this to be a nice day out to lunch without some drama between us or some drama springing up," Mikayla answered. "And to be completely frank, Charlie, I'm not one of your social work experiments from your line of work, okay? I am supposed to be your friend. How dare you try to psychoanalyze my life when you can't even keep a damn man?"

Charlie put her hands up. "Really? That's how we doing now? Just blow for blow with words? You're right. I have no right. Just don't call me when shit goes bad, Mikayla, because it will."

Emerson cleared her throat. This was a losing battle, and it was either keep on pressing forward with them fighting, or encourage them both to back down for now.

"Let's just agree to disagree and have a nice time," Emerson placated.

Charlie threw her hands up. "Yup. Let's just fake our way through lunch. It's up to you, Mikayla. But if anything ever happens to either one of those girls as a result of this bullshit that we know is going on, I swear"—Charlie spoke with her hands spiritedly—"there will be hell to pay for everyone involved. I will not sit by and have to deal with the guilt of this bullshit later. "

"That's it! I've had enough. You've done all of us a disservice by inviting me here and pulling this bullshit today, Charlie. I thought you were my friend, my sister. This isn't the time nor the place for this shit, but like always, you're in the midst of drama. I think you like to create it so you have something to do with your life, you know, seeing that you don't have kids and you claim you don't have a man. Let's not talk about how evasive you've been lately. Yeah, all focus is on me, but what have you been up to?" Mikayla lashed out, her upper lip quivering. She watched as comprehension washed over Charlie's face.

"You're right. I'll just go back to my non-life and mind my business while you stay getting your ass beat and putting your kids at risk of growing up like you did with a missing mother," Charlie shot back cruelly.

"Charlie," Emerson gasped. "Please, stop," she whispered harshly. They had already started garnering sideways glances and hushed whispers around them.

"Fuck you! Fuck the both of you!" Mikayla boomed, standing up from the chair so abruptly she sent it crashing to the ground, which really got stares and murmurs from other restaurant patrons.

Emerson clutched her chest. "KayKay, sit down and stop it," Emerson whispered harshly, immediately embarrassed by the scene.

"I won't sit down and break bread with fucking backstabbers," Mikayla hissed. She really needed what she had in her purse. She had to get out of there.

"We're the backstabbers?" Charlie scoffed. "Better check a mirror. Or better yet, check your household."

"Like I said, fuck you," Mikayla replied. With that, she stormed away from the table and headed back through the restaurant. All eyes were on Emerson, Charlie, and Mikayla. This wasn't exactly how any of them had envisioned their meet up turning out. Sometimes love and friendship hurt, and this was one of those times.

Emerson shot to her feet. "Nothing to see here. We're fine," she said, chuckling nervously as she moved quickly to follow Mikayla.

Charlie tilted her head toward the direction Mikayla had gone in. "Follow her if you want, but I'm not. Nothing I said today was wrong. It was all out of love."

"You need to learn that fucking timing is everything, Charlie," Emerson scolded before she rushed out of the restaurant. As soon as Emerson stepped outside, she heard her name being yelled. She froze dead in her tracks. Her eyes went wide, and her mouth dropped open. She sucked in her breath and instinctively threw her arm up to shield her face. It was too little too late.

"Emerson! Emerson! Is it true you left your husband for a woman?" a paparazzi reporter screamed as she ran straight toward Emerson with her microphone jutted in Emerson's face.

Emerson couldn't move. Her entire body went numb. Her mind was telling her to run, go back in the restaurant or rush away down the street. How had she missed these sneaky bastards? She was too busy arguing with her friends to notice the world around her.

"We also heard that you've been hospitalized in the past for suicide attempts and bipolar disorder. Is that true? People all over the net are saying you went crazy because you've been living a lie all your life. Is it true you were always a closet lesbian, married to hide in your own closet?" the pudgy-faced tabloid reporter pressed.

Emerson's pulse quickened, and she could literally feel her face filling up with blood. This was what she'd been trying to avoid after becoming an internet sensation with her blog and vlog and Instagram page. Her entire platform would be ruined now for sure. Emerson could just see the publishers who were courting her snatching back their offers when they found out she wasn't actually a divorced damsel in distress on the rise.

"Oh God," she gasped. She shifted her weight from one foot to the other. She looked up and down the street, trying to remember where she'd parked her car. She needed an escape.

"Where's my car?" Emerson mumbled, moving in circles, literally. Mikayla was long gone. This was partly her fault. And fucking Charlie's too! Emerson's head spun. This was sort of what it was like when she was off of her meds. Hysteria. Confusion.

"Eme, what's going on? Did you catch her?" Charlie asked, walking up on the scene.

Charlie's voice snapped Emerson back to reality. Emerson let out a long, relieved sigh. "Charlie! Where, um, where did I park? We have to get out of here. These buzzards found me here, and they're not letting up."

"Everyone is saying that all of the things you represent as your social media influencer presence—divorcee on the rise, strong feminist, women's empowerment ambassador—is fake, Emerson. So tell us, are you a closet lesbian who has been hiding your new love interest? Do you suffer with mental illness because of it? Was your entire marriage a sham and lie?"

Charlie opened her mouth and eyes wide. "What the fuck?" She couldn't believe her eyes or ears. Lesbian! New love interest! Charlie whirled around, almost as taken aback as Emerson.

Emerson shook her head in disgust. "You see what I mean? Why I never want a scene? These people are relentless, and they'll ruin my image at any cost just for a fucking story," Emerson huffed. "Let's get out of here."

"Is it true your husband found out about your affair with the woman?" the reporter screamed out, pushing her microphone toward Emerson again.

Charlie's jaw rocked feverishly. At least six cameras clicked and flashed at the same time. "Get the fuck out of her face! Back up! Y'all acting like she Beyonce or some shit! It is not that serious," Charlie barked, shielding her cowering friend with her body. "Get away! It's not that serious, you fuckers!"

"We have pictures of you and your new love, Emerson! We plan to post them to TMZ tonight! Are you going to continue to deny everything?"

Emerson's ears rang. Her left foot beat against the ground. Another surge of flashes exploded in front of her.

"Let's go." Charlie grabbed Emerson's arm and pulled her down the block.

The reporter didn't stop pursuing them. "Is your marriage over because you had an affair with a woman? Are you a closet lesbian? Just answer the question. All of your followers who are of the LGBQT community want to know, Emerson! We want to know who you really are!"

"Fuck this," Emerson grumbled as she picked up her pace.

"Emerson! Wait! You might want to hear this! We have pictures! We also have your hospital records. Do you want to clarify any of this? All of the stays in the psych ward?"

Emerson bristled. The reporter's words had given her pause. She stiffened and stopped moving for a few seconds like someone had splashed ice-cold water in her face. Emerson's hand slid from Charlie's and fell limp at her side. Her face paled. She felt like she was in one of those bad dreams where she'd woken up only to find herself in front of an audience, buck-naked and exposed. Everything she'd try to keep private was being exposed. Her worst fears were coming true.

"How dare they?" Emerson gasped, barely getting enough air into her lungs to get the words out. Tears welled up in the backs of her eyes. They had taken things too far. Emerson turned slowly to see the female tabloid reporter waving what appeared to be a medical document in the air—Emerson's personal medical records. There was only one person who could've gotten those with the way the privacy laws were set up.

"It's all right here. Did your ex-husband know about your history of mental illness? And what about your secret love affair with a woman? This is your chance to speak up for yourself," the reporter offered cruelly.

"Bastards," Emerson croaked, her legs weak.

Charlie grabbed her elbow. "Come one, Eme. Don't fucking listen to these crackpot-ass piece-of-shit tabloids," Charlie said, helping Emerson stay on her feet. The cameras flashed as they ran to Emerson's car. The reporters stayed hot on Emerson's heels. She had nowhere to run, nowhere to hide. Her life felt like it was over.

Emerson finally slid into the driver's seat of her car, slammed the door, and with shaking hands, locked herself and Charlie inside. She whipped her head around as the merciless reporters banged on her car windows and the hood.

"Let's get the fuck out of here," Charlie commanded. "This shit is crazy. I have never seen no shit like this. Maybe I didn't realize just how big you were on the internet, Emerson. I had no idea it was like this." Charlie looked out of the windows in shock and awe. She actually felt like she was sitting in the car with an A-list celebrity the way those half-baked reporters were hounding them.

Emerson had tried to tell everyone, but no one seemed to believe in her like she believed in herself. Emerson gripped her steering wheel until her knuckles paled. She had listened to the reporters screaming the words "divorce," "lesbian," "love affair," "mentally ill," "suicide," and "bipolar disorder." With each cruel question and blistering accusation, Emerson felt like someone was stabbing her in the heart. She'd worked so hard to build her name and her brand. Now it was all crumbling, and so was her mental stability. She felt it.

"Move!" Emerson screamed, her hands trembling as she laid on her horn. She had finally come out of her daze. She threw her car into drive and stepped on the gas. The car lurched forward, causing the cameramen and reporters to scatter for safety.

"Stay away from me! Stay out of my fucking life!" Emerson cried out as she accelerated away from the curb, tires squealing.

Charlie looked on, shocked into silence. It was apparent to her in that moment that she and all of her friends, just a couple of girls from Baltimore, were living secret lives.

Chapter 14

Emerson

Emerson groaned awake and stretched her sore arm out, blindly feeling around on her nightstand for her ringing cell phone. She placed her hand on the phone, slid it off the nightstand, and clumsily raised it to her ear.

"Hello," she grumbled without opening her eyes. Her head pounded. She still hadn't recovered from everything that had happened two days before with that tabloid reporter and Mikayla running out on her and Charlie at the restaurant. After that day, Emerson had tossed and turned and popped her anti-anxiety drugs, and nothing had seemed to help. What had bothered her the most was how the tabloid had gotten her medical documents. Emerson had reasoned that it was probably Macy, the person Emerson shared attorney-client privilege with, or Emerson's mother. And she didn't think her mother would do something so cruel. Instagram had exploded with the story about Emerson being a lesbian who had only married for the purpose of hiding her sexuality and being mentally ill. It had made her physically sick to read.

"Emerson," the voice came through the phone. "Emerson, I need to speak to you. I need to see you. I'm sorry."

"Macy?" Emerson's eyes popped open at the sound of Macy's frantic voice. "What? What do you want?" Emerson closed her eyes tight. The pain in her head intensified immediately.

Macy was rambling and speaking so fast. With the fuzziness of sleep still clouding her mind, Emerson couldn't understand anything.

"Wait. Wait. What? I can't understand." Emerson sat up, barely able to keep her head up. She felt like it would roll off of her shoulders.

"It, um, it was me. I . . . I was mad. I'm sorry," Macy said, stumbling over her words. "I was just upset with you. I didn't mean for this to turn out like this. I'm sorry."

"What? It was you? What?" Emerson knew exactly what she was getting at, but she still played dumb. Emerson could hear Macy take a deep breath and blow it out. "You did what?"

"I told you before, Emerson, I can't live without you. If I have to ruin everything just to make you be with me, so be it. I want to be the one who helps you pick up the pieces, just like after the divorce. I want to be the one holding you and being there for you. I left her, for God's sake. I gave up everything for you," Macy said in an eerily calm voice. She sounded deranged, like some kind of stalker. Did women really stalk other women?

Emerson's heart began hammering against her breastbone so hard it took her breath away. She listened and could tell that Macy was crying. Macy was supposed to be the strong friend. Emerson shook her head, disgusted. If what Macy was saying was true, she'd tried to destroy Emerson's life.

"Macy?" Emerson gasped, finally saying something amid the confusion in her head. "Why are you doing this? What did I do to deserve this?"

"It's me, Emerson. Not you. I just want to be with you," Macy replied, her voice shaky.

"But we can't. I explained this to you already," Emerson said, exasperated. "It's not . . . it's not what I want. I care about you as a friend, but I never said we would be together."

"Well, I recorded us, Emerson. I have something to show the world. Once I realized you might be playing me for a fool, I needed to make sure I had something. Proof that I wasn't crazy. Proof that you loved me and you said it. You meant it. I know you did. You're living a lie, Emerson. You're living a fucking lie," Macy said, raising her voice at the end.

Emerson could hear the emotions rising and falling in Macy's tone. Emerson shivered. She'd never experienced anything like this. She'd been with Mason all of her life. "Okay, Macy. Let's just talk about things, think everything through," Emerson said, gripping her phone so tight the veins in the top of her hand popped to the surface. "Let's try to talk and be reasonable here."

"Go ahead, talk, Emerson. I'm listening. I've always been the one who was reasonable. You're the only one being unreasonable," Macy replied, her voice cracking.

Emerson pressed her phone against her ear, but she couldn't find any words to describe the chaos going on inside of her. If Macy were in front of her in that moment, Emerson probably would've wrapped her hands around her thin neck and choked her to death.

"Hello? Are you there? You can't be at a loss for words. Not the ever-popular vlog queen Emerson Dayle. You talk for a living now, so start talking," Macy said angrily. The mood switches were apparent, and they made Emerson cringe.

"Macy, I'm just trying to figure out why you're doing this, to me of all people. We've been friends so long. We've had some good times, and we were there for one another through some bad times. I thought we had a real friendship," Emerson said, taking at stab at trying to get sympathy.

There was a short pause. Silence.

"Macy," Emerson said tentatively. "Why?"

"I need you, Emerson, that's why. You changed your phone number so I couldn't call you anymore. Is that how you treat someone you claim to love? Even if you only love me as a friend," Macy said with animosity. "I know what we had didn't mean shit to you. I see that now. But if you know anything about me, you know that I won't give up without a fight, a real fight. I'd rather take you down than to see you with anyone else. I mean that."

"Macy, what we shared was something that happened. You were there. You know that it just happened. I didn't mean to lead you on. I never said we were going to be a couple," Emerson said flatly. "But we can—" she started.

"Shut up! You led me on! And more than once! You fucking came back for more and more! I told you that I loved you! I left my girlfriend for you! You played with my fucking life! I can't eat. I can't sleep. I can't work!" Macy boomed, losing it before Emerson could complete her sentence.

Emerson gasped. Then there was silence and the sound of Macy's heavy breathing.

"I . . . I'm sorry, Emerson. I didn't mean to . . ." Macy stammered, quickly changing up her mood again. "I just want to know if you ever had any feelings for me. All of the times we made love, the nights out, the days in, what were you feeling? How could you do this to me? To us?" Macy's voice cracked. She sounded like a totally different person, which scared the hell out of Emerson.

"Macy, you sound very unstable right now. Please, maybe you need to speak to someone," Emerson said calmly. "I know how that could be, feeling all alone and like . . . like this."

"Fuck!" Macy yelled. "Just listen to me! I need to see you! I need to be with you! I just need five minutes, that's all. C'mon, Emerson, if you ever cared anything about me, just see me. Please! Fucking see me right now!" Macy ranted.

"Oh, my God," Emerson gasped. "Goodbye, Macy. You need to really get some help. Don't call this phone back," Emerson said, her voice shaking. "I don't want to have to get the police involved, Macy."

"Wait. Please," Macy groveled, having another shift in mood. "I just need to see you. I need you to know that I love you. We can work things out. Please, Emerson, don't just shut me out. You're all I have left," Macy whined, suddenly completely calm.

Emerson rubbed her arms to try to get the hairs to lie back down. She was terrified. "Macy, you should probably get some help. You really don't sound good. Like I said, I never led you to believe anything other than what it was. Now, I have to go," Emerson said levelly.

"Wait! Goddammit! Wait! You can't do this to me!" Macy barked right before Emerson finally disconnected the line.

Emerson sat on the side of her bed and put her head in her hands. Her stomach swirled with waves of nausea, and her head throbbed even more now. This was not the way she wanted to wake up after the week she'd had. Emerson stopped for a few seconds and swiped her hands over her face. "What the fuck?" she huffed, breathing out hard.

She was startled by a loud, resounding knock on her bedroom door. Everything had the ability to make Emerson jumpy in that moment. Emerson turned toward the door and stared for a few long seconds. It took her a minute to remember she was at least in the safety of her home with the doors locked and windows shuttered. At least Mason had been good for that when he lived there— he always made sure they had the best security systems on the market.

"Are you there?" Emerson's mother called to her from the other side of the door.

Emerson sighed, stood up on weak legs, and padded over to her bedroom door. "I'm here," she said softly, opening the door.

"I heard you talking, and you sounded upset," her mother said, but the question was there in her tone. She moved farther into Emerson's bedroom. Her mother looked around as if she expected to find another person inside. "Are you all right?" her mother asked, finally turning to face her after a quick inspection.

Emerson contemplated lying, but at that moment she needed to tell someone. She put her hands over her face for a few seconds.

"Emerson? What is it? Are you feeling okay? Do you need me to get anything?" her mother shot rapid-fire questions at her. Emerson could hear the worry in her mother's voice. It never took her long to conclude that Emerson was on the verge of crisis. Sometimes Emerson thought her mother felt better when she was in crisis because it would give her mother some purpose in her life.

"No, no. I'm okay. I'm just a little shaken up by a call I got," Emerson said, flopping down on the side of her bed, her legs too weak to keep moving on them.

"A call?" her mother asked. "What kind of call? Is everyone okay? Did something happen?"

Emerson put her hand up to stop the questions from spilling from her mother's mouth. "Nothing happened, yet."

"Yet?"

"Mom, just let me get it out, okay?" Emerson huffed.

Her mother closed her mouth abruptly and shook her head in agreement.

Emerson sighed. She didn't even know how she'd tell her mother about this without telling everything. She lowered her eyes to the floor. "It's Macy. I don't know what's gotten into her," Emerson said, sighing heavily again. "She's . . . she's stalking me, I think. She sent some information to the tabloids about me, and now she's tracking me down even after I changed my number. She has a lot of connections, and she told me she wouldn't stop unless . . ." Emerson stopped short of telling her mother the whole truth.

"What kind of information about you? You told me you changed your number for business purposes. Connections? Emerson, what is going on?" her mother said, worry lacing her words.

"It's complicated, Mom. It's a lot to explain, but she was so unstable on the phone that it has me worried a little bit," Emerson replied.

"Is she angry at you about something? Did you pay her for her services with the divorce? I mean, why would a woman who was your friend start stalking you, Emerson?" her mother pressed.

"Mom! I don't know! Okay, let's just drop it. She called me, and she went from angry to sad to happy to mad. I've been around people like that, manic people. I just need to sort it out," Emerson snapped, getting back to her feet so she could pace the floor.

"Oh, goodness, Emerson. This sounds serious. Now I'm worried about you. Please, be careful. Maybe you should go to the police and let them know she's not stable. You must still have connections with the police department, I mean, through Mason. Right? Please," her mother pleaded.

"I knew you'd get worried right away, but I'm okay," Emerson assured her, although her heart knocking against her breastbone said otherwise. She wasn't okay at all. Her stomach was lurching, and her brain felt like someone had fried it on a skillet. "It's probably nothing. I'll try to reason with her."

"It's stalking, Emerson. That means there is no telling what else she will do. She knows where you live. The places you go. Emerson, please. There is no reasoning with an unstable person, and you said yourself that she sounded unstable on the phone. Please, let's just at least make a police report. Let's call Mason and see if he can help. Please," her mother begged some more.

"No! We will not call Mason or anyone else for that matter!" Emerson snapped. Her mother jumped back a step.

"I'm sorry to snap at you," Emerson quickly recovered. Contacting Mason was out of the question, and she needed her mother to know that. That would be all Emerson needed to make matters worse—her ex-husband involved in a sordid love mess she got herself into with a woman. Emerson knew that Mason would surely investigate and find out what had happened between her and Macy. Emerson tried to convince herself she didn't care what Mason thought, but that wasn't true. After the divorce was finalized, Emerson felt like she'd always be in a competition with Mason. She never wanted him to know she was anything other than 100 percent happy. And, in some ways, Emerson wanted to think he was suffering without her.

"It's okay, Mom. I swear. I'll be fine. I don't think I need to file a police report, especially not with Mason. Macy is probably just upset because she's under a lot of stress. I know her. It's all talk. She will calm down. That is probably the last I'll hear from her," Emerson assured her, although she wasn't even sure herself.

"I don't know, Eme. I don't have a good feeling about that woman. I never have," her mother said uneasily.

Emerson took a shaky breath. "Macy wouldn't hurt me," she said in a low whisper. "She said she loved me as a friend. That has to count for something." Even as the words left her mouth, Emerson wasn't so sure she believed them herself.

Chapter 15

Charlie

"Keep your eyes closed," Mason said, holding on to Charlie's shoulders while he led her forward. "And don't peek, Miss Nosy Body."

"I'm not. I swear," Charlie giggled. "But don't let me fall either, Mason. You know me and heels have a limited-time kind of relationship."

"Would I ever let anything happen to you?" Mason replied. "I would never let one hair on your perfect little head get hurt," he said reassuringly. Charlie's insides melted. Mason was so perfect. She was finally in love with Mr. Right.

"Okay. When I count to three, you can open your eyes," Mason said, halting her movement.

"Oh, my God, Mason. You're killing me. I'm too nosy for surprises," she complained in her fake whiny voice.

Mason laughed. "Now one, two, three," he counted down.

Charlie finally opened her eyes. She sucked in her breath. "Oh, my God, Mason, how . . ." she gasped. "How did you do this?" Her eyes filled with happy tears, and she could hardly catch her breath. The entire room was covered with wall-to-wall roses. There had to be a thousand roses. But it was the message in the center of the floor spelled out in rose petals that really brought Charlie to tears. She had to be dreaming. Her legs were so weak they threatened to give out. Never in her life could she have imagined it.

"Well?" Mason said, putting his face close to her ear from behind. "What do you say?"

"Yes! I will be yours forever," she huffed, hardly able to breath. She had never in her wildest dreams believed this would be happening to her.

Mason picked up her off her feet and spun her around and around. "You're so damn perfect, Charlie Dixon. And I'm so damn lucky," he said.

Charlie closed her eyes and relished the moment, but in the back of her mind, she was asking herself, *Charlie, what are you doing? Do you remember he is Emerson's ex-husband? How can you do this and not share it with your best friends?*

Everything was happening so fast. Too fast to be believable in Charlie's mind, especially because she had stopped believing a long time ago that she deserved to be happy. Mason put her down on her feet, and Charlie was so head over heels she almost buckled to the floor.

"There's more," he said, grabbing her hand and leading her through his place.

"I don't deserve you," Charlie said, on the verge of tears.

Mason turned and pulled her into his chest and held on to her. "I know you may be thinking things are moving very fast, but with love, there is no time frame. You deserve everything, so don't ever let me hear you say that you don't. You're the best thing that has ever happened to me. I never felt like this inside, Charlie," Mason said. He used his hand to make her look him in the eyes. "Never."

Charlie melted against him, closed her eyes, and just lived in that moment. That was where she wanted to be forever.

***

To Charlie's great surprise, Mason had an entire evening planned. After the wall-to-wall flowers and asking her to officially be his girlfriend, he'd laid out a beautiful purple Donna Karan dress and a pair of Valentino pumps for Charlie to wear out so that she didn't have to go to her apartment to change. Charlie was beside herself. What planet had sent this man? Never before in her life had she had a man with one ounce of Mason's thoughtfulness, attentiveness, and just overall caring. Was this everything that Emerson had given up? Charlie felt slightly sorry for her friend for losing such a gem of a man. Charlie kept secretly pinching herself to make sure she wasn't dreaming and that this perfect fairy tale was really happening with her as the main character.

A few hours and two lovemaking sessions later, Mason held on to Charlie's arm proudly as they approached the front doors of District ChopHouse. On the ride from Baltimore to DC, Mason had told Charlie that he'd stopped caring about hiding their love. Although that seemed noble to Charlie, now as she walked with him out in the open, she couldn't help but keep her head hung low to avoid being seen by anyone they might know. Charlie knew that this love felt good to her, but it might not feel good to Emerson. Charlie had played it over and over in her mind how she'd explain to Emerson that it was something that just happened. Charlie had even prayed for guidance on what to say when the day came. Still, she knew in her heart she was wrong.

Charlie was still shell-shocked by the media buzzards who had invaded her and Emerson that day at the restaurant downtown. It was like nothing Charlie had ever experienced before. Those tabloids were relentless just for a story. Before that day, Charlie had thought she'd understood that Emerson was a little in the spotlight, which might have opened her up to public scrutiny. But what Charlie had witnessed that day had seemed so over the top for what she'd thought was a D-list celebrity at best. Emerson had tried to tell them how wildly popular she'd become, but Charlie had definitely underestimated her friend's celebrity. That was, until that day. Charlie shuddered now just thinking about it. She knew that kind of life wasn't ever going to be for her.

Charlie held on to Mason. Just as they got to the front of the restaurant doors, Charlie noticed a man rapidly walking up on them. "Are you Charlie Dixon?" the man asked, winded and clearly out of breath.

Charlie's face folded into a confused frown. She opened her mouth to ask who the hell he was, but before she could utter a word, the strange man pulled out his cell phone and snapped pictures of her and Mason arm in arm. Charlie tried to quickly unlatch her arm from Mason's, but she knew that the man had already gotten several pictures of them hooked together. Anyone who'd see those pictures would be able to tell they were on a date.

Charlie threw her arm up to shield her face. "Oh, my God! Stop it! Who are you? Stop it!" she shouted. She was immediately brought back to the day with Emerson. But why her? Why now? Charlie was confused as hell.

"What the hell?" Mason grumbled as stepped in front of Charlie to shield her from the camera flashes. "Get the hell away from her before I have you arrested! Get the hell out of here!" Mason boomed, pushing the man roughly in the chest. The man's trench coat flapped in the wind. He looked like a typical television private investigator.

Charlie flinched at every flash of the camera. Mason pushed the man again and went to grab his cell phone from him, but the man turned swiftly and started to run. Mason started after the strange man, but Charlie grabbed on to Mason in the nick of time. There was no telling what Mason would've done if he'd gone after him and caught him.

"Mason! Don't!" Charlie held on to him so tight her fingers ached. "You have way too much to lose. Not over me. Not over him. He could have a weapon or God knows what."

"What the fuck was that all about?" Mason spat, his chest pumping up and down. "That was just weird. Who would send a fucking PI after you?" he huffed, straightening out his clothes. "Are you all right?" he turned and asked Charlie.

"I . . . I don't know," Charlie stammered. She instantly regretted that they didn't do their usual and meet up separately. She had no idea why anyone would want pictures of her. She wasn't Emerson. Charlie's stomach cramped, and her head felt light.

"Too fucking weird," Mason said, still seething and looking down the block in the direction the man had run. "I don't think, in all my years as a cop, I've ever experienced a stranger just putting a fucking camera in my face for no reason and taking pictures."

"Well, some reporters had taken pictures of me with Emerson a week ago when we met up for lunch with Mikayla," Charlie confessed, grabbing Mason's arm to calm him down. "I don't know if that was the same people or what. Maybe they thought I would be with her, I don't know," she continued. "But now there are pictures of us out there. Not just pictures, pictures of us together." Charlie shook her head. "That's not what we wanted. It's not how we want her to find out. We have to figure shit out, Mason. We have to make sure we are doing the right thing the right way."

"Look, she's going to find out sooner or later, Charlie," Mason said, grabbing her hand as they both finally calmed down enough to make their way inside the restaurant. "You're going to be with me forever. I'm not going anywhere, no matter what Emerson finds out. She will have to know, and whatever the fallout is, we will deal with it together," he said with feeling.

"Oh God," Charlie blurted, fanning herself. She rushed back out of the restaurant doors to the sidewalk curb. She bent over and threw up her guts.

Mason was right behind her. "Damn. Charlie, are you all right?" he asked, holding her hair back. "Don't let this make you sick. I promise, it's going to be all right," he comforted her.

Charlie tried to stand up, but she bent over again and threw up some more. She was sick to her stomach. She panted and held her midsection. The pain was crazy. She felt like her legs would give out at any minute.

"Don't do this to yourself, baby," Mason comforted her, using one hand to rub her back. "Everything will work out. I swear. I'll take it all on me."

Charlie hurled some more. This time if felt like just the acids in her stomach were coming up. She didn't know why her life always had to be so complicated. Finding love was supposed to be a happy thing, not a thing that sent you throwing up your brains on the street while everyone watched. Finally, Charlie felt like she had nothing left in her stomach to come up. She slowly straightened up and adjusted her crumpled dress. She backhanded the sweat from her forehead and patted her own face.

"Oh goodness," she panted. "I'm sorry. I don't know what . . ." She choked out her words, too weak to get it all out in one breath. "That never happened to me before." Charlie could tell that her makeup was crazy looking after that, and her face felt flushed like she had a high fever. "I just don't feel good at all," she rasped, her throat sore from vomiting.

"Let's just leave then. You're in no condition to eat or celebrate," Mason said, holding on to her to make sure she didn't faint. "Besides, I don't want to have to kick anyone's ass out here tonight. I just have a feeling that this is not over."

"I'm sorry, I ruined it," Charlie apologized. "It was all overwhelming, I guess. I haven't been feeling like myself for a few weeks now, honestly," she confessed.

Mason touched her face and moved her hair out of the way. He kissed her forehead. "No need to apologize. I was trying to be over the top anyway, when really all I wanted to do was be at home, in bed, with you," he said, making a confession of his own. "We'll have a million opportunities to go to dinner. But right now you look like you need a shower, some peppermint tea, and some me." He laughed.

"Well, I guess this is good night and back home," Charlie said, lowering her eyes. "I can't believe I ruined it. Always me."

"You mean this is the start of a good night," Mason said, reaching out for her hand so he could guide her while they walked back to the car. "You could never ruin anything for me, Charli Baltimore."

Charlie smiled at him weakly. She didn't know how to feel. They walked back to the car in silence. Charlie was thinking all sorts of things, and she imagined that Mason was too. Who were they fooling? This thing of theirs couldn't end in anything but disaster. Charlie got chills just thinking about the many ways this would end up. She was going to lose either her best friends or the man she'd been waiting for her entire life.

Mason drove home with Charlie in complete silence. Charlie felt terrible about how the night had turned out. Mason had worked so hard to show her the love she deserved. She felt like she'd trampled all over his efforts.

"If you're worried about someone seeing us together, don't be. I'm going to take care of it, and we will let it out when you're ready," Mason finally said, noticing that Charlie had put some mental distance between them. "I'll follow your lead from now on."

"Maybe I should just be alone tonight," Charlie said barely above a whisper.

"I respect that," Mason said. "But there is no way I'm letting you go up alone. I'll take you up, and then I'll leave."

Charlie wanted to scream, "Who is this godsend of a man? Who is this? Do I deserve him?"

When they arrived at her place, Charlie's legs felt like two lead poles as she slowly walked toward her building a few paces ahead of Mason. The hairs on the back of her neck stood up. The beautiful dress Mason had bought for her suddenly irritated her skin and made her feel like she was wearing a burlap sack. There was something eerie in the air. It was like a premonition, but Charlie couldn't place it. She'd only felt like that a few times before, and every time she had, something bad had happened. Charlie couldn't shake her sixth sense kicking up. She shivered and picked up the pace.

Charlie's stomach still swirled with nausea. She felt like she was being watched, and suddenly her skin became covered with goose bumps. *Why do I feel like this?*

Mason ran ahead of her and got to the door before she could reach out for the door handle. "Let me," he said like the real gentleman he was.

Charlie smiled. It was a fake smile, but still, she gave him a smile. Charlie went to step past Mason into her building when she heard her name.

"Charlie? Charlie Dixon? Is that you?" the familiar voice called out.

Not again! What the hell is going on? Charlie froze in place, her mouth slightly open and her heart threatening to jump out of her chest when she turned toward the voice and saw who it was.

"Anna? What . . . what are you doing here?" Charlie gasped. She was literally one second from blacking out and hitting the floor. Charlie backed up against the door for support. This couldn't be happening to her. Was she dreaming? This nightmare just kept getting crazier and crazier by the minute.

"Shit," Mason huffed and sucked in his breath like he'd seen a ghost. He immediately sprang into defensive action. "Anna, listen to me." He put his hands up. "Before you get all crazy, let us explain. Let's talk about this like adults. Everything is not what it might seem."

Emerson's mother rushed forward like a bull on the charge. She finally came face-to-face with Mason and Charlie like they were all getting ready to square off in battle.

"What are you doing here with her? You're my daughter's husband, you bastard. I know bullshit when I hear it, and I certainly know it when I see it," Emerson's mother asked and accused all in one breath. She balled her hands into fists and scowled so hard extra lines cropped up on her face along with her wrinkles.

"Ex-husband," Mason corrected her quickly. "And we can explain. It looks worse than it really is. Just listen."

Charlie seemed a little shocked and thrown off when Mason said that. Was he going to deny her now after he'd just said he didn't care who knew? Charlie's head felt like it would explode. She knew just how overprotective Emerson's mother could be, and in this case, rightfully so.

"I don't have to listen to anything you have to say. I want to know from her what the meaning of this is." Emerson's mother rasped, pointing and turning her attention directly to Charlie, who'd already started shaking and crying.

"I . . . we . . ." Charlie stuttered through her tears. She knew there was nothing she could say to make the situation any better. They'd been busted. Period. No amount of lying was going to clean it up. Why else would Charlie and Mason be dressed to the nines and entering her building together at night? Even a blind person would be able to tell they were out on a date. Anna was no different.

"I can't believe you, Charlie. I can't believe either of you," Emerson's mother said, shaking her head. "I am so disgusted I can't even find the words. The ink isn't even dry on those divorce papers and you two already . . . I can't even fathom what kind of sick people would do something like this to someone they both claimed to ever love," she spat.

"Just listen to reason, Anna," Mason said evenly. "This has nothing to do with Emerson. And this was not the case before the divorce, so let's just be clear I never violated my marriage and neither did Charlie. Neither one of us really owes Emerson anything here." He was so calm and collected.

In a seemingly knee-jerk reaction, Emerson's mother swiftly reached up and slapped Mason across the face. "Don't you dare say her goddamn name. You don't have the right," she hissed. "You owe her everything! All of her sacrifices and all of the years she spent shrinking so you could grow! You're a bastard for this, Mason Dayle!"

Mason put his hand up to his cheek and bit down into his jaw. Charlie moved between them. "Anna, please," Charlie pleaded. "I know you're angry but—"

"I don't want to hear anything from either of your filthy, lying mouths. Is this why you divorced my daughter? Huh, Mason? So you could sleep with her so-called best friend? You both are dogs, not worthy of shit and especially not worthy of my daughter," Emerson's mother spat. "Is this about jealousy? Huh? Revenge? Huh, Mason? You wanted to hurt her, so you slide under this snake?"

Charlie's legs wobbled, and she felt sick again.

Mason noticed that Charlie was starting to look green around the gills. "Can we just go upstairs and talk?" Mason asked, still trying to hold onto his composure. He looked like he was one minute from punching his ex-mother-in-law in the face. He had spent years honing his negotiation and mediation skills. He needed to use them right now to the full extent.

"Oh, upstairs? Is that what you call it? How many times have you been upstairs talking, Mason? I should've known that day in the hospital when I saw you two on the elevator looking like two guilty dogs. Do you know what this could do to Emerson if she found out? This could destroy her. My daughter could get sick over this, you fucking piece of shit," Emerson's mother barked, her voice rising and falling with apparent hurt.

"I don't want to see either of you near Emerson. Do you hear me? She can't find this out because it would simply destroy her, and she's going through enough! In fact, fake best friend, I came over here to find you," Emerson's mother said, turning her attention back to Charlie. "Imagine that. I came to rally her best friend to be by her side. Emerson is going through a tough time, and she happens to need her friends right now, you conniving whore. I came here to talk to you about helping me help her, and this is what I find? This is what you've been doing, instead of checking up on your so-called best friend? Sneaking around with her husband, you bitch?" She jabbed her finger in Charlie's face so close Charlie could feel it ever so slightly on the tip of her nose.

"We didn't mean for it . . . ." Charlie said, throwing her hand up to her mouth and stumbling backward. She shook her head from side to side and tears danced down her cheeks.

"Shut your lying mouth!" Emerson's mother said. She squinted her eyes into dashes and moved in on Charlie for the kill. "You always were jealous of Emerson. I warned her about you many times when I first met you. I knew you right away. You were a broken little girl who couldn't stand to see others happy, with jealousy and envy floating around you like a dark cloud. You hated my little girl because she had me and her father. And you had no one. I remember, Charlie. I remember how your mother hated you and let you know it every chance she got. I remember Emerson telling me that you were so desperate to find love you'd accept it out of a trashcan. You hated your own life, and you always resented Emerson for hers. So how ironic is it that you'd tried to steal her life now? I'm not surprised at all. Women like you slither around other women's husbands and break up happy homes every single day. I've been there, and you know what? Bitches like you don't deserve to even breathe," Emerson's mother said cruelly.

Charlie jerked back as if she'd been bulldozed by the words. She actually felt her heart breaking, and the pain caused her to clutch her chest. Charlie shook her head no as she sobbed. She couldn't speak. Those words. Those truths. They had all incapacitated Charlie. She wasn't usually one to lose her voice or mince her words, but in that moment, she was a helpless little girl again. She closed her eyes so tight she gave herself a headache. Things came swarming back to her mind.

"You ain't nothing, Charlie. All your life I knew you wouldn't amount to shit. Ain't no man ever going to love you. You hear me? Not one. Ain't nobody ever going to love you. You was tainted from conception! You think a man could love you when your daddy ain't give a fuck

about you? Who else you got but me? Who else going to want a throwaway like you?"

Charlie listened to her mother that day, all of the days before that day, and all of the days after. She felt like somebody had hit her in the chest with a wrecking ball. Charlie couldn't catch her breath. A flame ignited on her face, and her cheeks burned. Charlie had had a ball of fire growing inside of her since she was a little girl, and that day it finally exploded. Her entire body shook. She couldn't stop her teeth from chattering. Charlie willed herself to stay still, although in her mind's eye she saw herself strangling her own mother to death.

"I hate you! I hate you so much! You're not my mother! You're not worthy of being my mother," Charlie screamed.

"Enough, Anna," Mason said, stepping forward.

His words interrupted Charlie's memories. Everything was swirling around her. Her life was like a tornado right now.

"I know you're upset, but I'm not going to let you keep this up. She doesn't deserve it," Mason continued. "You're saying things you don't know anything about."

"Oh, I know all about it. You don't know her, and that's the problem. Let's face it, Charlie. You'll never be as good as Emerson, and all you will ever be is a rebound for him and Emerson's sloppy seconds," Emerson's mother said flatly, sending her last insult hurling at an already-wounded Charlie like a rock upside the head.

Mason frowned and stepped closer to Emerson's mother. But he didn't have to say anything else. Charlie had finally had enough. She started to storm off, but before she did, she had to say something in her own defense. She cleared her clogged throat and homed in on Emerson's mother.

"I know that you think I'm the worst person in the world, and that's okay, but we can't help where and when we find real love. You of all people should know that. You should also know that I've always loved Emerson, and no matter what happens, I always will. You're wrong. I never envied her. I've always admired and loved her. But now I love Mason, and I won't apologize for that. I know you'll think the worst of me, but I will not give up what I've found here. You said I grew up in a loveless home, and you were right, so understand that now that I've found real love for the very first time in my life, I will fight for it. I will fight to the death of me for it, and I don't care who thinks I am right or wrong. I know what is right for me and this . . . this just happens to be right," Charlie proclaimed honestly, her voice trembling.

"We'll see about that. I'll see about all of this. You just wait," Emerson's mother shot back. Then she swiftly turned her back on them both, ready to leave.

"Anna," Mason called after her. Emerson's mother paused, but she didn't turn around. "You know that Emerson and I weren't good together. You also know that I tried with her and our marriage. I did more than try, and you were a witness to it. You can say whatever you want, but you know that I am not a terrible person. You know that for sure. This, what we have, me and Charlie, this is real. If you know anything about me from all the years you've known me, you know that I am not a liar. I never lied to you, I never lied to Emerson, and I am not lying to Charlie," he said with feeling.

Emerson's mother never turned around. She stormed off, taking what she knew and Charlie and Mason's fate with her in a fury.

As soon as she was gone, Charlie's knees buckled, and she fainted.

Chapter 16

Mikayla

Mikayla held her left nostril closed as she used her right nostril to inhale the small mound of white powder laid out on a pocket mirror in front of her. She winced as the drugs hit her system. Her eyes snapped shut by themselves, and her body went limp for a few seconds. She slumped over, nearly kissing the floor.

Mikayla exhaled through her mouth and shimmied her shoulders. This was the boost she was going to need to muster up the courage for the day she had planned ahead. She peeked out of her bathroom door to make sure Charles and the kids were gone. She could hear her mother and brother stirring downstairs. They were waiting for her. Today was the day she'd been looking forward to since they'd arrived. The day she would finally get rid of them once and for all. She hoped.

Mikayla took one last long look at herself in the standing floor mirror in her bedroom before she stepped out the door. She went downstairs.

"Let's go," she droned.

"Don't be so happy to get rid of us, sis," Damian said. "I remember there was a time when you wouldn't let me out of your sight. Now it's like you never want to see me again," he said, putting his hand over his heart like he was hurt.

"My life is just different now. You of all people should understand that," she replied.

"Different or fake?" Damian replied. "Either way, once we do what we got to do today, I'll forgive you, and your secret will be always safe with me," he said, raising his right hand but smiling sinisterly at the same time. "You can trust me just like I trusted you to take care of me all these years," he said, smirking.

"I still can't believe you let her put you up to this," Mikayla whispered harshly to her brother. "I never asked you to do anything for me back then. You did it because you wanted to. I always kept money on your books, and I supported you the best I could from here."

"Somebody got to look out for me. You sure didn't do what you said you would do, sis. You never visited. Was it too much to ask for you to break from your perfect life to come see your baby brother who made the ultimate sacrifice for you? Nah, you just didn't care enough," Damian replied.

"I may not have visited, but I always kept money on your books, so don't tell that lie. I did what I could, Damian. I know you know that. You're under her influence," Mikayla shot back.

"Would it have been too much to visit the person who took the rap for your crime?" Damian rasped. "Look, I can ruin you. Let's not go there. Let's get this over with so everyone involved can go on with their lives," he said, raising his hands. "I just want what's owed to me, really. And I'm probably entitled to much more."

"Yeah, because if we keep talking, nobody wins. Nobody wins when the family feuds," Mikayla's mother said, stepping from behind Damian.

Mikayla was startled by the sound of her voice. Her mother still had a way of reducing her to a helpless child. Mikayla exhaled and prayed for the best. She wasn't sure what she would encounter at the bank. All of the accounts were in Charles's name. He doled out money to Mikayla in amounts he thought she should have. He provided for her and the girls' every need so she wouldn't need lots of cash on hand. It was another form of control.

Mikayla sat in front of the bank for a few long minutes before she prepared to exit her car.

"You've been a thief all your life. This won't be anything for you," her mother said snidely. "You remember how you used to steal from me all the time? Time for payback, I guess." Her mother snickered evilly. The sound was like nails on a chalkboard to Mikayla's ears.

"Fuck you," Mikayla hissed. She slammed the car door so hard even she jumped.

Mikayla's hands trembled as she passed the check and the forged "power of attorney" form to the teller. Sweat poured down the side of Mikayla's face, and her heart galloped in her chest so fast it made her feel like she'd been running in place. Mikayla said a silent prayer. Mikayla hoped she'd done a good job of forging Charles's name.

"Are you okay, Mrs. King?" the teller asked, looking up from the paperwork, her eyes roaming Mikayla's sweat-drenched face.

Mikayla swallowed hard and exhaled. She was talking to herself. *Calm down. Calm down. Calm down.* Mikayla shook her head up and down. "Oh, I'm fine. Just left yoga class," she lied, smiling nervously. She fanned herself and then used the back of her hand to swipe away the mucus she felt about to run out of her nose. Just that fast, she needed to get high again.

"Will it be much longer?" Mikayla asked. "I'm just kind of in a hurry. Got to pick up my children." Her nerves were seriously on edge.

"Charles King," the teller read from the computer screen. "Your husband? He owns the Pulse, right? The club?" the teller asked, seemingly starstruck.

Mikayla relaxed a little bit. "Yeah. That's our place," Mikayla replied, shifting her weight from one foot to the other. She just wanted the girl to hurry up.

"I love going there. It's always live up in there," the teller continued, making small talk as she processed the check and began counting out the money.

"That's good. Keep coming," Mikayla said, smiling weakly.

Finally, the teller looked up and paused for a minute. "With this amount, I'll have to get a bank manager to sign off on it. It'll be just a few more minutes. You can have a seat until they call you," the teller said, smiling brightly.

Mikayla felt like someone had sucked all of the air out of the room. Her head spun. Was this a trick? Were they secretly calling the police or, even worse, calling Charles on her? Mikayla had to think quick. She didn't take a seat like the teller had asked her to. Instead, Mikayla paced in a small, tight circle. She actually had to bite down into her jaw to keep her teeth from chattering.

"Mrs. King," a pretty, young black woman with a friendly smile called to Mikayla.

Mikayla stopped moving and rushed toward the woman. "Yes," she answered, clearing her throat when she realized how shaky her words sounded. "I'm Mrs. King."

"It's nice to meet you. You can follow me," the woman said.

Mikayla didn't know whether to run for the door or follow the woman. She looked around to see if anyone else might be watching her or if there were any signs that they were stalling her. Something about every sound inside the bank made Mikayla's stomach churn. The clicking of computer keyboard keys, the sounds of people's voices, everything seemed amplified. Mikayla's own labored breathing even assailed her ears. She felt like she was being led to the gas chamber. It was almost like everyone in the bank knew she was doing something wrong. Mikayla could hardly walk straight as she entered the little office space with its glass window walls.

The bank manager closed the door and rushed past Mikayla to her desk. "Have a seat," the woman said, still smiling like she knew something that Mikayla didn't.

"I, um, just need to make this quick. I have an appointment," Mikayla said, getting to the point. She looked at the clock on her cell phone for a little emphasis.

The woman, still smiling, nodded. Then her face got serious as she took her seat in front of her computer. "I understand," she said as she typed something into her computer. "It's just that we need to verify things since we always deal with Mr. King and haven't had the pleasure of meeting you or dealing with you," she said, nodding.

"Okay, but what else do you need? You have the signed power of attorney. Charles has been sick," Mikayla lied. She didn't know if she was making things worse, but at that point, she was all in anyway.

The woman kept nodding and smiling, but that didn't stop her from pecking away at her keyboard. "Usually with this amount of cash we get a heads-up," the woman said, turning her eyes toward Mikayla.

Mikayla felt a flash of heat explode in the center of her chest, not to mention the buckets of sweat rolling down her back. "Well, I didn't have time, and you have all of the proof you need. You also have my ID and know that I am Mrs. King."

"I understand, but we have to have a second layer of approval. I am just the first."

Mikayla's ears rang like tiny bombs had exploded around her. She moved to the edge of the chair and thought about bolting out of the door.

"My husband has been banking here for years. I know all of his identifying information, and I have power of attorney. I can't help but think I am being profiled because we are black, and they are using you as a token to do it," Mikayla shot back. She used the only thing she could think of to distract her. It was kind of bad, but it was all she could think of to throw the bank manager off of her trail.

"I'm really sorry, Mrs. King. Let me see if I can get the approval faster for you," the woman said nervously.

Mikayla's legs swung in and out, back and forth as she waited for the woman to return. She looked at her cell phone again. She'd already been inside the bank long enough for the police to show up. The fact that none had come was a good sign.

"Good afternoon, Mrs. King."

Mikayla popped out of her seat like a jack-in-the-box. She came face-to-face with a tall, redheaded white man. He was smiling.

"Hello," Mikayla managed, although her racing heart made her feel like she didn't have enough breath to even speak.

"I'm Thomas Barker. I'll be doing your next level of approval. I hope you understand that all of this is for your and your husband's protection," he said.

Mikayla cleared her throat. "Can you make it fast? I really, really have to go."

"Yes, ma'am. I'm going to try my best," Thomas said, picking up the stack of papers and looking through them.

Mikayla swallowed hard. Her heart throttled up, and her mind raced. She flopped back into the chair, her wobbly legs feeling like they would give out at any moment.

"Hmm," Thomas moaned as he read the paperwork, looked at something on the screen, then turned back to the papers.

Mikayla coughed loudly, hoping she could be a distraction. "I'm sorry to rush you all like this, but with my husband being away and all . . ."

Thomas and the woman both shot looks in Mikayla's direction at the same time.

Mikayla immediately realized what she'd said. "I . . . I mean, being away sick like this. Having him away from the home has been very hard on all of us," she said, cleaning up her lie.

"I can imagine," the woman said, averting her eyes from Mikayla.

"Okay, well, I think we are all set," Thomas announced, thrusting some paperwork in Mikayla's direction. "We'll just need you to sign here."

Mikayla couldn't believe her ears. She let out the longest, most exasperated breath ever. She grabbed the pen and could hardly hold on to it her hands shook so badly. She didn't want to count her blessings just yet. For all she knew it could still be a setup. She scribbled her name.

"I'll get the cash," the woman said, rushing out of her office. The man followed her. Still unsure, Mikayla watched as they left together and had a furtive conversation. Mikayla watched everyone who passed, still making sure no police suddenly rushed in to arrest her. After a few minutes, the woman returned with a black pouch. She sat down behind the desk and pulled out the stacks of cash. She counted it all out in front of Mikayla and made her sign another paper.

"What is this now?" she asked.

"Oh, this is a suspicious activity report. We always have to file these for any transaction over ten thousand dollars. It's nothing, just protocol," she replied.

Mikayla didn't like the sound of that, but she was too far gone to turn back now. She signed the paper. The woman pushed the cash toward her. Mikayla quickly snatched the money and furtively stuck it down into her oversized bag.

"Thank you," Mikayla huffed. She flashed another shaky smile.

"No problem, and sorry about all of this. It's just policy," the woman said, smiling.

"Uh-huh," Mikayla replied as she left the office without turning around.

Mikayla rushed out of the bank like she had just stuck it up at gunpoint. Her nerves were fried, and she needed a hit so bad her body ached all over. She looked up and down the usually busy downtown Baltimore street to make sure Charles wasn't somewhere buzzing around. Mikayla knew she'd be caught red-handed if Charles saw her anywhere near a bank. Mikayla didn't have access to Charles's accounts at all. She still hadn't figured out how she'd get out of it once Charles found out she'd taken that much money from his retirement account. Mikayla had dug through his things and found out about the different accounts he kept hidden from her. She also knew that he didn't check that particular account that often. That would buy her some time. Mikayla was on borrowed time in all aspects of her life, it seemed.

"Damn. I thought you went in there and got locked up or something," Damian joked as Mikayla flopped into the driver's seat of her car. "Thinking about you getting locked up. Now ain't that a thought," Damian said, being a smart-ass.

Mikayla's entire body was tense, and she didn't need to hear anything from his smart-ass mouth. "It took as long as it needed to take. We are not talking about chump change here," Mikayla grumbled. She dug into her bag and quickly retrieved the big envelope with the cash. The faster she paid her mother and brother, the faster they got out of her life for good.

"This is everything you asked for. The plane tickets are in the email," Mikayla informed them.

"No, sis. This is what we asked for, for now," Damian replied, smiling slyly at Mikayla.

Disappointment flashed in Mikayla's eyes. If she had a gun, another gun, she might've taken it and done the deed again.

"Well, there's no more where this came from," Mikayla grumbled. Between dealing with Charles's abuse, her mother's and brother's constant harassment, and the fact that she still needed to call Charlie and apologize, Mikayla felt on the verge of mental collapse. Being in the hospital and getting her hands on those pills had saved the day and offered Mikayla a new way to cope. When Mikayla snorted, she felt uncharacteristically happy and even invincible. All of the negative aspects of her life seemed more tolerable when she was high. Mikayla even had an extra pep in her step. But her supply was running low, and that would be another challenge she'd have to face soon. It was scary to imagine. When she wasn't high, everything seemed to spiral. Like now, Mikayla felt agitated, and her body felt achy. Her moods swung like a pendulum—one minute she could be sad, depressed, and so weak she'd be on the brink of tears, and the next minute her patience could be so brittle she felt like she could actually kill someone.

"Take the money and have a nice life," Mikayla said.

"How much is this?" Damian asked just to be a bastard.

"A hundred thousand. Exactly what you asked for," Mikayla replied, scowling.

"Damn, big sis. You weren't playing," Damian teased, smiling as he flicked through the crisp bills. "Seems like it's all here." He leaned over the seat and reached out like he was about to hug Mikayla.

Mikayla recoiled and avoided his touch as if he had a disease. "It's too late for niceties now. You all came here, and for these past few weeks, you've extorted me, harassed me, and threatened me. I don't ever want to see either of you again." Mikayla felt her heart break saying those words to her brother. She couldn't care less about her mother, but at one point in life, she'd loved her brother more than anyone in the world. He'd made the ultimate sacrifice for her, and she wouldn't forget it, but under her mother's tutelage, Damian was a different human being. He wasn't the baby brother she remembered before he'd gotten locked up for taking a murder wrap for Mikayla.

"Not so fast," Mikayla's mother said. "Money can't get rid of the blood that courses through your veins. You can play house all you want, Mikayla. We are still your family, reminders of where you come from."

"This time we asked for this amount, but that might not be enough," Damian followed up matter-of-factly.

Mikayla's heart sank, and her nostrils went wide. She thought that kind of money was enough. Anything more was going to be impossible. Charles would surely notice the next time. Mikayla still didn't know how she'd get out of stealing from him this time.

"You know I can't get my hands on any more cash. I'm already going to have to explain this missing money when Charles finds out," Mikayla whined, biting down into her bottom lip. "Why are you doing this to me?" She was crestfallen.

The yearning in her body to get high, to escape, was becoming stronger the longer she sat there without a hit. The anxiety she felt not being able to get more money to get rid of her mother and brother made her legs involuntarily swing in and out. Her brother shrugged his shoulders, and her mother shook her head at Mikayla.

"Nobody ever told you to start stashing cash the minute you married a businessman? The minute you were with him, you should've been putting some of it aside in a secret place. How could you be any daughter of mine? I thought you'd be smarter than this. I just don't understand you, a pitiful, pampered princess wannabe letting a man control you with his wallet. I guess you always have been kind of simpleminded and stupid," her mother snapped cruelly.

Mikayla's bottom lip quivered with a mixture of hurt and anger. She couldn't even argue with the truth. You'd think a girl who'd grown up fending for herself would be smarter than this. But Mikayla wanted to be comfortable. She didn't want to have to scrap all of her life like she'd done in the past.

"I suggest you work it out. Because we might be back, sis," Damian said, picking up where his mother had left off.

Mikayla bit down into her jaw and pulled her car onto the street. She drove like her car was on fire. When she pulled up to BWI airport, there were no pleasant goodbyes between Mikayla, her mother, and her brother. In fact, Mikayla stared straight ahead as they exited her car. She refused to acknowledge them.

As soon as her back door slammed shut, Mikayla peeled away from the airport like she was being chased. She drove around to the waiting area lot and threw her car into park. Like a dog waiting for a treat, Mikayla quickly dug into her bag for her medicine. Her hands were shaking so badly she could barely get one of the pills out of the bottle. Mikayla pulled a small pill cutter from her pocketbook and shakily placed two pills into it. She quickly squeezed the little plastic device until she cut the pills in half. Then she shook it so the pill pieces would move around and she squeezed again, crumbling the pills into even smaller pieces. Mikayla continued to cut and shake until the pills were finally crushed into powder. She opened the top of the pill cutter and dumped a small heap of the pill dust onto the back of her hand. Mikayla's mouth was watering, and her nose was wet inside as she lowered her head and used her left nostril to inhale the drugs.

"Ah," she exhaled, throwing her head back and squeezing her eyes shut as the potent formula hit her brain like a hard kick to the head. Mikayla knew that the quick shot of pain she experienced at first would subside after a few seconds. She kept her eyes closed and rested her head back on the car seat as the drugs took effect. Mikayla's lips curled into a lazy grin, and her head lolled to the side. She was happy again. No, she was downright euphoric. Mikayla giggled out loud for no reason.

"I am ready to take on all of you fuckers and even my piece-of-shit husband and whatever he wants to fucking dish out today," Mikayla said out loud.

Mikayla rode home with her music blasting and feeling good. But the faster her high wore off, the more horrible and ashamed of herself she felt. Mikayla was grateful she hadn't gotten busted at the bank. But the walk of shame out of the bank, knowing that she had stolen from Charles, had been enough to make Mikayla want to bury herself alive.

When Mikayla pulled her car into her driveway, she saw her phone light up with a text message from Charles. Her heart sank. Charles had made it back home before her. There was no telling what he might know. Mikayla was terrified to go inside. She looked at the phone and forced herself to read the text.

I know what you did, Mikayla. Your brother left me a letter telling me everything. You are not who you say you are, and you are a danger to our girls. If you return, I will have you arrested.

In an instant, Mikayla's whole world crashed in around her when she read those words. She'd tried for years to hide. She'd done everything her mother and brother had asked, and still they betrayed her in the worst way. Mikayla read the words from Charles over and over again. She was suddenly reminded of her reality. She closed her eyes for a few long minutes and was thrust back to that fateful day.

"No! Please!" Damian begged, gagging from the mixture of snot and blood running over his lips and into his mouth.

Mikayla cowered and shook, too injured herself to think. The salt from her tears stung the open wounds on her split lip. But that was the least of Mikayla's pain. Watching her brother be hurt was worse than anything she could endure physically.

Another slap across the face almost snapped Damian's neck from his body. He was ten, but he was as skinny as a bird. Their foster parents fed them when they felt like it. It showed on Damian more than it did on Mikayla. The hit landed with so much force, blood and spit shot from between Damian's lips.

"Please, beat me, not him," Mikayla groaned through her swollen lips. "Please. He didn't do anything wrong. It was all me. I swear," she rasped.

"Oh yeah? It was your fault? Well, look at what you've done," their foster father growled evilly.

"Agh!" Damian let out another painful scream.

Mikayla couldn't even stand to look over at her baby brother. She sobbed at the sight.

"Mikayla!" Damian screamed as more body blows landed on his frail ribcage.

"Damian! I'm sorry! I'm so sorry!" Mikayla wailed. She knew she had to do something to save them both.

Mikayla looked around, and she spotted the silver gun that their foster father often brandished in their faces to scare them. It sat on the kitchen counter after he'd put it down to put hands on her and Damian.

"I have to get to it," *Mikayla mumbled under her breath as sweat beads ran a race down her entire body. Her nerves made her knees knock together, and her heart thrummed so hard she felt nauseous. Mikayla backed up slowly while her foster father went to town on Damian with the belt and his fists. Mikayla held her breath as she finally reached over and grasped the gun.*

You got it! You can save him! *Mikayla told herself.*

"Get off of him," *Mikayla finally said, her voice trembling.*

Her foster father turned toward her and laughed. "What the fuck you think you doing with that?" *he snarled.*

"I'm not joking. Let him go. I'm telling you now, I will do it. I swear to everything, I will use this," *Mikayla said through clenched teeth. The muscles in her skinny arms burned as she kept them extended in front of her.*

Her foster father laughed dismissively again and smirked like he didn't take Mikayla seriously at all. "What? What you going to do, little bitch?" *he chuckled evilly.* "You shoot me, you shoot this little dumb nigga you call a brother."

Fire flashed in Mikayla's chest. "Let him come to me and I'll put it down," *she said in an eerily calm voice.*

"You ain't going to do shit, little girl," *he spat with his face curling into an evil, contorted snarl.*

In that moment, Mikayla knew she was facing off with the devil. He'd been coming into her bed since they'd arrived at that home, and she'd had enough. Damian had tried to help her fight back, and now it was her fault he was being abused. In that moment, Mikayla saw his mouth moving, but suddenly she couldn't hear him anymore. Her nostrils flared, and she swallowed hard.

"Shut up and let him go," Mikayla growled breathlessly. Her chest heaved, and her jaw rocked feverishly. Her hands shook so badly the gun wavered slightly in front of her. She didn't want to shoot anyone. She just wanted him to let Damian go.

"Just let him go and we will leave," Mikayla said. Her even tone of voice completely contradicted the raging inferno burning inside of her chest. Mikayla didn't know why with a gun pointing at someone she was so calm, and that scared her more than anything.

"Nah, I ain't letting nobody go nowhere," her foster father hissed. Then he slapped Damian so hard his head whipped violently to the left.

Mikayla swayed on her feet. She was going to have to kill him. She could feel it all down in her bones.

"All I want to do is leave. End this. Nobody has to get hurt," Mikayla spoke calmly, another last-ditch effort to end it without his death. Her insides were going so crazy—churning stomach, racing heart. She felt like she would throw up any minute. Their mother had put them in this situation, and Mikayla hated her for it. Mikayla felt her knees buckle a little bit. If she could have just lain down and curled into a ball and cried for hours, she would have.

"So are you going to let him go?" she asked, the gun pointing right at her foster father's chest.

"Psh," he scoffed. Then he did something Mikayla hadn't expected. He threw Damian to the floor with a crash and started toward her.

Mikayla's eyes flew wide, and she adjusted her grip on the gun. "Stay back!" she screamed.

He didn't listen. Her foster father glared at her, shook his head, and advanced on her.

"Get back, I said!" Mikayla screamed, moving backward. She slid her right pointer finger into the trigger *guard of the gun. Her foster father laughed again, an evil cackle that caused tight goose bumps to crop up all over Mikayla's body. Sheer fear was what moved her in that moment. She closed her eyes and squeezed.*

Boom. Boom. Boom. Boom.

Damian let out an ear-shattering scream. Mikayla fell backward. Neither one of them uttered another word. The smell of the gunpowder immediately settled at the back of Mikayla's throat. The scent of raw meat permeated the air. She coughed. Damian gagged.

"Give it to me. I did it," Damian said. "I'm a little kid. I won't go to jail for life," he said, taking the gun from Mikayla's hands. She let him. That was the last thing she remembered before tons of police showed up.

Mikayla flinched as she snapped out of the nightmare. "Why?" she cried out. "Why me? Why can't I just be happy?" She lowered her face into her hands for a few seconds. Mikayla let out a round of exhausting sobs—a combination of hurt, confusion, hatred, love.

"Agh!" Mikayla slammed her fists against her steering wheel, finally feeling anger over all other emotions. What about her girls? They were her entire life. They could hardly be without her for a week, much less forever. "No!" she screamed out. Her first instinct was to rush inside the house and get her children, but she knew that this time Charles might kill her. And then who would her girls have? Mikayla's hands trembled fiercely. She raised her head and looked at herself in the rearview mirror.

"Disgusting. That's what you are Mikayla. Disgusting," she murmured, backhanding the snot rimming her nostrils. "You didn't even think about those babies, the consequences, nothing." Her high was totally gone now. Her stomach swirled with nausea. There was no way she could go inside. Not alone. Now that her mother and brother were gone, Charles would be back to his old self.

The thought terrified her. She picked up her cell phone and dialed out.

"Come on. Come on, answer," she mumbled, her legs opening and closing restlessly. Mikayla sat up straight in her seat when the line finally connected. "Hey, Charlie, it's Mikayla. I need to see you. Yes, sooner rather than later," Mikayla said, closing her eyes and letting the tears just flow. "I need to figure some things out, and I know you can probably help me," Mikayla said, finally relenting. She said a silent prayer that Charlie could help her.

Chapter 17

Emerson

Macy and Emerson stared at one another for a few long seconds. Emerson sucked in her breath and felt a hard lump form in the back of her throat. She couldn't believe her eyes. Macy looked nothing like herself. Gone was her friend's usually put-together image. Macy's eyes were bloodshot, like she hadn't slept in weeks. She had lost a significant amount of weight, which showed in her scrawny cheeks and neck. Her hair looked like it hadn't been combed in days. Macy's clothes also weren't sharp like usual. She wore a rumpled blouse that seemed out of place with her dirty jeans. She wore sneakers that looked 20 years old. The Macy Emerson knew wouldn't be caught dead going outside dressed like that, let alone walking the streets. Macy was a high-paid attorney, and she had always made sure she stepped out of the house dressed neat and crisp.

"Macy?" Emerson croaked, hoping this was a bad dream and that her eyes were deceiving her. Her heart felt like it had crumbled to dust. She stepped back a few paces. She hadn't been expecting Macy to be lurking outside of her house this time of morning. Emerson had purposely been leaving very early in the mornings to take care of business so that she could be back before dark, just in case.

"Can we talk inside?" Macy said, her voice soft and mellow.

Emerson was trying to stay as calm as possible to ensure that Macy stayed as calm as possible. She thought for a few seconds. Her mother wasn't home, which meant she'd be alone inside the house with Macy. But the sight of her neighbor watching them made the decision for Emerson to go inside. She couldn't afford for her neighbors to start talking about her too. The tabloids had done enough damage with their information.

"Okay," Emerson said tentatively. "But I have a really important meeting that I have to get to, so we will have to make it quick," she said. Emerson backed into her door, refusing to turn her back on Macy. Macy followed her inside and closed the door behind her.

"Emerson," Macy said sweetly, smiling. "I'm so happy to see you. You look beautiful as usual," Macy said, awkwardly tilting her head. She rushed toward Emerson with her arms stretched out in front of her. Emerson shrank back and put her hands up defensively. Macy halted and looked at her strangely.

"Macy, let's not," Emerson said, keeping her voice soft. "Let's not act like things are normal between us. Let's just get to the point of your visit," Emerson said. Emerson was suddenly drawn back to the last time she had seen Macy. The crazy things Macy had said. The crazy way she had proclaimed love, although it was nothing like that in Emerson's eyes.

Macy dropped her arms in disappointment. Her eyes went dark. She ran her hands through her wild hair. Emerson could tell Macy was trying to keep herself calm.

"Okay, Emerson. If that's the way you want to be. I was simply trying to give you a hug," Macy replied, her jaw rocking back and forth feverishly. "I guess I'll just get to the point of my visit then," Macy continued, pulling a large envelope from under her shirt. It had been stuffed down the front of her pants. "Thought you'd want to see these," Macy said, pushing the envelope into Emerson's chest.

Emerson stumbled a little bit, shocked by Macy's abrupt touch. "What is this?" she asked incredulously.

Macy chuckled. "Open it, Emerson. Don't always try to find the easy way out of everything, damn," Macy snapped, clearly annoyed.

Emerson swallowed hard and went about opening the envelope. She pulled out several eight-by-ten glossy photographs. Emerson shuffled the photos one at a time. She stood her ground, although her stomach was in knots and her heart banged against her breastbone. She squinted at the pictures and then shot Macy a look that could slice a diamond in half.

"Where did you get these? What does this mean?" Emerson said barely above a whisper. She could barely talk. The room felt like it was spinning. Her hands trembled. Her heart squeezed so tightly she felt like it would just stop any minute and she'd be dead on the spot.

"I told you I was going to prove to you who was really loyal to you. I told you, I am the only friend who truly loves you," Macy replied. "And that's not all. Your dear, dear mother knew about all of this the whole time. She knew about all of it. When I had them followed, I saw her confront them. She's known for weeks now," Macy said with a sickening satisfaction in her voice. "I guess your so-called best friend and your ex-husband were stabbing you in the back this whole time. Yet you want to turn your back on me, the person who loved you the most."

Emerson couldn't show Macy that she'd won. Emerson felt like the ground had crumbled under her feet at the sight of Mason and Charlie together, but she had to stand her ground. Giving Macy the satisfaction of knowing she'd hurt her was not an option. "This doesn't matter to me, Macy. He's not my husband anymore," Emerson lied. In actuality, her heart was shredded. She couldn't believe her eyes, but she had to keep her composure.

"But he was your husband. I bet they've always been fucking. There's no way they could be that in love that fast," Macy said, reminding Emerson of the obvious.

Emerson felt defeated. She didn't want to do this with Macy. She couldn't believe that Macy was actually hiring private investigators to seek out information to hurt her.

"Please leave me alone, Macy. If you really care about me like you say you do, why are you doing these things to destroy me?" Emerson said, her voice cracking just like her resolve.

"I needed you to see," Macy said, her voice rising. She moved a few steps closer to Emerson. "I needed you to see who really cares about you. Don't you see, Emerson?"

"Okay, and I've seen. The damage is done. Is there anything else I can help you with?" Emerson asked dismissively. She was dying inside. But she had to stand firm. She had to get rid of Macy. She needed a moment to be alone. Those pictures had cut her deep inside, so deep she didn't know how much longer she could keep it together. Not Charlie! Of all of the people in the entire world, not her first best friend. Charlie and Emerson were like Oprah and Gayle, Laverne and Shirley. They were like sisters. How could she? Emerson fought hard to keep the tears painfully welling up in her eyes from falling.

"C'mon, Emerson. My life is a mess without you," Macy begged pitifully when she realized her hurtful information wasn't going to get her any closer to Emerson. "All I want, more than anything, is to be back with you. I gave it all up for you. The job, the relationship, the money, everything. I just want you back. I've been trying to speak to you. I've been going completely crazy without you. I need you. Please, let me help you through this tough time," Macy groveled. She moved in close again.

Macy being so close made Emerson uncomfortable. She was scared and angry and confused and hurt all at once. Emerson didn't know what to do next. She needed to get rid of Macy. She needed to be alone for a minute.

"Macy, you can't be serious with this shit. I never said I loved you! We fucked, okay? I'm tired of being nice about this! It was just a fuck for me, nothing more. I didn't lead you to believe I wanted to be with you. I'm not a fucking lesbian!" Emerson barked, her caramel face turning almost maroon. "I don't fucking love you! Now get out of my life!"

Macy paled slightly, seemingly genuinely shocked by what Emerson had said. She began breathing hard, almost beastly.

"Macy, I think you should leave," Emerson said, taking a few steps backward, realizing she might've gone too far with her words out of sheer and raw emotion.

"So that's it? You're going to act like I'm not here pouring my heart out to you?" Macy growled, moving closer to Emerson. Once again, Macy's mood took a drastic swing.

"I said just leave," Emerson replied flatly. Before she could react, Macy reached out and grabbed her neck roughly.

"Macy! Get the fuck off of me!" Emerson said through clenched teeth. Macy clamped down tightly on Emerson's neck.

Emerson flailed her arms, struggling to get out of Macy's grasp. Emerson had certainly underestimated Macy's power. Emerson gagged under Macy's grip.

"Get the fuck off of me!" Emerson said, gagging out her words. Macy seemed to have the strength of a man in that moment. Emerson knew that when people snapped that happened to them—a strength beyond regular abilities. She'd been around a lot of people who she'd seen this happen with. Emerson's heart punched at her chest. Her body became engulfed in heat.

"Just listen to me, Emerson. Just hear me out," Macy said as she continued to squeeze Emerson's neck with so much force Emerson thought her esophagus would crumble.

Emerson resisted and scratched at the tops of Macy's hands, but she couldn't loosen Macy's grasp. Emerson felt herself getting lightheaded, and the more she struggled, the less air she was able to get.

"Let go, please," Emerson gurgled. Macy clamped down even harder. Emerson lifted her foot and tried to stomp on Macy's foot, but she missed.

"Stop fighting me, Emerson," Macy whispered like a madwoman. Emerson could see the fire of pure evil flashing in Macy's eyes. Emerson squirmed and continued to claw at Macy's hands. The more she clawed and moved, the harder Macy gripped her neck.

Emerson's entire body was ablaze—a mixture of adrenaline, fear, and anger. Sweat drenched her face.

"All I wanted was you. Was that so hard? You selfish bitch! I gave you the best of me! I made sure your divorce went smoothly! I was there for you when your friend got hurt. You're ungrateful and fucking hateful," Macy growled.

Tears streamed Emerson's face. Fear was choking her even harder than Macy's hands. Her breathing became labored. Her head felt like it was about to explode. Emerson didn't know how much longer she could hold on to her consciousness.

"Please," she rasped out a whisper. She dropped her arms and decided that maybe if she stopped fighting, Macy would come to her senses.

"I will let you go," Macy hissed, increasing her grip even more. "I will fucking let you go to hell forever. That's the only place you're going to go if you don't want to be with me."

Emerson's legs began to give out, and her body began to go limp. "Please," she gurgled one last time. She looked up into Macy's crazed eyes, pleading with her own eyes.

Suddenly, Emerson felt herself hurtling to the floor. She hit it so hard it felt like something at the base of her skull cracked. Emerson gasped for air as small squirms of light exploded behind her eyes. She was literally seeing stars. Her body went limp. She could hear, but she couldn't move or speak.

"Oh, my God! Emerson, wake up. I'm sorry," Macy gasped, quickly falling down at Emerson's side.

"Get . . . away," Emerson croaked, her body shaking all over. The pain shot through her head and down her spine. She was sure with the hit to the head she'd taken she would be paralyzed. Emerson felt her heart shatter inside of her chest. Never in a million years would she have expected Macy to hurt her like this.

"Get out," Emerson growled in a hoarse whisper at first. "Get out! Get out! Get out!" she screamed, her voice going so high it itched the back of her throat and intensified the pain in her head.

"Emerson, I'm sorry! Wait! I didn't mean to . . ." Macy pleaded.

Emerson struggled to her knees. She fell back down twice before her head finally felt strong enough. She crawled toward the door, trying to get away from Macy as fast as possible. Her head throbbed, but she knew she needed to get outside. She made it out onto her porch with Macy scrambling behind her. Emerson couldn't take the chance of Macy attacking her again.

"Police! Somebody call the police," Emerson cried out, right before her world went black.

A few hours later, Emerson heard her mother's voice. "Oh, my God! Emerson! I came as soon as they called!" Anna cried, her arms extended in front of her. "I told you this might happen. I knew we should've gone to the police before. This is so crazy. I was worried sick."

Emerson hugged her mother. "I'm fine. It's a small bump on the head," Emerson assured her. "We have much more important things to discuss," Emerson said dryly.

"Okay, what is it, honey?" her mother asked, averting her eyes, which told Emerson that she knew exactly what it was.

Emerson closed her eyes for a few seconds and breathed out. "Did you know about Mason and Charlie?" Emerson asked bluntly.

Her mother blanched. She flopped down on Emerson's couch and fanned herself. "I didn't know for sure," her mother replied.

"If you're going to lie to my face, just leave and don't ever come back," Emerson spat, then turned her back on her mother and prepared to walk away.

"Wait, Eme," her mother called after her.

Emerson paused, but she didn't turn around.

"I saw them one night," her mother said.

That caused Emerson to turn around to face her. "And?"

"But I couldn't say for sure if they, you know, were together," her mother lied. Emerson glared at her mother.

"So why didn't you tell me you saw them?" Emerson asked, suspicious.

"Because you were already dealing with a lot. If I wasn't sure, I didn't think it would be worth upsetting you. I know how these things can upset you and make you relapse. I just didn't want to see that. Mason is not even worth it, and neither is Charlie," her mother rambled, her words rolling out quickly like she had to get it off her chest or else. Emerson knew when her mother was lying, that was how she sounded—like a child in big trouble.

"So for your own selfish reasons, you hid from me that my best friend was fucking my ex-husband? Does that even make sense to you? Didn't you think it would hurt me more to know that my own fucking mother hid something like that from me?" Emerson boomed. The yelling didn't help the pain throbbing through her head. Emerson felt dizzy and almost fell.

"Eme!" Her mother rushed over to her and grabbed her arm. "Sit down, please, before you hurt yourself even more."

"I don't know who anyone is anymore. Everyone and their fucking secret lives," Emerson said gruffly, fighting back tears.

"You know who I am. I am always your mother first. Protecting you is my job. I will do it at any cost," her mother said. "I would've told you in due time. It just wasn't the right time."

"Nothing is ever the right time for you," Emerson snapped.

Her mother took the words on the chin but kept her cool. "I just think you need to let it go. Neither one of them is worth having you," her mother said.

"You'll say anything to keep me where you want me," Emerson shot back cruelly. "But truth be told, I don't trust anyone. Not even you." Emerson got to her feet, and although her head was swimming, she grabbed her car keys.

"Emerson, you're in no condition to drive," her mother said, standing up to get in front of her.

"Don't make me fight you. You know I've done it before, and I'll do it again," Emerson said. "Now get out of my way. I have business to take care of."

"But look at you, Emerson. Your hair, your face, everything is a mess from the incident. At least sleep on it. At least give it a day if you're going to confront them. Take your medication. I can see that you're out of it right now," her mother pleaded.

"Really? You're worried about how I look or what I'm going to do? If that were the case, you wouldn't have let me find out like this," Emerson shot back. "Now get the hell out of my way!" Her booming voice startled her mother.

Her mother let out a long sigh and shook her head. "Just let me get you some help," her mother pleaded one last time.

"The only thing you can do to help me right now is stay the fuck out of my way," Emerson said through gritted teeth. With that, she pushed past her mother with so much fury Anna almost fell over.

"Just be careful, Emerson. I don't want you getting hurt, mentally or physically," her mother said somberly.

"At this point, I don't have shit else to live for anyway. Either way, this ends with me locked up in jail or locked up back in the mental institution, because I can't deal. My life is over either way you slice it," Emerson said with finality.

Chapter 18

Charlie

Charlie circled the floor inside of her apartment fifteen times in two minutes. Her insides were dancing with nerves. She looked over at her coffee table. It had three bags filled with what she needed. *Who goes to three different stores and buys all of these?* she asked herself silently. "You, that's who. Now stop being a coward," she spoke out loud. She walked over to the coffee table slowly, like a poisonous snake was waiting for her in those bags.

"Here goes nothing," Charlie huffed, snatching the bags up and rushing to her bathroom. Charlie dumped the contents of the three bags into the middle of the floor. She shook her head at how many different types of tests were available nowadays. Back when she was a teenager, there was one—plus or damn minus. Now Charlie stared down at so many with all the high-tech shit on them she couldn't even decide which to use first.

"Ugh, shit," Charlie grumbled, frustrated with the double wrapping on the first test she picked up. Charlie's hands shook so badly she had to use her teeth to open the silver foil packaging. Her hands were so sweaty even that was a chore. It probably didn't help that her heart was racing, too. Her nerves were so on edge that she couldn't keep still. She had been holding her pee just for the test, and that didn't help either. She did the pee-pee dance in circles until she finally got the test in her hand. Charlie's shoulders slumped, and she blew out a windstorm of breath. Suddenly her cell phone ringing interrupted everything. Charlie ignored it at first, but it rang again.

"Shit," Charlie huffed. She pulled up her panties and grabbed her phone.

"Mikayla?" Charlie grumbled into the phone. She wasn't expecting to hear from her. "What? Wait, just calm down," Charlie said, her heart suddenly throttling up at the sound of Mikayla's frantic cries.

"Do you need me to come get you?" Charlie asked. "Okay, I'll be there."

Charlie hung up, and at first, she whirled around in confused circles. But she still had to pee. Charlie took the open test, peed on it, and set it on the bathroom counter. She didn't have time to wait for the results. She'd see them whenever she got back. Right now, she had to go save Mikayla.

Charlie rushed into the restaurant, moving like her feet were on fire. Her palms were drenched in sweat, and so was the back of her shirt. She spotted Mikayla, and immediately her heart rate sped up. The half-cocked nervous smile on Mikayla's face quickly faded when she saw the sheer terror in Charlie's eyes.

Mikayla stood up and greeted Charlie with a tight hug. Immediately they both started crying. They held on to one another for longer than normal as both had all sorts of things running through their minds. Charlie was the first to pull out of the hug.

"I just have to say this, KayKay. You look like shit," Charlie said honestly.

Mikayla put her hand up to her mouth and hiccupped a sob. "I can't do it anymore. I didn't know who else to call. Emerson was not answering her phone," Mikayla cried.

"What happened?" Charlie asked. "I mean, I know what's been going on, but why now? Finally?"

"I think if I go back, he will kill me this time," Mikayla answered almost breathlessly.

Charlie closed her eyes, and more tears came dancing out of the sides. She was way more emotional than usual. "So what are you going to do?" Charlie asked, shaking her head. "And the girls?"

"I don't know. I'd have to fight to get them back, but he told me I wouldn't win," Mikayla said through tears. "I'm lost, and I think he will have me arrested."

"Fuck him! Arrested? Why? Those are your kids," Charlie said, her voice getting loud. Her blood was boiling.

"Shh." Mikayla put her hand up. "No, I stole from him," she confessed.

Charlie sucked in her breath and put her hand on her chest. "How much?"

"A hundred thousand," Mikayla said.

Her words dropped like bombs in Charlie's ears. "KayKay, my God," Charlie gasped. "For what? Why?"

"I wanted to get rid of them, Jewel and Damian. That's what they asked for." Mikayla cried some more.

"Fucking bastards," Charlie grumbled.

"And something else," Mikayla said in a low whisper.

Charlie tilted her head.

"This." Mikayla opened her balled fists and dropped her pill stash on the table. "I need to kick it. I can't even try to get the girls back unless I kick it."

Charlie let out a long, exhausted breath. "Oh, Mikayla," was all Charlie could muster up at that moment. Charlie knew that Mikayla wasn't lying about needing help. She looked terrible. Her hair was slicked back in a sloppy ponytail that was held together with what appeared to be an office rubber band. Her eyes had rings around them so dark it looked like someone had punched her in

208 Katt

both eyes. Her clothes—a pair of jeans and an oversized T-shirt—were so rumpled it looked like she had been sleeping in them for days. Charlie's heart was breaking seeing it. It was obvious Mikayla was in a great deal of distress.

"We can go back to my house. We can go there and at least call Emerson over, and we three will work through this together," Charlie said.

Mikayla put her hands up. "I don't want to put y'all out, Charlie. If I weren't so desperate, I wouldn't have called. I know that Emerson and you probably hate me after last time. I know you all blame me for staying so long and not fighting back. Trust me, I am feeling the same way right now," Mikayla said pitifully. "That bastard Charles has done some things to me that were lower than low. But now, taking the girls from me, he has left me with nothing. He is trying to destroy me. I just need some support. I have been getting high for the past three months, and I have nothing left. No friends. No family. No husband. No home. No money. Nothing left but my little girls," Mikayla sobbed.

"You have me and Emerson," Charlie gasped, softening at the edges. "I had no idea it was this bad, and I'm so sorry. Why didn't you get honest with us sooner?"

"It's not easy to admit you have nothing left," Mikayla confessed.

Just then Charlie's cell phone vibrated. Her heart jerked when she saw Mason's pet name. She snatched the phone up off the table.

"Stay right here," Charlie instructed. "I have to take this really quick."

Charlie rushed away from the table and out the doors. "Mason," she huffed into her phone. "Don't come to the house. I have to bring Mikayla there. Yes, I'll explain later. I have to go."

Charlie returned to the table and extended her hand to Mikayla. Mikayla looked up surprised.

"Let's go," Charlie said, smiling.

Mikayla cracked a small smile and put her hand into Charlie's hand. Charlie helped her get to her feet. "We got this. We have been through far fucking worse, and we will get through this too," Charlie assured her.

"Thank you, Charlie," Mikayla whispered with more tears springing to her eyes.

"No thanks needed. We are Baltimore girls. We are built fucking tough. Remember that," Charlie proclaimed.

"Fucking tough," Mikayla repeated.

Charlie stepped aside to let Mikayla walk in front of her. She felt her heart breaking into a million pieces when she looked closely at her best friend. Mikayla was in pretty bad shape.

Chapter 19

Emerson, Mikayla, Charlie

Emerson's hands shook so badly she could barely drive her car. At every stoplight, she closed her eyes and took in a breath and released it slowly. She was trying to make it to Charlie's house without crashing. Every time she thought about Charlie and Mason's betrayal, Emerson felt a stab in her gut.

"How could she?" Emerson roared, slamming her phone into the steering wheel over and over again. After a few seconds, she went very still. She stared blankly out of her windshield until cars behind her began laying on their horns. Charlie was supposed to be her best friend. What happened to the girl code? If a dude was ever dating your friend, he was automatically off-limits to you. Well, it made him even more off-limits if your friend had been married to him! Emerson's insides churned with anger every time she thought about the pictures Macy had thrown in her face. She'd seen Charlie wrapped around Mason's arm. She'd seen them kissing in his car. Tears streamed down Emerson's face. It was true, she'd divorced Mason, but that didn't change the fact that Charlie had betrayed her, broken their code.

Emerson parked her car at a hydrant in front of Charlie's building. She didn't give a damn. She scrambled out of her car and stormed into the building like a gusty tor-

nado. Emerson raced to Charlie's apartment and pounded the door so hard the side of her hand hurt. Emerson
shifted and moved in circles in front of the door, waiting.
"She better answer this fucking door. So help me, God,"
she mumbled. She had a thing or two to get off her mind,
and she was not going to let Charlie off the hook without
a face-to-face confrontation.

She'd seen Charlie's missed calls on her cell phone.
Emerson wondered if Charlie knew that she knew already. Charlie had called Emerson repeatedly over the
past few hours. Emerson figured it was because Charlie
had found out that Emerson knew about her affair with
Mason. Emerson put her ear up against the door for a few
seconds before pounding the door again.

Emerson pounded the door like her life was about to
end if she didn't get inside. The side of her fist ached, but
she wouldn't stop pounding. Sweat wet her hairline and
curled her hair into fine balls at the base of her forehead.
Appearance be damned at that moment. Emerson was
on a mission. Her heart threatened to escape her chest
through her throat. Everything around her buzzed loudly.
That was her rage playing out in her ears.

Mikayla yanked Charlie's front door open so fast and
hard she stumbled back a few steps. She couldn't understand who would be banging like the police about to
conduct a raid.

"Girl, what the . . ." Mikayla immediately swallowed her
words when she saw Emerson's red-rimmed eyes, hair
like a wild bird's nest, and heaving chest.

"Eme? What the . . . What's wrong?" Mikayla screamed,
shocked at the sight of the third member of their trio in
front of her. Emerson's chest rose and fell like a beast on
the attack. She had jagged black lines of mascara running
down her cheeks, making her look like a bad version of
the Joker from the last Batman movie. Her fists were

clearly balled, and her nostrils opened and closed like a bull on the charge.

"Where's Charlie?" Emerson growled hoarsely. "Where the fuck is she?"

Mikayla's already-big, round eyes were about to pop completely out of her head. She hadn't ever seen cool, calm, collected Emerson Dayle look like this. Emerson was the sounding board of the group, the usually level-headed one with all of the good advice. She was usually the one with her shit together. Not today.

Mikayla wasn't a fool. She stepped aside to let this bull in a china shop move past her.

"Charlie is in the kitchen. Eme, what is the matter?" Mikayla asked again, her eyes still wide as saucers.

Emerson stormed into Charlie's house and past Mikayla, refusing to answer her question. Emerson could hear what she thought was laughter coming from the kitchen, and the sound assailed her ears like nails on a chalkboard. Charlie had to be on the phone, and with whom? Who would be making her giggle like a schoolgirl? The thoughts swirled in Emerson's head like a double-eye hurricane. Emerson felt herself floating. She was having an out-of-body experience, and this usually happened when she was off her square.

"Why, Charlie?" Emerson boomed as soon as she crossed the kitchen's doorway in a fury.

Emerson had assumed correctly. Charlie was on her cell phone. The sight of her crazed friend caused Charlie to end her call without another word to whoever was on the other end. Charlie's face flushed and her mouth dropped open slightly. "Eme, what's—"

"Out of everybody, I never thought you! You? You, Charlie? You were supposed to be my best friend! I was there for you when every single nigga crushed you and your heart. I was there for you when your mother turned her fucking back on you and called you a whore! I was there for you when you were on the streets of Baltimore, bed hopping just to have a warm place to stay! And you turn around and do this to me? You don't have respect for the code? Our code? You fuckin' bitch!" Emerson rat- tled off so breathlessly her head felt light. Her body shook uncontrollably.

Charlie's eyes filled with tears. She put her hands up in front of her and shook her head. She knew this day would come. She had wanted to explain it all before it blew up in all of their faces. It was too late for that now. "Eme, wait," she started. "I can explain."

But Emerson couldn't hold back any longer. The dam of reasoning in her mind had finally broken, and red-hot rage rushed out so fast and furious it flooded all of her senses and sensibilities.

"Urgg!" Emerson growled. She rushed into Charlie so wildly and unexpectedly that Charlie's body went crash- ing to the floor with no way for her to break her fall. The back of Charlie's head hit the hard ceramic kitchen tile with a loud, sickening crack.

"Oh, my God! Emerson! Stop!" Mikayla screamed, rushing over to the body tangle that was her two best friends.

"Why, Charlie?" Emerson screamed through tears as she wildly slammed her fists into Charlie's face. "Why didn't you tell me? Why would you do this? You are not my fucking friend! You never were!" Emerson shouted through tears, suddenly growing weak.

Charlie's eyes were shut, and her head hung to the side limply. Blood leaked out of her nose and drained onto the floor. She was defenseless against Emerson's attack.

"Emerson! She looks really hurt! You have to stop! Please." Mikayla grabbed at Emerson's clothes, trying to pull her off of Charlie. It was too late. Charlie looked dead. Blood covered her face and drained out of her left ear.

"Why did she do this to us?" Emerson managed, allowing Mikayla to pull her off of Charlie. Emerson fell to the side of Charlie, sobbing.

"We were best friends! She knows what I went through! She lied to me every single day for the past six months!"

"Oh, my God! She won't wake up! Call 911," Mikayla screamed through tears. "I don't care what she did! You can't just kill her, Emerson! We are sisters! This is a sisterhood! You can't just kill her!"

Emerson threw her hand up to her mouth and gagged. She was frozen as she looked over at her lifeless friend.

"Charlie! Wake up!" Mikayla yelled, shaking Charlie's body. "Help! Help! Oh, my God! Charlie! Wake up!" With her body trembling fiercely all over, Mikayla lowered her ear to Charlie's face. Mikayla felt breath on her cheek.

"She's alive! Oh, thank God!" Mikayla cried out. She grabbed Charlie's cell phone and dialed 911.

"Please! Help! My friend, she's been attacked. She's unconscious, but she's breathing," Mikayla huffed hysterically into the phone. Tears poured down her face, and she could barely answer the operator's questions.

"Um, she was, um . . ." Mikayla stammered, looking over at Emerson. She didn't know what to do—choose to give Emerson up or lie to the operator. "She was attacked, and she fell really hard and hit her head. Please hurry. I don't think she will make it if she stays here like this much longer," Mikayla cried into the phone. If help didn't arrive fast, Mikayla didn't think Charlie would recover. There was so much blood Mikayla felt woozy herself.

The ambulance and police made it to Charlie's apartment in less than six minutes, but it felt like an eternity to Mikayla. Emerson had run out. She had gone and left

Mikayla all alone. Police officers seemed to flood every inch of Charlie's apartment.

"Mason," Mikayla said, relieved when she recognized a familiar face in the crowd. She could tell he'd been crying too.

"What happened?" he managed, clearly trying his best to be strong.

"Emerson, she had . . . maybe she was having an episode," Mikayla said, shaking her head as she relived the horror all over again.

"Emerson did this?" Mason asked, his nostrils blowing open.

Mikayla nodded. Although the EMTs had already rushed Charlie past her, Mikayla could not stop shivering. She couldn't concentrate on Mason's questions. She could see his mouth moving, she could even hear the sound of his words, but she couldn't comprehend them.

"Mikayla, are you listening. Did Emerson say anything? Anything about why she did this?" he asked.

Mikayla shook her head and lowered her face into her hands, sobbing. "It was so terrible. Emerson was like a crazy person, and she just attacked Charlie. She kept screaming at her, saying she betrayed her and the code," Mikayla bawled.

"Did she say anything before she left?" Mason asked.

Mikayla shook her head no. "This is all my fault," Mikayla cried.

"What do you mean?" Mason asked.

"Charlie, she was distracted. She never saw Emerson coming, and I didn't even warn her, even after I saw how crazed Emerson was," Mikayla lamented.

"It's really my fault," Mason said softly, lowering his head. "I . . . I've been with Charlie."

Mikayla's head shot up, and her brows crumpled down the center of her face. "What? What do you mean?"

"Charlie and I fell in love. It wasn't planned, Mikayla. Honestly, it just happened, and she's the best thing that has ever happened to me," Mason said.

"But how could you?" Mikayla said, backing away.

"I feel awful this happened, but I don't feel bad about loving Charlie," Mason said. "I've got to go to the hospital. My men are going to have some questions for you. They need to find Emerson."

Mikayla opened her mouth to say something else, but Mason rushed away so he could follow the ambulance. Mikayla felt all alone again. She wished she hadn't given Charlie her stash of drugs.

"Excuse me, ma'am," a tall, bald white man said as he approached. "I'm Detective Lattimore. The officer told me that you were the one who witnessed this attack. Can I speak to you for a few minutes, please?"

Mikayla looked at the detective through her swollen and red-rimmed eyes. She was sure she probably looked like the one who'd been attacked. She sure felt like it.

"Yes, I was the witness," Mikayla answered apprehensively. She felt like she owed Emerson something. In a way, Mikayla now understood Emerson's attack. That kind of deep-rooted hurt could cause you to kill someone. Mikayla fully understood that.

"Ma'am, I know these types of situations are always hard. Is the victim any relation to you?"

"She's my . . . one of my best friends," Mikayla answered. She wanted to scream and say, "They're both my best friends!"

The detective wrote fast on a little notepad. "Do you live here with the victim? Were you visiting?"

"I, um, she . . ." Mikayla stammered. It was still a bit confusing for her. Technically, at the moment, she would be staying with Charlie, but it had just happened, so she wasn't actually living with her. Mikayla closed her eyes and breathed out. "I was here visiting. She came and picked me up shortly before everything happened," Mikayla replied. She didn't want to tell the detective she was going to be living there and why. All of that was too personal to share.

"Ma'am, I want you to think very carefully and answer as truthfully as possible. Why would the perpetrator want to hurt your friend?" Detective Lattimore asked.

Mikayla blinked a few times, and it became obvious to her that the detective didn't know what Mason has just told her. Mikayla shifted uncomfortably. She swallowed hard.

"Now, ma'am, I know it's difficult, but in these situations, you can't protect anyone by not telling us everything. Do you understand?" Detective Lattimore said point blank.

Mikayla took a deep breath and inhaled. Her heart was like a jackhammer in her chest. She didn't want to see Emerson go to jail, but she also didn't want to lie right to the detective's face. She shook her head slightly and closed her eyes for a few seconds.

"You understand?" Detective Lattimore asked, bending his head so that he was eye level with Mikayla.

"No, um, I mean . . ." Mikayla stumbled. She was in the middle. All she could think about was how much Charlie's actions had directly affected Emerson and caused all of this. But Mikayla also had to consider that Emerson had no right to do what she did. Charlie could've died. God only knew how permanent her injuries would be now.

"She found out Charlie was with her ex-husband, and she came over and confronted her. Things just got out of hand," Mikayla blurted before she lost her nerve. The detective raised an eyebrow at Mikayla.

"But I don't know where she is. She ran out, and I swear I have no idea where she is," Mikayla said quickly.

"I guess that would be a motive. Who is the 'she' you refer to?" Detective Lattimore pressed.

Mikayla closed her eyes and swallowed the hard lump that was now sitting at the back of her throat. She could see Emerson's face in her mind's eye.

"Ma'am?" Detective Lattimore urged, looking at Mikayla expectantly.

"Emerson Dayle," Mikayla said, her voice barely above a whisper.

"Emerson Dayle as in wife of Detective Lieutenant Mason Dayle?" Detective Lattimore clarified. He put his pen down and stopped scribbling on his notepad. All of the air seemed to rush out of the room. A few officers stopped moving around the apartment and stood seemingly rooted to the floor.

"Yes, my other best friend, Emerson Dayle, ex-wife of Mason Dayle," Mikayla replied, closing her eyes. She said a silent prayer for Charlie and Emerson. This situation was a double-edged sword, because Charlie deserved justice, but the price would be Emerson's freedom.

"You have the wrong person! Get off of me! I will have all of your jobs! Do you know who I am?" Emerson barked as the officers surrounded her.

"Ms. Dayle, we have a mental hygiene warrant for you, so you need to cooperate," an officer said, waving the papers in Emerson's face.

"Who sent you? Whoever sent you is lying! They are just trying to get back at me! This whole story was made up!" Emerson screamed.

"Yeah, yeah. That's what all of the crazies say when we try to bring them in," the officer said. "Let's just make this easy and not hard."

220

Katt

Emerson looked around, and she knew she couldn't
win if she tried to fight. She still didn't know how they
knew where to find her. That place was a secret between
her and Mason when they were dating as kids.

Hushed murmurs of speculation passed among the
nosy passersby as they watched Emerson get escorted
away.

"Hey! That's Emerson Lovely!" someone screamed out,
recognizing Emerson as her internet personality. Emerson wanted to die on the spot. Her life was over. Then
she saw her mother fighting through the crowd that had
gathered.

"Mommy! Tell them they have the wrong person! Tell
them," Emerson shouted.

Her mother let out a sob. "I'm so sorry I had to do this,
Emerson. It breaks my heart, but it is what is best for you
right now," her mother cried.

"You bitch! You bitch! I should've known this was all
your doing! You just want to be in control of my life! You
were never happy for me! I swear when I get out of here,
I'll get my revenge. You'll be out of my life forever!" Emerson screamed, threatening her mother.

Her mother doubled over and sobbed as she watched
them cart Emerson away. "I'm so sorry. I failed you. I'm
so sorry."

Epilogue

Emerson, Mikayla, Charlie

Charles was taken aback when he opened the front door and came face-to-face with Mikayla and her police escort.

"Are you losing your mind? I told you not to come back here and—" Charles said.

He didn't get a chance to finish his sentence before Mikayla pushed past him so hard he stumbled. Mikayla continued into the house.

Charles noticed the police officers with her and backed down from trying to physically stop Mikayla.

Mikayla stalked through the house and headed for the staircase.

"Zuri! Kai!" Mikayla screamed. "Mommy is home!"

Mikayla hadn't made it to the top of the stairs before her girls came bounding out of their room.

"Mommy! Mommy, you're back!" they cheered, rushing into Mikayla's arms. They seemed to have grown so much in just a few weeks. Tears immediately sprang to Mikayla's eyes and her heart melted.

"Oh, my babies. I've missed you both so much," Mikayla cried, holding her daughters so tightly that her arms started to ache.

"But Daddy said you were gone forever. He said you left us and that you didn't care about me," Zuri sobbed.

"No, I would never leave my babies behind. Never. I just had some things I had to take care of. Mommy was sick for a while, and I had to go to the doctor to get better," Mikayla replied honestly. "You both are my life. You know that I can't live without you."

"Don't leave us again," Kai demanded, squeezing her mother a little tighter.

"Never," Mikayla answered through sobs. "How have you been? You've both grown so tall. And I love your hair," Mikayla rambled, trying to lighten the mood a bit. The girls clutched their mother like they didn't believe she wasn't leaving again.

"You can't take them. You need to get whatever you came for and get out," Charles growled from the bottom of the stairs, interrupting the mother-daughters reunion.

Mikayla's mood quickly changed. Her tears suddenly dried up, and her facial expression darkened. She stared down the enemy, ready to do battle. The line in the sand had been drawn when Charles tried to take her children from her, the only thing that mattered in her life.

Mikayla had tried to prepare herself for the moment when she and Charles came face-to-face, but nothing could have readied her for the way her heart slammed in her chest. Anger radiated into her face, making her flush.

"Okay, girls, go to your room while Mommy and Daddy talk. I'll be right there," Mikayla whispered softly to her daughters. They both looked at their mother pitifully and then down at their father warily.

Charles headed up the stairs in Mikayla's direction. She was going to face him head-on, just like she'd planned in her discussions with Mason and the police officers he'd arranged to escort her there. Already the look of shock on Charles's face was priceless. He clearly wasn't expecting this level of bravado from Mikayla, who'd always been so afraid of him. She had never stood up to him in the past, and the few times she'd tried, he'd always come out the victor.

"Just where the fuck do you think you are going?" Charles snarled, trying to grab Mikayla's arm. Mikayla wrestled her arm away and stood toe-to-toe with him. A sinister smile curled on her lips. Charles did a double take at his wife. He had not seen her look this good in months. And he'd never seen her so sure of herself and so bold. Mikayla's skin was clear and glowing. Her makeup and nails had been professionally done. She wore her natural hair pulled back into a classy chignon. Even her clothes—a loose fitting sheer tunic, a pair of distressed jeans, and Jimmy Choo pointed-toe pumps— was a big change and highly flattering to her slightly rounded figure.

"This is my house. That's what I'm doing here. And I am going to my bedroom to take a nice, soaking bath. After that, I am going to climb into my king-sized bed, flick on my sixty-five-inch television, and watch some reality TV," Mikayla answered, waving the court order in Charles's face. "And you, according to this, you have to vacate the premises for the safety of me and the children."

"What the fuck is that supposed to be? You think some piece of paper gives you any rights?" he scoffed.

"It's more than a piece of paper. And, yes, it gives me my rights back. In fact, it points out rights that I didn't even know I had because I have spent so many years being brainwashed by you and that evil bitch of a mother of mine," Mikayla shot back.

"This is not your house. I don't give a fuck what your paper says. This place was bought with my money. You don't have a fucking dime. You ain't never had shit without me, and you still don't. You are hood trash and always will be. I guess what they say is true: you can't turn a hood rat into a housewife. You are still just a little, poor, struggling daughter of a drug addict. You wasn't shit then, and you ain't shit now," Charles spat maliciously, swiping at the papers in her hand.

Mikayla steeled herself against his words. Mason and her new counselor had warned Mikayla that Charles would try to break her down with words. They said it was because Charles was really a weak, insecure man who degraded and abused women to make himself feel more like a man.

"Yeah, yeah. Those harsh words used to hurt me. Not because I believed them, Charles, but because I loved you. I stayed in this marriage, not just for the money, but because I wanted to be with you," Mikayla rasped, her jaw stiff. "Oh, and about me not having a right to be here because you bought this house with your money, well, that's where you're wrong. Maybe you should have used your money to get an attorney to explain the laws to you. This house is our marital house. When you bought it, we were already married, so it doesn't matter if you paid for it with your money or mine. It is considered communal property. It is where we built our marriage. Therefore, it belongs to us both. But because it is on record how you beat my ass and put me in danger, now I can kick you out," Mikayla said confidently. Charles began to argue, but Mikayla cut him off with an angry wave of her hands.

"I don't want to hear your flimsy insults and mean words. That shit doesn't work on me anymore. And before you even mention it—because I know that it's coming up—that prenup you had me sign that says I'm not entitled to any financial support is basically null and void. It was filled with so many holes it won't stand up in court. You will definitely be paying me spousal support. Especially with all of your abuse so well documented. So go ahead and pack. The police are here to make sure this goes down without incident," Mikayla concluded with a satisfied grin on her face.

As she turned away, she let out a long, silent breath. That was the hardest thing she had done in years. She rehearsed this very moment with Mason and the counselor least ten times before she felt she could handle the situation well enough for it to go smoothly.

Mikayla glanced over her shoulder as she walked toward her bedroom. "Close your mouth, Charles. Something might fly in it."

She knew Charles wouldn't give up that easily. She knew he was super competitive. She was expecting more.

"Guess what, bitch? I have proof that you stole thousands of dollars from me. I will put your ass in jail before I let you get one red penny of my hard-earned money," Charles hissed just inches from her face.

Mikayla took a deep breath and smiled. "I've already taken care of that. Turned myself in, made my own police report, and will have my day in court. My attorneys figure that, given all of the extenuating circumstances, I will probably get two years' probation, maximum," she said.

Charles tried to grab her, but she quickly sidestepped him. She dug down into her purse and grasped the little silver .22-caliber Smith & Wesson revolver. Mikayla aimed the gun at Charles's head.

"You ain't got no more chances to abuse me, Charles. Not physically or mentally. Now you go ahead and leave in peace. Or I can call those officers downstairs to come and take you to jail. Either way, you will not abuse me and send me running back to drugs," Mikayla rasped through her teeth.

Charles put his palms up in surrender. "You got this for now. But I ain't done. I don't give up that easily," he said as he slowly backed away.

"I don't give up that easily anymore either, Charles," Mikayla said with finality as she watched her husband backpedal out of her bedroom.

"Only two more snakes left to take care of," Mikayla muttered as she flopped down on her bed, exhausted.

Charlie examined herself in the long wall mirror that hung on one side of her bedroom. She turned sideways and smiled. She rubbed her stomach and turned to the other side. She smiled again.

Charlie inhaled and exhaled loudly. Her anxieties about everything hadn't changed since the day she found out. Her shoulders went slack, and her lips curled downward. It was no use. The fear of being a terrible parent invaded her thoughts all day every day. She was eighteen weeks pregnant, and she still couldn't bring herself to be all the way happy when she was alone. Mason was overjoyed.

No matter what Charlie did, she somehow always felt a deep sadness about everything that had happened. During her last doctor's visit, she'd been informed that the baby was due on Emerson's birthday. Charlie thought that was the cruelest joke the universe had played on her yet. She missed Emerson, and she felt terribly guilty about everything that had happened. She loved her friend deeply, but she still couldn't control who she'd fallen in love with.

Charlie quickly shrugged into her fluffy baby blue chenille robe. Her stomach growled loudly, and a round of kicks from her baby followed. Charlie giggled. "Little boy, have some patience. Please don't be like me," Charlie spoke to her belly.

"Who you talking to?" Mason said, creeping up on Charlie. She started and turned toward him.

"Didn't I tell you to stop creeping on me?" Charlie asked jokingly.

He grabbed her into his arms and held her tight. "You mean Daddy creeping," Mason said, letting his hand move to her belly. "I'm always going to be a Daddy creep, believe that."

"You better damn not, before we have a runaway baby at five months old," Charlie said, then chuckled.

"So is today the day?" Mason asked, changing his tone to serious.

Charlie pulled away from him. Suddenly her belly felt painfully tight. That's what always happened when she thought about it. "Yes. Mikayla is going with me. Since you helped her get everything fixed for her and the girls, she said the least she could do was make sure that I got the chance to apologize properly to Emerson."

"I think it's a bad idea. Emerson could've caused you to lose the baby. It wasn't even about me. Her mother said she was already spiraling out of control way before that," Mason said, his tone kind of argumentative.

"Emerson was my friend way before you were my man. I owe her this, Mason. We have a code. I violated it. Do I regret my life because of it? No. No, I don't, but the least I can do is talk to her," Charlie replied, getting a bit argumentative too.

"And if she's off her meds and attacks you in your condition, then what?" he asked.

Charlie fell silent for a few seconds. She had thought about it over and over. What if Emerson got so mad she wanted to see her lose the baby? It had played in her mind, but she wasn't going to back out of going to see her.

"It won't go like that," Charlie said weakly.

"You even sound unsure about it," Mason said, shaking his head. "Let me at least send a car to sit outside just in case."

"No. Seeing the police would really take things to a different level. She's not a monster, Mason," Charlie argued, rolling her eyes. She started past Mason, and he grabbed her arm. Charlie stopped and looked at him.

"If anything ever happened to you, I would never forgive myself, Charlie. You're the best thing that has ever happened to me, and I don't just say that as a cliché. I mean that shit with every fiber of my being. Baby aside, I need you like I need food and air," Mason said with feeling.

Charlie moved into him and melted against him. He stroked her hair, and she closed her eyes and let him hold her.

"You're the best thing that happened to me too, Mason. You have no idea what it is like to make it to thirty-five and never have had anyone love you until now. This feels like a totally different life for me. I thank God every day for you and now for our little bean. Nothing is going to happen. I am going to set this straight so that we are free and clear to love each other for eternity," she said.

Mason leaned down, and they kissed, sealing the deal that they'd be together forever.

When Emerson's mother opened her front door, Charlie and Mikayla stood nervously awaiting her reaction to them being there.

Anna's eyebrows shot up, and her mouth went round with surprise. She was definitely surprised to see her daughter's so-called friends at the door, after everything that had happened.

"You two have some nerve," Emerson's mother scoffed. She stepped out of the door and pulled it behind her but all the way closed.

"Ms. Anna, we just need to make things right. We love Emerson, and we believe everything can be solved with communication," Charlie said, stepping up.

"Please. If after today Emerson says she never wants to see us again, we will leave and never look back," Mikayla followed up.

"I don't want her upset. I think you two should—"

"Ma, who is it?" Emerson called out and pulled the door open.

Charlie, Mikayla, and Emerson's mother all turned their attention in Emerson's direction. It was too late. She'd seen them, and they'd seen her.

Emerson looked flawless. The time in the hospital and with her new spiritual counselor had served her well. Even in a pair of simple joggers, a plain fitted white T-shirt, and her hair braided, Emerson looked beautiful enough for a magazine cover.

"Hey, Eme." Mikayla was the first to break the ice. "We really need to come inside and talk to you," she said.

"Did you plan this?" Emerson said through gritted teeth, confronting her mother with her eyes ablaze in anger. "Did you set me up?"

"No, I wouldn't do that. I had no idea . . ." her mother answered almost breathlessly.

Emerson folded her arms across her chest defiantly. "Sure seems like a setup to me," she pressed on.

"Trust me, Eme, I wouldn't spring something like this on you," her mother assured her. Emerson twisted her mouth and rolled her eyes.

"It was us. We had to come and make things right, Emerson. We love you and miss you," Mikayla said, reaching her hand out toward Emerson.

They all could tell Emerson's blood was boiling. She didn't need this kind of drama after all she'd been through.

"Just give us a few minutes of your time, and if at the end you don't want to see us again—" Charlie told Emerson.

Emerson stormed into her house. "Come in," she grumbled to her unexpected and uninvited guests.

Charlie let out a small gasp. Mikayla smiled and rushed through the door. They found Emerson pacing the floor of her living room, her hands on her hips, waiting for them.

"What the hell are you two really doing here?" Emerson asked, wasting no time with small talk. "You can't just pop back up in my life like this, no warning, nothing. You both did me dirty," Emerson spat. She needed to make sure they knew that one of them stole her ex-husband and the other one turned her in to the police.

"Emerson, please. I know you're furious with us, but everything has an explanation. We wouldn't even be here if we didn't love you. We can't just write off over twenty years of friendship just like that," Mikayla said on the verge of tears.

"Emerson, I love you, and that has never changed. I can explain it all. I swear I didn't mean for it to happen the way it did," Charlie said, tears running down her face.

Emerson changed her tone and angry body language slightly. She could see that her friends were being sincere. She knew them better than anyone.

"Why didn't you both call first? I mean—" Emerson started.

Mikayla put her hands up in a placating gesture. "We just weren't sure if you'd agree to see us, and we needed to see you. Life has been hell thinking that you'd never speak to us again. We've both been through things that we are used to having you right by our side through," Mikayla said pitifully. "That bastard Charles put me out of the house. He tried to take the girls from me. He almost left me with nothing. I had been getting high and had gotten to the point where I had nothing left. I had to dig out of all of that without you, Eme. It was hard, and I needed you," Mikayla sobbed.

"Oh, my God," Emerson gasped, softening. "I had no idea. I'm so sorry too, for everything. I . . . There is really no explanation for what I did," Emerson said, hanging her head.

"Don't hang your head. You don't have to do that with us," Charlie instructed, moving closer to Emerson. "I just want to share with you that I would never do anything to intentionally hurt you."

Emerson looked at Charlie's face and then down at her protruding belly. "Congratulations, I guess," Emerson said tentatively. "Is it, you know . . ."

Charlie lowered her eyes to the floor. "Yes, the baby is Mason's," she said softly.

Emerson swayed a little on her feet but immediately lifted her chin and chest. "I'm glad someone finally gave him that family he's always wanted," she said.

"Listen," Mikayla stepped between Charlie and Emerson. "We are all going through things. Now, more than ever, we need each other. We need our sisterhood. We have to stick together, show loyalty to one another. Sometimes sisters fight or don't always agree with one another, but we can't be dragged down by these disagreements," Mikayla lectured like a mother hen.

"I get that, but she also lost all her rights to my friendship when she betrayed me. And honestly, I told myself that I wasn't ever going to deal with her in life," Emerson said firmly, wavering back to being angry at Charlie.

"You don't have to be her friend, but let's at least have this sit-down and hear each other out," Mikayla said. "We don't let years of friendship go just like that. I mean, you did things to her too. She could've died."

Charlie and Emerson locked eyes for a brittle few seconds. Emerson couldn't lie to herself. She felt her heart breaking into a million pieces when she looked closely at her former best friend. She missed Charlie so much.

"Let's sit down and talk," Mikayla instructed both of them. "I know this is not easy for either of you. Charlie, I think you should start. You owe Emerson an apology first and foremost about breaking the code," Mikayla said, playing mediator.

"I don't want her apology. What don't you get, Mikayla? This is not like she stepped on my toe and didn't say excuse me. She slept with my husband and is having his child. She kept that secret from me for almost a year. I will not forgive her," Emerson snapped stubbornly.

"Correction, Emerson. She slept with Mason after he was no longer your husband. Now I understand that it's a sore spot for you, but let's just make sure the record is set straight. This all happened after you had already said you hated him, never wanted to see him again, and had divorced him, not while you were with him. Let's deal with the truth, even if it hurts," Charlie recounted, using her fingers to make her point.

"Does it matter when you slept with him? It was against every girlfriend code in the world. A friend's ex-man, ex-husband, all of it is off-limits," Emerson said matter-of-factly.

"You chose—" Mikayla started, but Charlie interrupted her.

"She's right, Mikayla. I kept a huge secret from her, but it was only to protect her. I saw how at first she was very emotional about the divorce, but then she became happy after the divorce. For the first time, she was living independently and loving life. I hadn't seen you that happy in years, Emerson. It was a lot to put on you," Charlie appealed.

Emerson's eyebrows shot up in surprise. "So your lies and betrayal were favors?" Emerson chuckled sarcastically. "You're funny."

Charlie turned toward Emerson with tears running down her face like a leaky faucet. "Eme, I am sorry. From the bottom of my heart, I am sorry. I can't say that enough. I am sorry you ended up hurt by actions that I took when I was falling in love for the first time in my whole entire life. But I wouldn't change a thing about what I did, because it gave me Mason. I won't go over it and over it, but I have never been loved before. He loves me. I hope you understand and can forgive me," Charlie cried.

"Really? That's what you're going with? You wouldn't change a thing?" Emerson shot back, hardening her heart.

"No, I wouldn't change a thing except for the way that you found out. I have been your friend since we were little girls. I saw how you seemed boxed in by your marriage. I took your side hands down. You had so many miserable years that I thought he was a terrible person. When you told me you were getting a divorce, I was overjoyed that you'd be free, finally. I knew how badly you wanted to break out and be your own person. I didn't plan this at all.

"Mason was the officer who saved me at the car accident. Everything just took off like a rocket from there. You know how much I've always believed in the power of love but had never been able to find it. You were there when my mother was always so extra hard on me. Never once did she tell me she loved me. You were there every time I thought I was close to being in love. Emerson, I am truly happy right now because, for the first time, I am over the moon. I never intended to hurt you.

"I should've told you that Mason and I had fallen in love, but I didn't know how. I was trying to figure things out when everything exploded. This love between Mason and me was not planned. It just happened. I know that sounds so cliché and rehearsed, but it's the God's honest truth. It was just perfect from the start, and I couldn't walk away. I knew he was your ex-husband, but I couldn't leave behind a love like this. I didn't have anyone to talk to, and I was embarrassed. Mason saved me in every single way. Emerson, the only reason I kept it from you was because I wanted you to be happy once and for all. It wasn't to deceive you. I have always loved you more than any other person in the world, and I still do. I put you before myself then, and I'm begging you to let me back into your life now. I want to share this with you," Charlie confessed, baring her soul. She rubbed her stomach at the end.

Emerson was sobbing. Her pride was telling her not to forgive Charlie, but her heart was telling her something else.

"I'm sorry for assaulting you," Emerson replied through her tears.

"I forgive you," Charlie said through her own tears.

"Let's all hug," Mikayla said, standing up.

They all embraced. "We are Baltimore girls, built tough," Emerson said.

Charlie and Mikayla giggled. "Baltimore girls, built tough."

"Ahhhh!" Charlie screamed at the top of her lungs as another thunderbolt of pain shot through her abdomen and radiated to her back.

"I think something is wrong," Mason shouted, a look of terror on his face. "What could it be?" he asked the nurse, his eyes as wide as marbles.

"It's labor," the nurse answered, wiping sweat from Charlie's head.

"Help me!" Charlie screamed out again, her face turning burgundy. Her body was dripping with sweat.

"What can I do?" Mason asked nervously, pacing.

"You can just support her, rub her head, and love on her," the nurse said. Everyone in the room wanted to laugh at Mason, but they refrained.

"Ahhh!" Charlie screamed again, arching her body on the bed, the pain stabbing her. Mason rushed to Charlie's side and dabbed her head with a wet towel.

"You have to get ready to push. I think we are there, okay?" the nurse told Charlie.

"I will be right here," Mason said.

"Argggh," Charlie emitted a scream from deep down in her throat. Charlie screamed again. This time feeling the uncontrollable urge to push, she did. Charlie bent to the side and vomited.

"Agggh!" Charlie screamed, bearing down.

"Breathe!" Mikayla yelled, holding Charlie's trembling left leg.

"You're doing so good, baby," Mason coached, stroking Charlie's hair.

"One more, girl. You got this," Emerson cheered, holding on to Charlie's right leg.

"Aghhh!" Charlie screamed again.

"I see the head," the doctor called out.

It didn't take but a minute for Mason to abandon his post and move to the end of the bed. "Oh, my God! Baby! I see him!" Mason yelled.

Charlie panted for breath. She was exhausted.

"One more push should do it," the doctor urged.

"Agggh!" Charlie growled and bore down, her chin to her chest.

"Here we go!" the doctor shouted.

As soon as the baby belted out his first screams, Mason hit the floor.

"Nurse! We need a bed for Daddy!" the doctor shouted.

"Just like a damn man," Mikayla said. Charlie and Emerson busted out laughing.

"I guess he ain't built tough," Emerson said.

"Definitely not," Charlie agreed, reaching out for her best friend's hand.

"I love y'all," Charlie said.

"We love you more," Emerson and Mikayla said in unison.